As the lights went out there was the whoosh of a stoner blast, but no ghastly pop-pop-pop that heralded impacted flesh.

Given Satcon's rotation the moon would come flooding in some time in the next fifteen seconds: that's how long I had to find O'Doul, so I yelled "Put that damn gun away!" as I rolled from the path of the expected hail of darts and drew a bead on the fading afterimage of the aiming device. "Good night, O'Doul."

THE TAKING OF SATCON STATION

THE TAKING OF
SATCON STATION

BY
BARNEY COHEN
AND JIM BAEN

A TOM DOHERTY ASSOCIATES BOOK

Copyright © 1982 by Barney Cohen and James Patrick Baen

A Tor Book

First printing: July, 1982

ISBN: 48-531-X

Cover Art by Howard Chaykin

Printed in the United States of America

Distributed by:
Pinnacle Books, Inc.
1430 Broadway
New York, N.Y. 10018

Prologue

"Please extinguish all smoking implements
and insure that your seat is in swing mode.
Also make sure that your tray table and
terminal are retracted, and that any packages
or carry-on luggage are securely webbed or
stored in the cabinet above your seat." It was
the soft voice of our cabin attendant, an un-
remarkably pretty girl of the type often
drawn to that sort of work.

I'm rarely caught by surprise by the more
predictable events of travel, so stubbing out
the remnants of the last of my complimentary
Fatimas, and checking to see that my orders
were safely tucked away in my pocket and
that my carry-on was webbed in tight with me
about covered the operation.

For most of the rest of the passengers on
MexAmerica and Pacific Skytrain 101, Lunar
Station Five to Constellation and local points

beyond (including an aerodynamic module tangenting to Los Angeles) the command produced a bustle and a scurry and a bumping of heads as people broke up card games and what-not and tried to sort themselves out and into the right seats. Two children traveling with one couple, delighted with Z-G and the confusion it was causing, did their best to sustain the chaos.

"We will be docking with Satcon Station's North Port in approximately one-half hour," said our attendant, now perched on what during the constant .2-G of the trip had been the ceiling, halfway up the aisle. Microphone in hand, preparing to get into her own harness, she was smiling at everyone and at no one in particular as she spoke. "Please remain in harness after initial docking. Immediately afterward we will be moved to a position on the outer rail and will take on .2-G. At that time you may feel free to unharness and leave your seats. Those of you continuing to Los Angeles"—I was in the aerodynamic module—"may either remain on board or visit our courtesy facilities in the North Port Mini Ring or on "A" Ring, Green Area. Both gift shops are unfortunately closed at this time, but many items, including Satcon Silica and duty free tobaccoes, as well as alcoholic beverages and recreational chemicals of all kinds, will be available via terminal order once we are on our way to Los Angeles. Those of you remaining on Satcon, we hope you enjoy your stay, and thank you for riding MA&P."

"Good luck," I mumbled to myself. As far as I could gather from the trip's hours of endless chit-chat I was the only passenger so blessed. For everyone else Satcon was just a stopover on the way to better things.

Up ahead the big particle engine fell silent and the chemical boosters began their pushing and nudging job, translated to us passengers as a series of Z-G bumper car jolts. Out the window to my right, Satcon Station rolled up into view. From five miles away it didn't look too awful.

Four 625-foot-wide rings of more or less eggshell white rotated on their common axes once every thirty seconds. Down their center ran a spine, a cylinder which extended a quarter mile outward into space, flaring at either end into low-G space docks. These counter-rotated so as to remain stationary for docking. They connected to the main station by mini-rings, one quarter the diameter and G of the main rings. In these .2-G mini rings were housed the main space port facilities and the "elevators" that eased you out of the port area and up to the .8-G spin of the adjacent station—vice versa when you were departing Satcon Station via one of its ports. Since the spine was aligned on Earth's axis, the ports and their mini-rings were called "North" and "South."

The four main rings of Satcon housed the factories, workshops, metal distilleries and what-not for which Satcon had once been famous. They were mostly abandoned now.

As we drew closer I could make out the four

major ring-to-ring access tubes which hooked up each ring to the next at the quarters of the lock, and the tacked-on postfab construction of several more-or-less self contained "inner" rings. Between these two "discs" the spine itself swelled outward, like a snake that had swallowed a watermelon, to a diameter of forty feet. It was here that Exxon had conducted the pioneer experiments in ultra-low-G composite alloy fabrication that had resulted in the invention of monocable, for which Satcon had also been famous.

These days Satcon was famous mostly for being old. Sad fate, but it happens to us all. Live to be eighty-eight and I don't care whether you won a Forster Prize or built a bridge across the Gulf of Mexico. They'll introduce you as "here's so-and-so, he's eighty-eight."

True experimental work had long ago moved on to newer and better stations. So had most manufacturing. Aside from some subsistence-level fabrication and farming, all that was left for Satcon was to be a way station, a cargo exchange facility—and of course to be a landmark, if that's the word, of the early Space Age. To be eighty-eight.

In 1989 its core, a strap-on booster, had been hurled up on a low-orbit mission of the "Space Shuttle." You don't believe me, look it up: Satcon started life as a spent fuel tank.

Five years later it housed the "long crystal" experiments, a year after that the space telescope survey, two years after that it became the dormitory for the men and one woman who built the first ring, the one that is now North Port Mini. Then it was boosted up to geosynch over Bogota and "A" ring was added. And so it went, growing by plan sometimes, revised plan sometimes, and by haphazard chance sometimes.

As Skytrain 101 drew within a mile I could begin to make out the helterskelter pattern of tubular appendages standing out from the rings, accomodations tacked on airlock by airlock at the behest of small companies who set up shop on the station as it grew. A sort of random coherence was the result, a slap-dash symmetry for the sake of rotational equilibrium.

A lot of people had made a lot of money on Satcon. In its heyday, when I was a kid, Satcon Station was the Queen of the Sky. She was beginning to show her age even then, not that a space-crazy kid would notice, but still, anything important that happened off Earth either embarked from there, took place there, or else stopped there to refuel (this was before fusion drive) on its way to destiny. Now Satcon was a wreck.

I had a certain amount of empathy (but very little sympathy) for the situation. My latest company physical had left me with thirty earth-weight pounds to drop if I wanted to collect my bonus. I wasn't thirty pounds overweight. I'm big boned. And I was forty. It's not easy to drop thirty when you're forty.

"Mr. Bockhorn?" the attendant's voice

whispered at me through the tiny speaker mounted up near the top of my harness. I pressed the answer button.

"Yes."

"Your paperwork is cleared through entry, so if you'll just pick up your luggage at—"

"I have no luggage, just carry-on."

"Is that experience talking or paranoia?" The smiling chatter of a skytrain attendant. Cute.

I had once taken a MA&P skytrain from Walt Whitman Station to Phobos Strip and had to wait three years for my genuine canvas overnighter to come back from the asteroids. But I didn't want to discuss it now, at least not via speaker and mike.

"We're both eating off the same soft salami," I answered and she didn't say anything right away but I could see her arching around, trying to get a look at me. To see if I was smirking, I guessed, to see if I had said something off-color.

"Then for sure it must be experience," she said with a smile, finally deciding that all I meant was what was right there on her manifest: that we both worked for the same company. I was relieved that she wasn't going to jump me for being lewd, but I'd've preferred it if she had at least winked.

"Soft salami," I chuckled to myself. Real carrier agent talk. Double entendre. It's a lonely job, fleet agent. It sends you far enough often enough that a steady woman, at least one with any sense, is out of the question. And low-G, as the astro- and cosmonauts never told us but know everybody knows, makes you so sexually labile that the merest glance from a pretty face can make you wish you never had to pay for it. And so the *double entendre*, based on the long discredited theory that if I talk dirty maybe she'll let me be dirty, becomes the basic male-female repartee, flirtation the fundamental male-female relationship, frustration the steady-state. I get as lucky as most guys, I guess, but as unlucky too. I put it out of my head, which was where it pained me least anyway.

The orders in my pocket instructed me to a Ms. T.J. Janes, Deputy Director of Station Security. It was from the first an odd kind of assignment. For one thing, this Janes lady was not a **MA&P** (pronounced **MAP**) employee.

A carrier agent's primary function is protecting the people and property of the fleet. It is a responsible job, and was especially so back then in the 2070's when the United States Space Command had all but pulled out the private sector. What with distances getting greater and greater, and property increasingly difficult to protect, the carrier agents of the Six Sisters (the really big space carriers: Chrysler-Pan Am, Japan Aerospace, Cosmoflot, Eurosky, MexAmerica & Pacific, and Freddie Laker) became the sherriff, the posse, and sometimes the judge and jury all in one. In short, we were the law. Still are, for that matter, but we try not to put it that way for read-out.

My rank, that date, was Fleet Agent. I had been one since the academy, two decades before. Fleet Agent is the infantryman of space security, a job that mainly concerns itself with the finding of work-contract truants and stowaways, a routine grind-it-out kind of job that most agents serve their apprenticeships on, and then either move up or out.

A few, like the several grains of salt that, shake as you might, never leave the shaker, have remained. I was one. In my case it had been a series of circumstances. As a youngster I had put the slug on a malfeasing superior. When he was later cleared on a technicality his malfeasance was scrubbed from his record, but my slug remained. I missed a few opportunities to upgrade to Detective Sergeant therefore, and by the time all the good busts and collars I was piling up began to balance out that slug I found that I had become "too valuable" to spare for higher duty, or, as my previous boss used to say, "Bockhorn has the optimum Fleet Agent's amalgam of skill, experience and maturity." Which I strongly suspected meant that out of a squad otherwise composed of wet-behind-the-ears academy grads, bucking second yearlings, and a few young turks, I was the only one his own age to go drinking with. I pulled all the "sensitive" assignments and remained a Fleet Agent.

I got to like it. It cost me a wife and family. Good woman but she saw I wasn't going anywhere and wanted better. As we'd only just tied the knot it cost me no children, thank goodness, and no loss of self respect either.

And truly, I'd become a very good stow pincher and an even better buster of tru's. I could interview my pants off, dogged-like if you know what I mean. I was a very good asker of questions, and an even better listener. A guy could snow all day and I'd always catch his drift.

Which brings us back to Ms. Janes, to whom my current section chief Perry Oxenhorn (yep, I was Oxenhorn's Bockhorn) had first begged, then ordered me to be polite, charming and discreet.

"But she's not even in our jurisdiction," I said.

"PfffGH," Oxenhorn answered, making that silly sound he does with his tongue when he doesn't want to go into a long-winded explanation. I forced it anyway, because I dote on getting if not giving background, and here's what I got.

While it was true, strictly speaking, that employees and equipment of the two dozen stations now scattered about Earth Space were under the jurisdiction of either the United States Space Command or SOVCOSMO, the fact was that since the Space Port Consortium was half owned by the Six Sisters, aid was often given on a lend-lease basis to any port or station that requested it. Satcon Station had requested a MA&P agent.

"I'm lend-lease?" I asked.

"PfffGH," Oxenhorn answered and then shuffled around some papers on his desk by way of showing me that he was busy and I left without the benefit of hearing him answer "Pfgfghf," or whatever, to my unasked question, the one about security mode.

My orders where marked "semi-hush" a ridiculous level which means roughly that if you ask me about my assignment and you're somebody I should be polite to I'll tell, but if not I'll just stay off your screen. It's crazy. If a thing is secret, bury it. If it isn't, print it out. I wanted some background on that. What I got was a skytrain ticket.

I packed my usual stuff, after removing the *same* usual stuff, only dirty, from my last trip, in my genuine leather overnighter. From the library compartment I removed four books. leaving only Dashiell Hammett's *The Continental Op*, which I hadn't finished, and added three Agatha Christies which I'd just received by laser launch from Philadelphia. Sure, all this stuff (and anything else since the burning of the library at Alexandria) would be available on terminal wherever I was going to wind up, and yeah real books can get expensive (I routinely sinkholed a tenth of my salary on my collection) but there was something about the yellowed, musty old paperbacks that added to a mystery. Something *besides* the missing pages, smart guy.

Our skytrain serpentined to approach the

North Port docks, close enough now to see men working on the ring nearest. The G-force of our deceleration began to ebb and the harnesses that held us began floating free on their pinions. By force of habit I touched a leg against the overnighter to feel for my M99 Stoner, the standard agent's-gun, a black, oval-barrelled, hand-held flachettegun whose stream of flesh-explosive darts could flay a man alive at fifty paces but would not violate the integrity of a vacuum wall hit point blank square. The Stoner bulged comfortably. Packed. Locked. Loaded.

Then I touched my armpit for another bulge, a 110-year-old, chrome skinned, ivory handled Smith & Wesson .357 Magnum. My baby. The dead-accurate Stoner with its pop-shot and Laimer (from Laser AIMER, remember?) might have been clever as hell. But the old Magnum with its thumb-diameter bore was positively cataclysmic. Unusuable inside where hull integrity was *primary*, except as a suicide weapon, outside, in Z or diminished G, it would have the power of a cannon, and a range of forever. I'd never fired it except in my fantasies, but, like the mystery books I carried, it reminded me, in those grinding days of busting truants and pinching stows, that I once had had a reason, fatuous and romantic though it may have been, for becoming a carrier agent.

I'm not complaining. Just trying to convey to you my state of mind upon arriving that day at Satcon Station. We bumped home and the attendant was instantly out of her harness and on the horn.

"Please stay in your seats until spin-G stabilizes and Satcon gravity takes hold."

It had.

Chapter One

Having been cleared through entry meant I could avoid the squad of twenty or so clerks and inspectors and general factota from the different authorizing agencies who, anywhere in space, filled the first half hour of each skytrain's docking with the questions and requests for credentials and the paying of fees and the stamping of stamps—rubber and electronic—and the affixing of signatures and printatures, all accepted resignedly by those who couldn't bear a break from being on board because they knew that an even larger squad of scribblers was hard at work in the cargo bays and no one could get off to sightsee or shop or whatever until both teams had finished anyway. The true medium of what Earth types for some obscure reason like to call "the space enterprise" was, and is, red tape.

As soon as our airseal was in place and our hatch popped I put all of that behind me and float-walked down the galley way, past the two kids now bawling to get off, up the corridor, feeling myself gain a bit of weight as I did so, to the waiting room where a dozen passengers departing Satcon for L.A. were themselves being stamped, signed, tithed and requested, and on through to the full .2G of North Port Mini Ring, from which I would ferry up to "A" Ring where Station Security had its offices adjacent to the Green Area to which our attendant had previously directed our attention. Got that?

The Mini Ring elevator doors opened. The car was empty. I pressed the "close door" button. Thirty seconds later the door closed. The motor whirred. I stared at the tattered grey carpet as the car picked up speed to take me from the Mini Ring to "A" Ring, where a full .8G (thought to be the "ideal" weight in the year 2020) held sway.

These so-called elevators are not ascensors necessarily—some of the smaller ones move inward and outward from the spine, most don't—they're just cars that move through the various access tubes that knit Satcon together. Presently I was aboard a car in one of the four "main lines." Had I wished I could have crossed in a straight line from North Mini out to "A" over to "B" to "C" to "D" and inward to South Mini without leaving the car I occupied. Instead, when the car stopped at "A" with a lurch and the smell of cooking lubricant I got off. I hadn't been on Satcon in years, twelve to be exact, and though it hadn't been pretty then, still it was a shock to have had to squint against the glare of the naked flouro that clung tenuously, as if to life, on the end of a wire in the elevator.

I was at the administrative area, a narrow hallway flanked by offices, cubicles, workspaces and whatnot, all a marvel of the miniaturization-minded cleverness of the days before the advent of cheap-boost macro-engineering. Clever, but cramped and dingy just the same. I checked the nameplates along the wall for an eighth of a mile spinward. "Hull Maintenance," "Health," "Agro," "Tenants Union Solidarity Committee," "Council for the Arts," "Safety." There I un-latched the door and walked in. A young man in a crew cut took his feet off the desk and tried to look alert.

"Station Security?" I asked, knowing it was somewhere in the "Safety" module.

"Whom do you wish to speak to?"

I handed him a piece of paper and he squinted through sleepy eyes at the names written there, mine and Lady Janes'. I glanced around his desk. Lock-boxed memory mod-ules were stacked on a shelf at his right. His incredibly elderly cathode ray terminal was on a shelf above his head, and a double-re-verse mirror brought the image down to him so that mike and typer were to his right and his printer was on his left. The scribble-sole work surface in between left him just enough room to squeeze in and out and, once he was in, vocoder dangling from his neck, the whole thing tended, I guessed, to lock him in. Very clever. I could never understand how people worked that way. He began pressing some buttons. I checked myself out in his "Are You STRAC" mirror. I hadn't seen one since training. Where but in security could you still be STRAC?

STRAC was an old NASA false acronym for "straight and correct." It had to do with uniforms and grooming and what-not. Space was once full of STRAC mirrors. The paint on this one was all but gone, but the outline of the old STRAC was still there. For m too; apparently I had activated the damn thing.

Now an arrow appeared, pointed to roughly where my head reflected, and the mirror asked "Hair neat and in place?" I was okay on the cap; I didn't wear one, and on the hair because I wore it so short it had to be neat. "Tie horizontal?" the mirror next asked. Okay again; didn't wear one. Hardly anyone did anymore. "Shirt buttoned up?" I was wearing an open-necked flourescent-red Izod under a blue-black flare-shouldered vest with matching slacks, bloused at the ankles. It was my standard plainclothes outfit. "Shoes shined?" The arrow now pointed to the bottom. Well, deck slippers with oversocks don't take a shine, so I was okay there, too. I sucked in my gut and stuck out my jaw. I was STRAC.

"Ms. Janes?" the boy said into his desk mike. "There's a Fleet Agent Bockhorn here to see you."

Whatever she said in response was said into his earpiece and I wasn't privy to it. All he said was, "Will you wait?"

I nodded. He indicated a small silicaform chair directly behind me and I sat down. My knees practically touched his desk. He shuffled some papers and then stiffened. I guess right that she was saying something into his earpiece. "You can go up now," he told me. "Third level, this stairway."

This "stairway" turned out to be an esca-ladder fixed on the wall behind the printer. I started up. Until you get used to it, "climbing" while the ladder pulls you is a bit like being dizzy on your feet. I plodded upwards. As I climbed past the second level a young woman behind a nearly identical desk set-up smiled at me. On the third level—no desk but a pair of chairs and a tiny coffee table—stood a tall, broad-shouldered brunette of about thirty. She wasn't smiling. Her hands were folded across a pair of exquisite breasts. Her hips, encased in the proverbial spray-on jump suit, were tilted at a comfortably enthralling angle. She had all the externals, but she left you cold enough to realize that she meant to do just that. "Bockhorn?" she said with a voice not as deep as mine but every bit as powerful.

I nodded.

"Will you follow me?" she said. I stifled a half dozen pulch funnies that I was just dying to tell myself and followed her around a corner, past another desk like the one down-stairs and into a larger office.

In Satcon terms, T.J. Janes' office was immense. It had two chairs and a couch. I dumped my overnighter and my shoulder satchel onto the couch and eased myself into one of the chairs. Janes remained standing, arms still folded, one hip leaning on the edge of her desk, her foot dangling slowly back and forth.

"It's a simple truant case," she said as if it weren't. "Here's a photo." She lifted from the desk a small sensaround and handed it to me. Pretty girl, twenty-two maybe, dark eyes, frizzy hair, open. Made you smile. Truancy was a thorny problem. People on work contracts would suddenly, for any of a number of reasons, burn out. They'd hoard a little, hide a little, then hole up somewhere to take off for a week or two. It raised hob with the tight work schedules. Locking them up for theft of whatever would, of course, have raised that much more hob. Sacking them and then shooting up and training their replacements was so expensive it was out of the question. Policy was to find them, scare them, rough them if necessary, and send them back to work. I hated that part of the job. I shook my head at the smiling photograph.

The girl's name was Lauren Potter. She was a relatively low ranking Port Authority worker assigned to station communications. "We have a weekly newspaper here," Janes said and swept a copy off the desk and at me. I took it. Standard smalltime weekly printout on recyclable monolar. "Lauren Potter is the editor," Janes said and moved around to sit behind her desk.

"When did she take off?"

"Two days ago. Monday. She didn't show up for work."

"Her quarters have been checked?"

"Of course."

"Why wasn't USSC notified? You're under Command jurisdiction. Wait a minute. I got this assignment yesterday. If this Lauren Potter didn't show up for work the day before that then you filed a truant report with girl out only eight hours. That a bit hasty?"

"There may have been foul play."

"Is that why I'm semi-hush?"

"You're semi-hush because your damn clerk wouldn't give me full hush."

"Why didn't you level with him? For that matter why don't you level with me? If there's a suspicion of foul play then it's not a truant case, it's—"

"Bockhorn! I am near my wits' end," she said, and despite the apparent stony calm in which her face was set, something made me take her word for it.

"Give me some background," I said in my most soothing way.

"Lauren was being followed. She was getting very nervous. Very upset. And the . . ." She put her slender, manicured fingers up to her eyes and rubbed them as she continued. "I didn't go to the Command because if Lauren *is* a truant I don't want her pinched. I asked for full hush because if she's in trouble, I don't want to aggravate the situation. I called right away because," she stopped, "because I felt I had to that's why. If that doesn't satisfy you then—"

"That's fine," I said quickly, not wanting to lose her. "From here on we're on full hush, unofficial."

"Thank you," she said and seemed to make too much a show of dropping her hands slowing to the desk in front of her. "I don't want Lauren stopped or brought in or interfered with in any way. I just want you to find her, ascertain that she's safe, and apprise me of her whereabouts. Clear?"

"Clear. How do you know she was being followed?"

"She told me."

"I can assume that your office is on her regular beat so that you and she know each other well enough to—"

"Bockhorn . . . she's my sister."

"Oh," I said.

"I am not being hysterical Bockhorn. I am not the hysterical type. I just know that something is wrong."

"Let's say there isn't. Can you give me some background on where she might have trued off to?"

"This station once housed 20,000 people. Now its down to a little over 5,000 people in the same space. She could be anywhere. If she could arrange some kind of access credential she could be off Satcon altogether. I've tried to put myself in her place but, I don't know."

"You're pretty certain she's on the run from this . . ."

"Guy . . . yeah I am," she nodded. "Oh wait. I also have this." She took from the desk drawer a small recodisc. On it, she explained, was a brief snatch of the man's voice. A telephonic mix-up had crossed her call to Lauren with his call.

"To Lauren?" I asked. She nodded. "Then Lauren knew the man?" She shrugged. "Did you recognize the voice?" I asked. She paused, either in thought or for effect and then said, "at first I thought so but no. When I abstracted the snatch that was clean, the more I played it the more my recognition factor receded."

"You normally have a good recognition factor?" I asked, not really kidding her.

"Yes I have. And the more I played the snatch, the less there was. There really isn't much there to go on."

"I'll give it a listen," I said and then, after getting a Lauren Potter printature and samples of her handwriting and voice, and hitting on Janes for all the background I could, I left for Lauren Potter's rooms, which were on "B" Ring, halfway round.

I decided to walk "A" Ring to the corresponding elevator just to get a better look at the terrain. It didn't improve any along the way. At the Green Area I sat down at the first picnic table and took out a Fatima; lit it.

I inhaled deep and hard. Maybe Janes *was* hysterical. Maybe this was going to be one of *those* jobs. I put her sister's voice sample next to the "mysterious" man's on the redwood table top and took out my pocket terminal. I pulled on the Fatima again, deep, and inserted the Potter disc. "Identify," I said. The readout on voice I.D. gave me no more information than Janes had. Standard personnel stuff. I inserted the other recodisc and got: "Insufficient phonemic material for voice I.D." I switched on the audio playback and listened to recodisc. A lot of nothing spun by and then: "S'cuse me."

That was all. I shrugged, stubbed out the Fatima, and continued my walk. I passed guys sprawled along the hedges sleeping off alky or chem. Charming place.

Lauren Potter's rooms turned out to be in a cantonement area still considered a good neighborhood. There were some families with little kids—tell-tale tricycles on the four foot square artificial lawns—but mostly it was a young-singles area, and to the right and left of the walkway were doors and windows painted with fanciful designs and surname renderings. I had the key to 1001-Potter so I twisted it in the lock and pushed in.

It was a two room flat on the third level (reached, like her sister's office, by a short escaladder), which meant that its roof was the inner surface of the ring; Lauren Potter's place had a skylight. It was a flat made for darkness and the enjoyment thereof. For a couple of seconds I allowed myself the pleasure.

The skylight afforded a view of the core of the station and the elevator tubes radiating out from it and the appendages constructed symmetrically on either side of nearly every surface.

The spacescape—right now the moon and Cygnes the Swan—rolled up in an an ever-changing backdrop behind it all. It threw a pale shadow on the floor, just enough to keep me from falling over anything. As I crossed the room to switch on the light the moon cartwheeled out of sight. Satcon is the smallest diameter, fastest rotating habitat in the sky.

You wouldn't think you could do much with the stamped aluminum walls of old Satcon, but you'd be wrong. Lauren Potter's were painted a light tan with the bracing stampings a dark brown, as if they were wooden beams. A large gold "L" hung on one wall next to a sconce of dried flowers. There were little bits of knick-knack here and there, mostly antique Satcon stuff from the grand old days, but also some Mexican onyx and a leaded glass of the Madonna and Child. And you just couldn't miss the two-foot-high teddy bear in red over-alls that sat on the floor next to the enter-tainment console. It was a big eyed bear, looked actually like an ursine Lauren, and it was worn from use. It was a working teddy bear. Jesus. The rest of the place was straight-on space singles.

Rattan mats covered the floor. The aluminum living room table, stamped and bolted, had been glue-inlayed with silacachips and on it was a small terra cotta cup bearing various brands of cigarettes. How much of this stuff had already been here when Lauren Potter had arrived to arrange it in so charming a way I did not know. Nor could I guess how much of it she had shipped in from elsewhere. That was an expense of course, and Potter was only a G-3 so even with an overtime load and some heavy off-hour differentials, her pay couldn't have amounted to more than 600IM monthly. I am always amazed at how people other than myself manage to live so apparently above their means. Especially young people. Resourcefulness, I guessed, and credit. So I didn't give the anomaly much thought.

The kitchen was well cared for but not overly tooled. And no whisk. How can you cook without a whisk? But it was only a one burner affair anyway and I guessed that Ms. Potter was a subsistence chef at best. The coldbox, empty but for two mean looking yellow apples, a couple of process tubes, and a nearly full jar of mayonnaise confirmed that. I checked the cupboards and found a simple service for four, a pitcher with a cow on it, a box of toothpicks, and a swizzle stick from a place called "Mr. Big's." I pocketed that.

The bedroom was decorated in Japanese modern, and contained nothing but a bed and a bud vase. The floor had been painted mahogany. On the wall was a single watercolor print of two horses; fillies, gamboling on the hillcrest. The closet was empty or nearly so. The one or two items I found in there—a work jacket, a cotton skirt, a single glove, and a knitted sweater—were all either stained or frayed or, in the case of the single glove, useless. That didn't agree with the shape of the rest of the place. Nor did another pile of shabby stuff I found in the bureau behind the horsey wall hanging.

I went back into the living room and sat down on the couch and rummaged through the cigarettes in the terra cotta until I found a Fatima and I lit up.

The terminal, which I'd saved till last, stared blankly up at me from the face of the coffee table. I flicked it on. The smoke from the Fatima curled up around my eyes as I began to play with the buttons of Lauren Potter's life.

As expected, an awful lot was scrambled, buried deeply in the access codes Potter had used for various areas of her computer day-to-day.

It takes a kind of touch to play with someone else's terminal. The central program is the same for everyone but the sub-routines each individual evolves are idiosyncratic in the extreme and virtually all personalized data are processed through those sub-programs. It is not just looking up what was purchased and where and who was talked to and how often and so on. It is more subtle than that.

For one thing, there are seven classes of access clearance from crypto down to civil. For another, certain job classifications demand specialized inputs. But mostly it is simply a matter of personality and computer literacy.

Some people scramble things that others print right out. Some scramble in a perfunctory way, easy to reassemble. Some slam an iron door. Then there's the operating level.

You can ask a terminal who I am and, depending on the operating level you're working on, get anything from name-rank-number to the chemical breakdown of my mortal coil. Certain people habitually work on certain levels, necessary or not, effective or not. Others are all over the lot; high-tech shoppers can be bubble-headed diarists. Then, there is style.

I'm not quite sure what I mean by style except that it is something we all have, like it or not. Look at it this way; there are a thousand ways to find the answer to any one question, each one different, and the patterns of the ways you ask your questions will tell you a lot more about yourself than any of the answers will. That's your style.

So, reading a person's terminal, really understanding it, can end up giving you a lot more than broken access codes and uncovered private entries. It can let you read a person's mind. It can let you *grok* a person. Sometimes, when the mood is right, I can do just that. I thought I did it with Lauren Potter.

As a fleet agent I had entry to her primary codes, so it only took about an hour of access breaking and unscrambling and plain guessing. I didn't get all of it. Maybe only 20 percent of it. But that was enough to sketch a picture.

I came up with a girl who loved her job at the news service enough to deeply protect every info-bit about it, sensitive or not, ditto for her sister. It also came up with a girl who, for the past week or so, had been going about life as if she planned to go truant. According to the retail receipts and traffic movements, she was getting ready to hole up for a few days, maybe a week. Classic truant profile. And, classically, it was now my lot to find her, roust her, scare her and get her back to her job a chastened and rededicated worker. But a few things didn't agree with that.

For one, her preparations had included everything but food. Truants always hoard food. Paying cash for something so basic virtually was an advertisement of truancy, and you couldn't eat on credit; what if your number was flagged? You couldn't exactly waltz into the employees cafeteria either. Number two, too much was gone from the room. All the clothes for instance. If Lauren Potter's missing wardrobe was as impeccable as the rest of her life, then the stuff I'd found had been left behind as a way of deep-sixing it, which meant that Lauren Potter had taken everything she wanted. I began to suspect that a lot of the rooms' spartan look owed itself to that too and as I sat sucking on my fifth Fatima, circles and squares of dust patterns began to wink at me from shelves and sills where other items taken by Lauren Potter had sat previous to her departure. Even the teddy bear, I noticed now, had two little clasps, one on its chest and one on its right arm. Perhaps a smaller, more portable Bear of Little Brain snapped into place there, a bear that Lauren Potter had taken, leaving the larger one behind. Spit.

I was disturbed that I hadn't seen them earlier but I went easy on myself and wrote it off to having been in such a hurry to get to the computer terminal, which was where I got still another argument against Lauren Potter having gone truant.

Going truant simply did not seem Lauren Potter's style. I didn't get that at all. She was simply too classy a kid. Maybe, I thought, that was why her sister had been so quick to buzz up MA&P when the girl turned up gone. She was no truant. I fumbled in my pocket for the recodisc that had the "s'cuse me" on it and inserted it into Lauren Potter's term. "Identify," I said.

"I'm sorry," the term printed out in electronic green, "civil level is not authorized for personnel search."

"Ah shut off," I snarled and I pocketed the disc again and took a last look around the place. It didn't argue of foul play. You can tell when a place has been neatened after a little rough house. The stuff may be all back in place but the scratches and gouges remain. This place had been neat from day-one. And there wasn't a hint to the contrary. Not a truant, and not a victim of a struggle. This case was getting interesting. It certainly was not "a simple truant case."

Maybe someone *was* following her. Maybe she got scared. Maybe a lot of things. But Lauren Potter left this room under her own steam. If, it turned out, that she was also under a Stoner then where was the ransom communication? A hundred complicated scenarios run through your head at a time like this. She's been murdered and shot off into space and the fiend has cleared out her place to make her look a tru. She's been kidnapped by someone who is bringing her to a place so far away we won't see the ransom note for a week. Too far out? Nothing is too far out to be gone altogether. So you log these things in the gray matter just to keep your mind open and also so that on the one case in thousand the solution turns out complex and colorful rather than simple and dull you can tell yourself, "See? I thought of that!"

I stubbed out the last Fatima in the terra cotta and prepared to leave. With most investigations, especially truant investigations, you really expect to get your answers from the subject of the probe itself, in this case Lauren Potter. And, as with most investigations, you expect those answers will turn out as simple as they can be. I was looking forward to them anyway. I closed Miss Potter's door.

It was getting dark. Late afternoon was becoming early evening, GMT, and the lighting of Satcon, that portion of it which was still functioning, shifted to display that in an artificial but still comforting way. Overhead lights slowly dimmed. Streetlights brightened. At least the ones that worked did. I walked through the garden at the edge of Lauren Potter's neighborhood and the dozen or so lights that lined the woodform bridge across the pond were all ablaze and reflected in the clear waters of the final-phase recycling pool. I tried to imagine Lauren strolling here, having her dinner on one of the benches rather than in her room, lying on the grass beneath the sunlamp. She had carved for herself such a pleasant little niche on dreadful Satcon. And now she was gone.

In my pocket I had several receipts and names from her term to look up and run down. I decided to put at least a dent in the list before turning in. Checking into billets would have killed off the evening so I shouldered my carry-on, hefted my overnighter, and trudged off.

At Parker's, the clothing shop on "C" Ring, a salesman remembered her face from my little mug shot and smiled involuntarily. "Pretty girl," he said. She came in often but he never saw her with anyone but another woman, "an amazon," as he described T.J. Janes, and he hadn't seen either of them recently. He told me a sad story about how declining sales had cut back his staff to himself and a part-timer. "An absolute ape of a welder," he bleated, "an ape." I agreed it was a pity that even private entrepreneurs were allowed no input in personnel selection for their own enterprises and left, juggling my luggage.

The matron at the beauty parlor did about as much for me. At the produce market a hispanic smiled at the sensaround and said he knew her. "Oh, yeah. She come in here maybe one, two times a week. She takes apples, kiwi, cabbage, this stuff here."

"Kohlrabi," I said, "it's another kind of cabbage."

"Oh yeah? She take that. One, two times a week. Most times with this big broad. Formidable. But not last week."

"She didn't come in last week."

"No she came in. Oh yeah. For this stuff. Kohl . . ."

"Kohlrabi, it's a kind of cabbage."

"Oh yeah. She come in and buys some of that but not with the big girl. With a guy."

"What kind of guy?" I asked trying not to look too excited, "What did he look like?"

"Oh yeah. Big guy."

"That's all?"

"*Real* big. Formidable."

We went round and round for awhile on how big was big and how formidable was this big guy, and finally I got out of the young man that the guy was a little bigger than me, light hair, dark blue eyes, "a nose like this" (flat), "and pink skin. Like an Irish, you know? Oh yeah!" And he had big hands. How big? "Oh yeah! Real big!"

I moved on. The Communication Section promised little since nearly everyone had long gone for the day. The two workers still there, an older woman who introduced herself as the advertising sales representative and a young man who, like Lauren Potter, was a reporter-editor. He expressed surprise that anyone should be asking after her. Especially someone with luggage. I had passed myself off as her uncle hoping to hear something about the big guy. I got this: "Today and tomorrow are her weekend, didn't you know that?" It was the older woman speaking. "Oh sometimes she comes in anyway—she's a very conscientious girl—but who would think it odd if she didn't?" Who indeed?

The young man, making gab, agreed that Lauren was very serious about her job. "You know," he said, "some of us, me I guess as well as anybody, we come up here just to get into space, you know what I mean?"

I did. I had.

"Well Lauren is space-gen," the young man continued. In the 2070's that still had clout. "She comes from Lunar somewhere. The question was asked of the older woman rather than me but I answered it anyway. "She's here," said the boy, "because she loves her job. I admire that." I nodded away. "With her background and talent she could be anywhere in Earth space. She could even have a safe birth Out there, if she wanted." I nodded some more. Then I pressed on for minutes of the same without turning up a mention of the big guy, or much of anything else for that matter, except that the kid obviously had a case on Lauren Potter and was too much in awe of her to admit it even to himself. I said goodnight and consulted my list of names as soon as I hit the door. A few more visits with people who knew Lauren Potter began to shade on the picture I had sketched on the term in her living room. Quite a girl.

"My but doesn't she grace de place?" said an old negro gent, burlesqueing himself or his job, or Space Treaty quotas, or his great grandfather, or something. He caressed the broom he was leaning on in the deserted employees cafeteria. That was all he said, but it about covered it.

My Lauren made her own clothes or else retailored or redesigned the things she and sister bought at Parker's; a not unnecessary task given that she was so small and sister was so tall. But she seemed to enjoy it. She had taught sewing for a while, as a volunteer at the Centenarian Center, helping the retirees to mend and make their own. The Centenary had been good to her. Maybe it was her way of paying back. They certainly loved her there.

Her main claim to fame was that she'd once launched a one girl crusade in the news service that pried the lid off a fruit labeling swindle that was going on Satcon. When I heard about it I seemed to remember something in the Lunar editions. It had turned out to be part of an Earth Space wide problem that eventually wound up in the Florida courts. I think the bad guys all got off in the end but that didn't diminish the effort put in by everyone who had dragged it in to begin with. Someone at IPI got a Halberstam for the story but there were a lot of people on Satcon who couldn't be convinced that the credit didn't belong to Lauren Potter. And this was more than a year later. Next stop, "B" Ring's .4-G inner circle where the old folks lived. They'd know Lauren Potter.

Lauren Potter had been on Satcon for a little over a year and a half. I knew that from T.J. and the personnel print out, but an old timer at the Centenarian Center remembered it up for me anyway. His name was Tarbox. His Lauren story was this.

She had come up to file a report on the treatment of the 100ers based on some guy, dead now, who had first come into space on the last mission of the last Enterprise-class NASA Space Shuttle. She was working then for Sunday, a weekly supplement, and was fresh out of Stanford, doing features and profiles and like that. "Met her sister right here, she did," Tarbox croaked, "and she stayed."

I must have registered some surprise because the old man leapt to cover for Lauren Potter as if she were a granddaughter. "Oh you know kids these days. Nobody stays in one place anymore." Actually "we kids" *can't* lose touch, now that the DataNet is complete. Not unless we want to. So it must have been an estrangement. But so what. I didn't press the point. "They'd lost touch somewhere back. But they found each other, right here on Satcon, and you know it turned out the luckiest thing for us? Her sister is in security, you see? And we were having a lot of trouble with the quality of stuff we were buying. I was on the procurement committee then, not now, now I just sit. But we weren't getting what we were ordering, what we were paying out for. What we were getting was cheated. On food and equipment, on medical, you name it. Well Lauren got the goods on them on the fruit, oh the fruit was bad. And so she did her story but she also got on the back of that Janes doll, the security lady, and she stayed on her till I don't know what happened but we began to get a decent shake. Now those two . . . Batman and Robin."

"Who?"

"Holmes and Watson," the old man tried.

"Gotcha," I said.

It was dark when I left the Centenary after sharing with the old man a Centenary dinner of stewed seaweed, mashed potatoes, a fried fishcake and a dish of peach halves in sugar syrup. Tarbox asked me for a couple of cigarettes, one for later, and I gave him the rest of my pack. He asked if he'd see me again and I said, "You never know."

You never do, so why say no?

I had six names left. One from my print-out, four from people I'd talked to, and one on a swizzle stick, Mr. Big's.

I realized I had been avoiding the last and my present urge to pack it in and quit for the evening was highly suspicious.

When the information you have presents a nice clear consistent picture, you sometimes hate to mess it up by finding something contradictory. I had a nice picture of Lauren Potter. Leave Mr. Big's until morning, I thought. But then I had a second thought. I had already decided that she was not the truant type. Also, that she was much too classy to split without leaving some word for those who loved her. That was my picture. Perhaps it was wrong? Maybe there was another side to the girl? Maybe she had split on a news story real fast, I argued for her, and she didn't have the time, or even the freedom to tell anyone. Maybe she was undercover? With all her clothes and half her bric-a-brac and a little teddy bear. Come on, Bockhorn, give us a break. I headed for Mr. Big's. I needed more background.

Mr. Big's was at the end of a long double-back to where I had started out: in the North Port Mini Ring. It was tucked into the narrow service area, diagonally across from the gift shop and next door to a cleaning service and a tool shop. It was a bar.

The distinguishing feature of the place was a four foot long holographic image of its name, written out as a signature, with a rotund, high hatted publican laying across the top of the thing. It hovered about a foot or so above the mirror that backed the small marble bar and gave the place the look of a New York City saloon of the 1990's. Except for customers at one table, the place was empty.

I activated the bar menu and pretended to scrutinize it while I listened to the table. A half dozen men, drinking beer or popping chem, sat around it arguing about somebody named Duffy Warren who apparently wasn't among them. The argument gave as good a picture as any of the bar and its clientele.

The men were all skippers and officers off the different ships and trains in the port. One appeared to be a skytrain man in civvies. That would make him a Six Sister man, though which line he worked for remained a mystery to me. The rest were all independent operators.

This was about the time when the indies were starting to become a real force. Using old and nearly derelict ships renovated from the garbage heaps of the Six Sisters, and then working their way up to small one- and two-car trains purchased new at discount yards, the independent entrepeneur had become a staple of station life, not to mention a menace to navigation, a threat to authority and order, and a pain in the collective butt of MA&P and the rest of the Sisters.

About all that kept the "tramps" even

nominally in some kind of order was the myriad of interspace regs with which they had to comply. One of them, bilging, had become a sore point on Satcon. That is what the argument at the table was about.

Rates of bilge had skyrocketed at the station. The men continued to pay, but they bitched mightily. They also talked about other ports of call, and avoiding cargos bound for Satcon. That's where the table divided into argument.

Half the men said that what was happening on Satcon could happen anywhere and if something wasn't done to stop it they would soon find port after port being closed to them by prohibitive expense. The other half just tossed up their hands and prepared to give up Satcon for lost. "And good riddance to this place," said a Scot, "I leave her to the big asses and spewing particles of the MA&P Skytrains and those bilious-blue Cosmoflots, may they waddle into Satcon's middle one day and split the whore in two." The table laughed until it became clear that nothing was funny.

That's when someone brought up Duffy Warren again, the man who wasn't there. Warren, it seemed, was going a third way. He was bilging himself, with a crew pressed man-by-man, day-by-day at dockside.

"And has he gotten his certificate yet?" one of the skippers asked, meaning had he been cleared by Satcon Port Authority for off loading.

He hadn't. His cargo of mariculture had

about another two weeks before it rotted in its hold. Warren had been tied up in port for nearly a month. "He won't pay," said an officer.

"He can't pay!" argued another, "Not and break even—forget about turning a profit —for his trip." Given the way indies operated, that meant there was a good possibility his ship would be confiscated for debt.

The fault, everyone agreed, was that instead of the three independent bilger companies that used to work North Port, there was now only one. "Big's hands are tied," said a skipper.

"Tied to that bilger company if you ask me," said another.

The argument steamed on for a minute or two longer, long enough for me to find out that Mr. Big was well enough connected to various parties in the Port Authority that he sometimes expedited the obtaining of the necessary certificates. At least he used to. Now he was either on the outs, as half the table maintained, or else, as the other half believed, on the *in*.

"It's on the table Big!" the skytrain man called out; it was a signal for all to rise and exit. A couple of them nodded to me on their way out. The rest were surprised to see me there and eyed me as if I'd heard something.

I swung around on the silicaform stool and faced the bar. I checked myself out in the mirror making the face I usually do, the one that accentuates my chin and furrows my brow. Not bad. I stopped before I got carried away with myself, and it was just as well because as I was reaching across the bar for a napkin and a couple of big blue low-grav olives a pair of curtains parted to my right and from behind them stepped a man who could only have been Mr. Big.

He had the appearance and demeanor of a quarter-ton elf; in the .2-G he moved like he was wearing ballet slippers. A few people move into a low-G environment and immediately start letting it all hang out. Bigelow certainly wasn't one. He was a *born* fat man.

He took the folding stuff off the table with the empty glasses and slid it into his pocket. Then he sidled behind the bar, this with some effort, and tapped out a no-sale on the antique digital cash register. Then he made a note on a pad, returned the pad to the tray with a flourish, returned the tray to the register with a bang and whirled to face me. "Do something for you?" he said and flicked his eyebrows. I made him to be somewhat more substantial than the twinkle in his eye was to have you believe. Mr. Big was a man who knew things. The trick would be getting them out of him.

I scanned the chemicals and the taps and ordered a pack of Fatimas and a beer, no carbos. He drew the beer. I got right to the point. "Seen her?" I asked, sliding the sensararound across the bar as he set down the glass. The beer sloshed lazily. He took up the face of Lauren Potter.

"Who's giving the quiz?" he twinkled.

"An old friend," I said and gave him a cock and bull story about having been a professor of Miss Potter's Earthside at Stanford and I was looking up all my old space-gens for a reunion but she wasn't using the name she used at school and all I knew about her was she lived on Satcon and hung out at Mr. Big's. It was a loud enough lie so that he could believe anything he wanted to believe.

"Pretty girl," he said.

"I didn't ask for a critical judgment," I said, "just some recognition. Besides, she's heavily committed, to a big bruiser. Irish. Maybe you've seen him?" He shook his head no, no, no.

"I dunno *perfessor*," Mr. Big said, "girls come and girls go. I run a bar, not an I.D. line up."

Had I hit a nerve? Sometimes you can aggravate a guy into telling you something and I wasn't above that sort of thing. I kept at it.

"Big crowd tonight," I said, scanning the four empty barstools and the half dozen empty tables. "Pretty girl and a big blond gorilla would be hard put to go unnoticed."

"It's crowded on weekends," Mr. Big said, and no matter how hard I tried—we did go back and forth for awhile—he just kept right on twinkling. "My name's Bigelow," he said, finally. "Yours?"

"Amos Stargis."

"Well Professor Stargis maybe I can help you and maybe I cannot, but let us give me a little test and see how I do, okay?"

He picked up the sensaround and hesitated a second to give me a chance to nod my assent, which I did, and he sidled back out from behind the bar and disappeared back behind the curtain whence he came.

I took a sip of beer. The curtain moved as if someone was behind it, perhaps taking a peek at me. I took another sip and turned to give whoever it was a good look. Presently the curtains parted and Mr. Big came back out with a frown on his twinkle. "Sorry, I seem to have failed I'm afraid. I thought maybe someone on the staff . . . but . . ."

"That's alright," I said and I took some money out to pay for the beer, but before I could slap it to the marble he said, "I'll play you for it."

"What's your game?" I asked.

He led me around the tables to an open area in the back of the bar. On one wall was a hundred-year-old Seeburg jukebox full of Johnny Mathis and Olivia Newton-John on real vinyl. On the wall opposite was a vending machine of smiliar vintage that dispensed beer-nuts and candy. And in the middle was a table for bumper pool. "You're on," I said.

I had misspent a good deal of my youth on the bumper pool tables of UCLA's Jerry Brown Student Center, but even accounting for the fact I hadn't played much in years, Mr. Big had me at a disadvantage. Clearly he played quite a bit. The table was about the only item in the bar showing any real wear. And when he drew his third shot I saw that he had picked up the impossible knack of playing the almost nonexistent antispinward drift.

It is really the odd little subliminal thing that here and there hints at the artificial nature of the gravity: the way water pours in a slightly distorted arc, the way a coin balances, and the way a pool ball, when properly played, can behave improperly, even accounting for low grav. While I was bumping bumpers, my rotund and chuckling adversary was weaving them. And all the time he was pumping me for Lauren Potter. I let on to be more interested in the game than in the girl and after a while he got the message, and quickly ran a few balls to finish.

I paid for two beers, though I hadn't finished the one, and prepared to go home. "May I make a suggestion?" Mr. Big asked as he shuffled back behind his bar and hit the cash register to deposit my two IM.

"Suggest away," I said.

"USSC is just up the way. The Command is not exactly the Royal Canadian Mounted Police but they might be of some service. The MP's. You know what I'm saying?"

"I didn't say the Potter girl was in any trouble," I said, playing the professor.

"I didn't either," Mr. Big twinkled. I know a curtain line when I hear one. I hit the bricks . . . or whatever.

Back on "A" Ring I followed the signs of my

room; they were shaped like old Holiday Inn
signs except they were painted blue and had
"MA&P Personnel Billeting" stenciled on
them in white. The route was also, according
to another set of signs, the way to the USSC
Main Station. I paid as much attention to
them as I had to Bigelow's advice about
dropping in at their Mini Ring booth.

There was something wrong about Mr. Big,
I thought. I was certain he knew Lauren
Potter, certain she'd been in there. Why would
he want to hide that? And why would he want
to know so much about my interest in the
matter. He certainly hadn't been very cool in
going about it. Maybe she had skipped out on
a tab? Or maybe it was just the lascivious
interest of a fat old man for a sweet young
thing he'd seen and lusted over in his saloon.
Bigelow made my skin crawl. Satcon made
my skin crawl. The USSC station was coming
up on my right. I debated with myself about
keeping the promise I'd made to T.J. Janes
about going full hush and Janes lost the
debate. I wanted to wrap this up and get the
hell out of this tacky place. I wanted all the
help I could get, quick. I turned USSC's latch.
It was locked.

A small note by the "assistance" phone explained: "We are out at the moment. In
emergency call LT P.B. Obermeier 68991 or
Master Sergeant Larry O'Doul 39478 or
68290." I laughed out loud as I punched up my
old friend O'Doul. He laughed out loud as he

let me in five minutes later, even carried my bags through the door for me.

We talked awhile about the old days, basic training, military training, the breaking of same. We had come up together in the Command, O'Doul and I. Military-police trained. For four years anyway. That's when he re-upped and I got out to attend Fleet Academy.

We had run into each other a time or two on different jobs and we'd always hit it off pretty good.

"Always good time. Expect same again," said O'Doul, a slab faced, no-necked monstrosity of a man who talked in the clipped pattern of a military communique. "Welcome Satcon. What brings?"

We yocked around a bit. I told him about my last case. He told me he'd been assigned to Satcon about six months ago and wasn't happy about it yet. I came to the point.

I took out my terminal and played "s'cuse me" for him. He shrugged and said he didn't think his equipment was any more sensitive than mine. "Play again," he said and I did. He seemed to be studying it. When it was finished he asked, "and who'd you say gave you this?"

"Didn't," I said, impossible not to pick up his banter, "promised full hush."

"Respected," he said. "Don't think I can help though. Insufficient phonemic material for positive I.D. You know 12 phonemes required for voice print to stand up in court."

"I don't need court-positive," I said. "I'm just trying to find out who the hell this guy is!"

O'Doul winked. "Against regs," he said as he inserted the recodisc into his master console. "Give it a try anyway . . ." He spoke to the machine. "I.D. check. All points. Insufficient material. Run anyway. Execute." There was a three second wait as the console digested and processed the meager voice clip fed into it. Then the screen began to print out, "Insufficient phonemic material to—" "Damn machine can't speak English."

O'Doul hit a button to stop it. Then slowly: "Court-positive not necessary. List possibles inversely on distance of last known location from Satcon Station." There was another three second delay and then the screen turned out 55 possibles in Earth Space, 9,337 on terra firma itself, and 7 in the rest of the system.

Too many names. O'Doul narrowed his instructions down to "Satcon Visitor" and the list narrowed down to seven possible. Then he got downright crude; narrowing that down to "Satcon visitor, present month, full ident," gave us this:

"Cobb, Harry W. Also known as Carr, Coyle and Cabino. Age: 40. Height: 75 Inches. Weight: 230. Hair: Blond. Eyes: Blue. Race: Cauc. Indentifying Features: none." I studied the picture in the upper left quadrant of the screen. "ARMED!! Should know: Ex-carrier agent (Fleet Grade) MA&P, Freddie Laker. Out of Service (Honorable) Jul 4 2060. Suspected ties to organized crime family of Caputo (Cocoa Beach-Titusville). Arrests for assault Jul 19 2061, Aug 1 2062, Feb 7 and Apr 18 2063, and Jun 20 2065. Arrest for manslaughter May 8 2067. Arrest for murder Sep 1 2069. For other arrests, lesser charges, see file 30M888-Cobb. Convictions: None. Repeat: ARMED!! No outstanding warrants. O'Doul cut the machine off in the middle of a prompt for 30M888-Cobb.

We printed out a mug shot. O'Doul looked at it with a sour face. "This yegg on Satcon?"

I shrugged. "I'll let you know."

"Do," O'Doul said, "I like to keep myself informed. Lt. in charge kind of a jerk."

"It's just you and him up here?"

"Had a clerk. Truant. Two months ago. Found out, week past, shipped to Belt on an indie. Awaiting repo now." Standing job assignment be damned, I had a certain amount of sympathy for a guy so fed up with Earthspace that he'd up and leave. True he would no doubt die out there; the Belt was rough. But then maybe he'd get rich first. Maybe even *instead*. I wished him luck. As for O'Doul, I wished him all I could wish the rest of us slobs. "Hang in there," I said.

"By thumbs," he answered, and closed the door behind me.

Walked briskly now to billets. Didn't notice further Satcon detritus or else had gotten used to it. Took five minutes for the voice in my head to stop sounding like O'Doul, by which time I was signing in at the MA&P employee quarters. The receptionist, a blue haired old bag in harlequin glasses, was pleasant and precise. I left a wake up call for ten hours and she spoke "0812" into her desk vocoder. I told her eight o'clock would be fine. There was a porter on duty but no one knew where he was. I carried my own bags, as usual.

From the look of the place I'd guessed right about the direction signs. The employees quarters were once a Holiday Inn. It had closed down sometime during Satcon's decline, and the MA&P hospitality people, recognizing a good layout when they saw one, just moved right in. The bed was nice and firm. I didn't bother to unpack.

I pulled down the bedside terminal, spoke in some names I wanted to go up against tomorrow now that I had the Cobb mug all printed out, and sent a scrambler back to HQ on Lunar Base Five. I included Lauren Potter's picture, her handwriting and her voice clip, also the name of Harry Cobb. If any MA&P agent knew of either's whereabouts the past week they were to contact me full hush, crypto scramble. Did all that as I got naked.

Then I laid back on the bed and spread my arms and legs out as far as they would go. Running around all day in multi-G had flat knocked me out. Besides, for us lunies .8G is not, repeat *not* "ideal," no matter how much high-G exercise we do. The bed pressed comfortably back up against me. Bliss.

My fading thoughts were of Harry Cobb and that cute little moppet-faced girl. If Harry Cobb was in the picture, Lauren Potter's sister had every right to be a little hysterical.

Chapter Two

0800 brought a reprieve in the form of a change of venue. When I unscrambled my messages I found that nobody knew the whereabouts of Lauren Potter, which figured, but that Harry Cobb had been seen yesterday at the Orion Fronton on Constellation. I'd never been there. It wasn't the kind of place one frequented on a Fleet Agent's salary.

I called Port Authority and got a place on a 1230 flight. Then I sent a scrambler to HQ requesting that they transfer me some credit and a room on Constellation.

My term flashed in phone mode almost immediately. "Show me," I said to the machine. "Do not acknowledge on-line status." The face of an impatient-looking Perry Oxenhorn appeared on the screen. "Put him on," I sighed.

"What's up Bockhorn?"

I explained to him why I was going and why

I needed the money, sparing him as many of the particulars as I could.

When you go into particulars with the boss it always brings up questions that you don't have the correct answers for yet. I spent a lot of my early years on the job explaining to superiors why my reports contained assessments and conclusions different from those I had told them I'd been working on. Spit. If there's a superior—from group head on down to squad leader—who doesn't like to tell the guy under him that he shouldn't make premature assessments, I've never worked with him. Of course you *must* make premature assessments, even if they're wrong, so they can lead assessment-by-assessment to something more closely approximating the truth later on. This job is nothing *but* making assessments.

If I had an Intermark for every case solved by the unearthing of a *tell-tale clue*, I'd be hard pressed to buy a decent dinner. Cases are solved three ways. Far and away number one is someone rats on a confederate. Number two, someone feels the pressure of an investigation and gives himself up. Three, the assessments lead to an inescapable conclusion. Clues are important only insofar as they force the speedy occurrence of any one of the above. The trick then is not in avoiding premature assessments. It is in avoiding sharing them with your superiors.

Oxenhorn seemed satisfied. He even told me to have a good time. I told him I intended to and he answered, "pffnGH." Ox didn't mind if you enjoyed yourself—as long as it wasn't on purpose.

The phone again. This time it was T.J. Janes. "I'm on the case," I said, over my shoulder as I repacked the overnighter, out of range of the visual pick-up. Having somewhat more at stake than Oxenhorn she was somewhat less satisfied with the quick brush. She pressed for details. I ran the name Harry Cobb through her and got no response. I didn't tell her who or what he was as I didn't want her unnecessarily agitated or I'd probably find a scrambler from Oxenhorn waiting at my destination. I thought it best not to tell her where I was going either.

I skipped breakfast at the employees' mess and took it down the ring at the old "Ho-Jo's." Eggs are eggs, most times, but nobody but Ho-Jo's makes a strawberry ice cream shortcake. I don't know why I eat like that.

At home, back on Lunar Base Five, there are a lot of idle hours for carrier agents between assignments. A lot of guys drink or chem. Most of them don't last. Others take hobbies. Harry Cobb used to write. Not literary writing; hand-writing, calligraphy, with a brush pen. He was good. He used to do birthday cards and desk plaques and award scrolls and stuff like that, and sell it. Me, I cook. Real gourmet. Well, I do the best I can with the stuff available Moonside. I mean, don't get me wrong, a lot of space-gen stuff is A-okay—its the lack of variety. You can't grow truffles in Moonrock. Still, I have a pretty good rep. I won a contest once—my *pomme de terre avec chapeaux,* stuffed baked potato to you. But when I'm out, every time I order something nice I wind up disappointed. So I stick with the junk I ate as a kid. A hot open chicken sandwich is always right there. You don't have to sweat out the hollandaise sauce.

The strawberry ice cream shortcake came quickly and went just as fast. I took out a Fatima and made a premature assessment. Lauren Potter is having an affair with Harry Cobb, whom she met at Mr. Big's. T.J. Janes, big sistering the deal, doesn't like it and is trying to bust it up. She's using a MA&P agent on a truancy charge to embarrass the girl and maybe piss off the guy. She didn't register on the name Harry Cobb because that's not the name he's using with Miss Potter. I stubbed the spent cigarette into the puddly pink remains of my breakfast, gathered up my carry-on, and made for North Port, ready to prove myself wrong as can be, but just as ready to be right on the nose.

Two hours later I was snug in harness, buried in Lady Agatha's *Murder in the Calais Coach*—I swear to God I guessed it on page twenty—and just as I finished, there was Constellation, cartwheeling gracefully up to meet us.

It looked better than its' postcard. It wasn't the newest of the stations; Nebula, which opened last year, was newer, but Constellation was still the grandest. Unlike Nebula which suffered a bit from the latest prol-utility rage that was sweeping space architecture, and making everything look a little like contemporary extrapolations of those awful old buildings that line New York Metro's Avenue of the Americas.

Constellation was classic optimal function-alism. It was a star station, five huge units that looked small because of the distance separating them: one globe, two cylinders, one that looked a bit like a chinese lantern (that one was a high-energy factory and need-ed maximum surface), and one Christmas tree connected by monocables, invisible at this distance, to a large central ring about which everything carrouselled.

It was good to be getting back to a geoform station if for no other reason than the breathing space it promised. Creating spin-G on the bolo model rather than the spinning wheel meant that each accomodation unit could be segmented perpendicularly to the plane of spin, creating floors that ranged far and wide in all directions to the limit of the radius of the unit. This produced an environ-ment difficult to distinguish from terrestrial buildings of similar size (about forty stories) except for the beneficial effects of the slightly lightened G: a poet's leap from the restrictive space of the circular station's endless hallway.

Of course there was another reason to smile

upon the contemplation of Constellation. One of the units circling majestically with its sisters—each of which bore the logo of a corporate heavy-hitter: I.G. Farben, Genen Tech, Pepsico, and U.S. Power & Minerals. The Christmas tree, of course was the Orion Fronton, the playground of space.

We sped past it silently on our way to port and I reflexively touched the Stoner and the Magnum. Another Skytrain had prior control ring port clearance and that caused us to back off and seemingly circle twice within the plane of the spinning shapes, like a roulette ball running counter to the wheel. Fantastic.

I was travelling under an identity, which meant I was no longer cleared through entry. So when the squad of ink-pad assassins came aboard I bit the bullet and complied. It amounted to filling out "Amos Stargis, age forty, immunized for everything, had chicken pox age twelve," maybe a dozen times. Then it was stamp, stamp, sign, sign, stamp, initial, sign, stamp. About as necessary as suspenders on a snake—and as useful. And forty of them could have been replaced by a coded-card slot. Ah, well, it makes jobs, I guess.

After a few perfunctory questions about my job—Amos Stargis, my low priority cover, is a public relations man from Intel in Houston—and my purpose—Stargis is usually "fact finding" but this time I used "vacation"—I was sprung from the ship and stepped into one of the transparent cars that ran from the port ring out to the five accomodation units along the monocables that held the place together.

The glass car was about as deluxe as you could want and cleaned and polished to a brilliance that made you examine your fingernails to make sure you were worthy. It held about thirty. There was another ahead of us, six more behind. A door before us opened and we slid forward a bit. It closed. A wheeze of pumps. Another door opened, a tiny puff of escaping air and like a bead on a string we silently glided out of the port into open space and headed for the Orion. God's heaven was all around us, above and below, pressing itself against the glass. We had just enough time to get past the ooh-and-ah stage and then another double set of doors opened sequentially. We had arrived. The glass doors opened and a moving-walk whisked us from God's heaven to man's, or at least one version of it: Orion Hotel.

It was big, it was bright, it was bejewelled. A leggy redhead in a sparkle-silver bikini hefted my carry-on from the desk to the elevator, down the deep-red carpeted hall, and through the door to my room, which sprang open with a whoosh at the touch of my thumb. I thanked her with a couple of Intermarks and my best smile. She palmed the I-marks and scissored out. I unpacked.

On the night table was a genuine two-dimensional ink-printed brochure illuminating the wonderful facilities of Orion Fronton with a request for you to put your terminal on Channel D for the full show. I ordered a hamburger from room service and flicked on the tour.

Eight separate casinos, 24 bars, twelve restaurants, four holo theatres, a dog track, a game park, two theme parks (Wild West, and World War Four), one Total Electronic Environment, and ten thousand guest rooms. Fade in bugles with fanfare: "And of course, the spectacular Orion Fronton, itself."

"Located in the Port Center, a fast and fantastic tram ride away, the fabulous Orion Fronton, queen stadium of the International Jai Alai Federation, accomodates 8,000 spectators in her grandstand, her two internationally famous restaurants, and the renowned Galleria high above the playing area. As you sit in heavenly one-half G, the finest Jai Alai players in the J.A.F. play weightless for your sporting pleasure in the electrifying six-wall mode that has made Earth Space Jai Alai the international pastime. You have watched and wagered on terminals in New York Metro, Kobe-Osaka, Jo-Berg, the capitals of the world and the worlds of space. Now see the game as it is meant to be seen, up close and personal at the . . ." blah, blah, blah, and so on.

I rang up the desk and asked for Harry Cobb's room and to no great surprise learned that no Harry Cobb was registered. The hamburger was prime and I put it away without a fuss. The beer could have been colder but I was quibbling. This place went right to your head in a hurry. I wasn't immune. Later maybe I'd risk the nearly inevitable disappointment of their *haute cuisine*. Right now I had work to do.

I decided to tour the casinos. Just a hunch that my luck was running plush. It was, but not the way I'd hoped. Two hours of wandering around with a thousand I-marks worth of chips—thank you Ox—left me plus 250 immers in black-jack winnings, but nothing in the way of a Lauren Potter or a Harry Cobb. I made another assessment. I was not taking this job seriously. I got down. Vacation time was over. I headed for the desk clerk back at the lobby.

My luck came back immediately. It was a man. I work better with men than I do with women. Especially than I do with the kind of women who were striding around *this* place. "Would it be too much trouble to get a look at your register," I jumped right in amiably, "I'm with Intel Public Relations and—"

The man looked up with a drawn expression that just begged me to stop, which I did. "Please," he said, "see the desk clerk." He indicated leftward with a jerk of his head. Craps. The desk clerk was a six-foot stunner with the eyes of an alley cat and the lips of a cosmetics poster. She was sitting behind a high desk so I couldn't see much else of her, but I could make a fair guess. I tried to keep my amiable, semi-chemmed smile intact. She matched it with one of her own. I asked to see the register. Still smiling, she replied that it was against hotel policy. I explained that I was a public relations consultant and I was on the make for a name drop or two for my client. She smiled, *that's nice*. I peeled off 25IM and she handed me the book, a genuine old-fashioned register book—the Orion was class—then walked quickly away from the desk so that it would not be her lookout if someone squawked.

I knew I wasn't going to find anything remotely resembling Lauren Potter or Harry Cobb. I was looking for something else, and I found it on the second page. Registered were a Mr. and Mrs. H.C. Cobbler, he's so clever that Harry Cobb, and they'd been signed into the book by the unmistakable hand of the calligrapher of Lunar Base Five. I returned the book. The desk girl returned immediately. I asked her to page Mr. Cobbler.

"I'll be waiting at the fountains," I said, but of course I strolled right on past the dancing waters and hid myself, detective style, against a potted palm across the lobby. I had a nice view of the desk from there. I waited.

Two women came up to the desk, asked something and walked away. An old man ambled by. Then nothing. Ten minutes went by, broken only by a young couple checking in. The girl at the desk started to make my page once again when a fortyish man approached the front and rang the bell. She stopped in mid voice and leaned over to the man as if she were asking him to repeat something she hadn't heard. Then she looked up, glanced over at the fountain, and then all around, and then shrugged. Perfect. Except that the man was not Harry Cobb.

She leaned over again and asked the man something else. He shook his head and left. He walked right past me, a confused look on his face. But not Cobb's. The girl did not repeat the announcement again. I walked back up the lobby to the desk and re-fixed my amiable grin.

I couldn't believe I'd come up empty. I knew that handwriting. And that name!

"Hello there," the desk girl smiled, eyes aflash, "I was looking for you."

"Did Mr. Cobb . . . ler show up? I must've missed him. I had to take a—" I had to take another look at that book and my hand was already fishing my pocket for another 25 immer and I was just hating having to pay twice for the same thing even if it wasn't my money. It was a matter of professional pride, which, it turned out, stayed intact after all.

"No-no," the girl said melodically, as if it were one word, "Mr. Cobbler called to say he'd be in the Fronton for the remainder of the afternoon. Would you like to leave a message?"

"Yes I would," I said, cheering up. "Tell him Herbie Peck was here; but I can't stay, see, because I'm checking out."

"Number?"

"Just a hello. We did time together Earthside at Lewisboro State Pen."

Her smile wavered just a trifle and then, suddenlike, turned genuine. "Sure Mr. Beck, will do."

I walked away snickering. With any luck this would be the last time old Harry used the name H.C. Cobbler.

Trams ran through to the Fronton in Port Center every two minutes. I had to run to catch mine, unwilling was I to put even the tiniest delay between myself and the little reunion I was planning with Harry Cobb. The glass doors closed. The station doors opened. We glided out.

I must admit that even for a jaded old spacer like myself the ride from the hotel to the Center was something special. The bubble car is transparent in *all* directions. So as you accelerate along the doped crystal monocable the effect is of sitting unsupported in the middle of the Big Nothing. Orion recedes, Center looms, and the rest of Constellation keeps its majestic whirling distance. Earth was eclipsing all but a clip-shot of Luna. Ninety degrees over, the bubble was almost opaqued by the Sun which glared, though not eye-burningly, through. Beyond that, well, the star-splashed universe beyond is enough to make even Bockhorn wax poetic. I'll spare you. But it was fantastic.

It being about the middle of the game-card, the car was pretty much empty, so dismissing the star-splashed, pin-wheeling universe I took time to think. And what I thought was this. I was still not taking the job seriously.

The man's got connections to organized crime, I reminded myself, and a record that filled up a screen. Add to that there was the chance he'd added kidnapping. But despite all the foregoing—and I supposed this was reason I was so light about the deal—I was looking forward to seeing old Harry again.

"Frontonnnnnnnn . . ." the disembodied voice announced over the intercom. I stepped out of the car, into the tram station, and bounced lightly over to the ticket rotunda. Attendance was automatically toted on a printout screen over the main box seat window. 6,873 not including me. I had narrowed my search down to one in that.

The fronton was arranged so that it spun independently and much faster than the rest of the Constellation configuration, hence the relatively heavy spin-G. Neat and very expensive trick, that. Along the walls were the betting windows, the two internationally famous restaurants and the Galleria, which it turned out was a pale impression of a Florentine sidewalk trattoria. The Z-G playing area was in the center of the Center, seemingly counter-rotating so that wherever you sat the rectangular glass playing box turned swiftly above your head. The rake of the chairs and chaises of the main grandstand brought you face to face with what was a really exciting kind of ball game, if you like that kind of thing.

Taking the speeding *peolotas* on crazy bounces of the ceiling and floor and walls, the floating *peloteros* really put on a show. But of course it was mostly for themselves. The great bulk of the people looking upward were here for the parimutuel windows. All they cared was that if they had a ticket for player number 6, then number 6, whoever the hell he was, should win the game and pay off on the ticket. Or if they had a 6 and 4 quinela, then 6 and 4 should flash up on the winners board. Or the trifecta or the boxed number or the SuperQuadrifecta Royale (available *only* at Orion Fronton), it didn't much matter who did what to whom with the *pelota* as long as the numbers kept being generated.

I watched the show for a quarter of an hour and got as bored with it as I could be so I whooped it up a bit and put down 5IM on number one in the fifth game. Then I started making my rounds.

At the first of the international restaurants —the *Côte d'Azur*—the bartender was pouring a rum and coke so I asked for the same. Didn't matter much as I rarely drink anything stronger than beer when I'm working, but the guy who was taking delivery was moved to speak, which was of course why I had so ordered to begin with.

"Drink rum and coke?" the man said.

"All the time," I said. He nodded. He was maybe my age, a little heavier set, definitely no better looking. He wore a New Orleans Red Sox hat and a jacket of genuine imitation vinyl. What such a guy was doing in such a classy joint I didn't understand. Still don't. "A lot of people," he said, "think its prol, working class, gauche, not too sophisticated, blue collar—"

"Yep," I said, indicating that I'd gotten his drift and that he might consider going on to whatever.

"Well you know what?" he said, fixing his drink with an uncertain stare, "it sure as hell is. They drink it you know," he said, indicating the *peloteros* bouncing around in the rectangle above us. "A game that's been played like that for five hundred years doesn't change so much just because you stick it up in Z-G. You'd think the space-gens would take it over, but they're still all Basque you know. Just like they been forever. Oh well, one of them isn't. One of them is Lunar . . . how come they don't have a third-world quota for Jai Alai?"

It was a test of my politics. "Maybe Basque is considered third world?" I offered. It didn't satisfy him, but then it didn't turn him off either.

"I've lost two jobs to third world quotas. Black and brown bastards. Either they don't want to work, just sit around and collect their money out of your taxes, or else they do, and the other bastards turn around and give them your job. Am I right?"

"You'd think in space," I said, "there ought to be enough jobs and money to go around." I didn't mean anything by it but to stir the conversation-pot. Still, I blush to confess, such sentiments had meant something to me, once.

"I lost my last job because of a safety ruling. They said I wasn't safe. Company couldn't afford robots. They went broke. I'm out of work now you know . . ."

He went on. I learned he was a space-gen, born on Lunar One. Also that he liked being on unemployment now better than he liked working. Also that he thought he was unique in that, "for a guy who isn't third world, if you know what I mean. But hey, why shouldn't I get a free ride now and then?" Why not, indeed?

He liked the Basque I had wagered on—Urrea at three to one—and as we lazed our eyes upward we could see that "four" —which was what he called Urrea—was in fact moving up on the board.

"I like him," he reiterated. He also liked the sensaround of Lauren Potter. He looked at it from all angles; even flipped it over and gandered the back. He whistled. "What a teddy bear," he said.

It was an expression I'd never heard but when I took the picture back I realized that was because it wasn't an expression at all, but an assessment. Lauren Potter did look like a teddy bear. No that's not quite right. She didn't look like a teddy bear at all. What she did was feel like a teddy bear or, as my great grandpa Buddy Bockhorn, the old Santa Barbara surfer, used to say, she gave off a lot of teddy-bear vibes . . . man.

The bartender agreed but he hadn't seen her either. My drinking partner asked for a second look but it was only to take a second look and so I thumbed my tab and walked out.

Up above me Urrea rocketed the *peolota* past some guy named "Little Gorichio," or "eight," and won up getting himself posted the winner, enriching me by 15 Eye Marks. Not a bad game at that. So I strolled to the windows. That is when I saw Cobb.

He was at the 25IM window, buying tickets for the next game, several of them. He said something to the man behind the lexite who said something back which seemed to annoy Cobb who swept up his tickets with both hands and turned to go.

The years hadn't changed Cobb much. They hadn't improved him at all. He looked leaner than the 230 that the mug print had made him, but he would have. A lot of Harry Cobb was hard.

Maybe he looked a little hunched over now, not from age or fatigue or anything like that, but bow-necked, the way you get when you're really onto yourself about something, pressing. The way he'd palmed the tickets and stuffed them in his pockets like they were silverware he'd just swiped off his hosts dining room table didn't speak real well for his mental state. Then, as he turned to go, his eyes locked, just for an instant, with mine. I smiled. He looked right on through me. But I mean straight on through! Then he walked.

The look was to haunt me for the rest of the case. There had been something crazy in it, something wild, something feral, hunted and hunting both. But the lock was broken.

I couldn't tell whether he really hadn't recognized me or had and was trying not to let on about it. He just wheeled and heeled, propelling himself up the aisle without much care for the people he moved out of his way. Some turned to watch him go. One guy, when his feet were back on the deck, made to go after him, but took a look and changed his mind. I, naturally, followed at what I thought would be a safe distance if, in fact, he had made me at the ticket window. I stopped at the entrance to the box seat area and let on to be scanning the crowd.

He turned down the center aisle and headed for the good seats, red plush chaises with little drink tables that folded out between them, and not once did he look back.

At the red section he went to a chaise, took out the tickets and fanned them out on the little table; then he took out a portaterm and laid it out next to the fan of tickets and started speaking into it and punching in numbers at the same time. The chair beside him was empty. But I was willing to bet my day's winnings on who'd show up to claim it.

I realized that the winning ticket was still in my pocket but it didn't bother me too much. I had switched games and, for right now, it looked like my lucky streak had switched right along with me.

The bell rang to signal the end of betting for the sixth game but it could just as well have been a cue for our teddy bear.

She came float-bouncing down the far aisle with a fistful of her own tickets and the same face I had sitting in my pocket, only better. And she was tinier than advertised too. Teddy Bear.

Cobb, craning his neck, saw her as she turned up the walkway to her seat. He didn't smile. But he didn't frown either. He reached up and took her tickets and returned to punching up his terminal. She sat down and watched him. He ignored her. So by and by she put her feet up on the chaise and lay down, eyes closed, like she was taking in some sun, ignoring the game that was now in furious progress above her. Cobb finished with his terminal and put it away. Then he leaned across to her and gave her a little peck on the lips and then lay back on his own chaise.

I patted myself on the back. I was right on the nose. But I owed T.J. Janes a little more sleuthing than a quick one-two to cover my first hunch, so for the sake of the report if nothing else I decided to stick around for the rest of the afternoon and call in over dinner. That meant I'd have to spend an extra day at the Orion, but a man has to put up with some inconveniences for the sake of his work.

I actually did scan the crowd on my way back to the windows to pick up my winnings from the fifth game. There were a few high rollers around in genuine-looking animal skins and pinky rings. There were a few like the guy in the Red Sox hat. Most were upper-middle types: managers, technicians, store owners, farm maintenance bosses. A face caught my eye. A young guy, maybe twenty five, who I knew from somewhere and yet didn't. Hard to tell with him, though; he was so nondescript. He wore a work hat, work gloves, work suit, work shoes, face to match. He could have been anyone or anything. But I knew him, or at least I'd seen him before, that face. He lit a cigarette and turned away from me to go. I turned away too. When I decided to look back he was gone.

I cashed in Urrea and hung around the windows for a while perusing pulch. There was plenty. Earth Space, even then, had much to offer a girl watcher, even one like me who'd been raised in the Bronx and educated at UCLA. But round about none were anything like the one walking up the aisle this instant: petite, feminine, cutie pie, little sister; pick one yourself. Teddy bear?

I have friends who hunt. They tell me there is a moment in the game when the quarry first draws close enough, and that this moment causes a hollow feeling at the base of what makes you a male. I hunt people, so to speak. I have felt that moment also. But never so strong as when Lauren Potter walked past me on her way to the windows. That was a moment I wanted to extend, if only for another moment and, since it wasn't exactly beyond the purview of my job, I decided to give it a shot. There was more to this Lauren Potter than met the investigative eye. I cashed in my winnings and fell in behind Miss Potter at the Ten IM window.

"Who do you like?" I asked wi.h the same smile and swagger I had shown to the desk clerk.

Lauren Potter turned around, checkeᵈ me out, decided to answer. "I don't really know," she smiled. "Who do you like?" If the tone was flirtatious it was general rather than particular. It told me more about her style than her interest in the guy talking to her.

"You mean that you don't know who you're going to bet on until you get on this line?" I asked, sounding interested in her, which wasn't hard. "Is that smart?"

"No," she said and her eyebrows arched up as if that had just occurred to her too. "But I can't tell who's good and who's not so good. Can you?"

I shook my head and pursed my lips and tried to let on that she and I were in some kind of benign conspiracy together to beat the system by knowing nothing at all about the game we were betting our money against. She giggled. My mouth got dry.

It is one thing to trust your instincts and quite another to understanding what it is you are trusting them to tell you. Let's analyze this: Why suddenly dry? Okay, we know that I'm not real great with pulch, and anyway lots of guys get nervous. We also know that the particular pulch in question was traveling with one rough customer. But I'm no marshmallow salesman either. Cobb may have been brawny enough to hold my attention, but nowhere near was he to drying up my squawker. I decided it was the girl.

"What's your name?" she was asking.

I laid out the Amos Stargis routine for her scrutiny and she seemed happy with it. "What's yours?" I asked, relaxing into the identity of the other person; it always seemed to loosen me up.

"Debbie Cobbler," she lied, "from Houston," she lied again.

"Me too—I'm from Texas, I mean," I lied. Wonderful conversation, real getting-to-know-you. "You on vacation?" I asked.

She nodded and stepped up to the window to purchase win tickets for numbers one, two and three, a one-two-three trifecta, and a boxed bet on one, two and three in all permutations. She peeled off a thousand IM to pay for the load.

"Bye," she said.

"Wait!" I said and quickly laid down a tenner, "three to win," and picked up my ticket. "That's a system isn't it?" I said, turning away from the ticket window to where she was standing, sorting out her handful of pink monolars. She nodded impishly. "Is it a secret? How does it work? Can you—"

"Is he bothering you?" said a voice. It was loud, but it was hard, too, an aural blow. It was designed to make you want to go away. It came from Harry Cobb, who was standing between the two lines of betters. I was about to go "Hiya Harry," and have a real good laugh when he stopped me with his: "Who's your friend?"

It was addressed to "Mrs. Cobbler," but it was meant for me.

"Amos Stargis, meet my jealous husband, Henry Cobbler."

I offered my hand. His stayed by his side. If she was attempting to soothe him with applications of gentle irony it wasn't working very well. "I was curious about your system. I—"

"It's a private affair," Cobb said evenly, "handed down from generation to generation. My family is very funny about it." To Lauren: "I shoulda told you that."

"Lissen, my line is public relations and I'm here on business which means I'm on expenses so if you two—"

"Nice meeting you Stargis," Cobb said and he took Lauren Potter by the arm and led her off.

"Catch you later," I shouted at his back. Cobb turned and glowered at me. I smiled as stupidly as I could. "Later," he growled.

They returned to their seats. She handed him her tickets and laid back and closed her eyes, thoroughly ignoring Harry Cobb who was busy again chatting up a storm with his terminal. Not once did he lean over to talk to her, about me or anything else for that matter. Still, I was sure he had made me. Positive.

When I turned around I saw that young man

again, the one with the face I'd seen before. Often, as an agent for a carrier, your very stock in trade is faces, names and faces, and rarely if ever did one elude me. But this guy was so standard-bred. I decided to give him a tumble.

Above my head a Basque gentleman named Flores was cutting a wide swath through the sixth game of Jai Alai and, as he was wearing the number that was printed in black on my ticket, it appeared I was still riding the seam of the beam.

I pulled out a Fatima, walked over to our friend, who I now thought of as *the face*, and asked him for a light. He looked at me like I was speaking to him in Bulgarian and he was listening in Eskimo. The boy was a tail. I read it from the top of his crew cut to the heels of his sock-covered slips. After a pause to collect his thoughts, he produced the necessary lighter.

"Are you following me?" I asked him clean and simple.

"Who *are* you?" he asked, trying to sound tougher than I suspected he was.

"You tell me," I said sounding even tougher than that.

He reached into his pocket and pulled out a cardfold and flipped it open. "J.A.F. Gaming Commission Security."

"Hmmmmn," I nodded, vaguely embarrassed. "You watching anyone I know?"

"You cleared to know if I am?"

"Thanks for the use of the flame," I said.

"Don't mention it," he sneered as if it was some kind of insanely clever comeback. I shrugged and walked off to the window to collect my winnings on Flores. The wages of sin come seldom without strings, but having forgotten that for the moment, I was prepared to pack it in and go home.

Cobb and Potter were away from their chaises. I made her at the ticket window. Him I didn't see at all. I lit out for the tram back to the hotel. There was a short line and no car, but the second man on that line was Harry Cobb. There was a small booth out by the station which sold tickets of all denominations to the late arriving and early departing itching for that extra shot, and the glass car pulled up with a *whoooosh*. I stepped inside and secured a seat with a view of Cobb at the "Courtesy Booth."

When it came Cobb's turn at the counter he did a lot of talking, took a lot of tickets, and peeled off a lot of money to pay for the privilege. The glass doors of the tram closed and I was *whooooshed* into space and to the hotel.

Back in my room I took a shower and a sun treatment and lay down naked on the bed, composing what I was going to say to T.J. Janes. Then I rolled over and spoke her access code into my term.

The screen showed her boy at the console downstairs. He gave me the secretary upstairs. I threw a towel across my most personal gear. She gave me Ms. Janes.

"Go, Bockhorn," she said.

"Okay," I exhaled.

"Did you find her. Is she all right." The questions were asked as statements, her expression as flat as her voice.

"Yes to both," I said. Then I must have paused, because my client said, "Bockhorn." Again, no interrogative lilt.

I said, "Your sister is alive and well Ms. Janes. I saw her this afternoon. I talked to her."

"You did."

"For a minute or two at the betting windows of Orion Fronton."

"Orion Fronton?"

"That's where I'm calling from, Ms. Janes. Does your sister often gamble, or is she on a flyer?"

"A what?"

"Lauren Potter, for reasons I have not ascertained, has taken up with a man who calls himself Henry or H.C. Cobbler but who's name of public record is Harry Cobb."

"You asked me about him."

"Right. This Cobb is a yegg, a bad boy. He's got no convictions but he's been accused of enough stuff so that plenty of the stain has stuck. You catch my drift? He's not wanted for anything that I know of but he's not the kind of company that our Lauren, from what I've gathered, normally keeps. But she doesn't appear to be kidnapped or anything of the sort, either. In fact she looks happy as a clam. Calls herself Debbie Cobbler, the misses. They kiss and hold hands, the whole thing. Unlike your sister, Ms. Janes, this Cobb fellow is no teddy bear; a peck on the cheek from him means something, if you know what I mean, and she's been pecking back. Now listen up because this is the thing—"

She didn't want to hear it. "You haven't detained her have you?" she asked. "You haven't told her who you are?"

"No to both," I said, "but here's the thing and you better listen to it. The yegg, this Cobb, appears to be betting some kind of system up here. I assume Lauren is not a frequenter of the parimutuels?"

"Come again?"

"What I asked you before, does she gamble? Does she game?"

"Never." Indignantly.

"Well she's going at it heavily now, with this system. It is something I have had neither the time nor the energy to figure out, and even if I did it would like as not prove out to be legal—there's no law yet except the mathematical ones against outsmarting the Gaming Commission—but that would be besides the point anyway."

"What *is* the point, Bockhorn?"

"That a Gaming Commission operative is tailing Cobb, or her, or probably both."

"What does that mean?"

"It means that if they are doing something illegal, if they are pulling strings somewhere or taking information, then maybe he'll tumble to it and so it means that as my client I feel duty bound to ask you what you want me to do. You sent me to find her. I found her. You wanted to know if she was safe. She's safe. At least as safe as a girl like her can be keeping company with a yegg like Cobb. But there's this new thing now, and I want to know what to do about it. Instructions, please."

"Wait there. Keep an eye on them. Follow them if they leave. I'm taking the next flight out."

"That's it?"

"That's it. And please hold your report till I get there."

"Pleasure," I said, and it was. It gave me still another night on the town, compliments of Ox. "See you when you get here. Ring up Amos Stargis."

"Who?"

"Me."

"Oh," she said, catching the drift. "Undercover."

"Hang it up," I said and she did. I punched up room service for another one of those prime meat burgers, and then personnel for an escort, red headed. Bockhorn was in the mood, and on the tab.

Chapter Three

T.J. Janes checked in at ten the next morning and I met her in Orion's Skybar Lounge for breakfast. Fantastic view of the other units of Constellation, backed up by a stately, pinwheeling universe featuring Earth, Sun, and Luna, in a two minute cycle. Very pretty, a stately gavotte; kubrickion. But the food's not much.

Janes picked over the California Buffet like she was trying to find the berry that wasn't poisoned, wound up with some carrot sticks, a mound of sprouts, steamed seaweed and several slices of protose bread. I had some scrambled eggs with fried chicken. I also did most of the talking.

"I let them run on their own from about five, that's when I called you, until maybe ten. Then I pulled their string."

Janes looked up with a mouthful of sprouts.

"I checked out what they were doing during that time. And it wasn't much. They left the fronton about six. Had dinner in their room. He made a call to Arizona but there was no answer. I have a man running down who was on the other end of that call, or supposed to be. You following me so far?"

She nodded.

"Then they came out of the room, went to Buccaneer Bill's, the clam bar on the seventh level, had some drinks and went to the casino next door, the Golden Nova, and dropped a lot of money playing roulette, or at least *he* did. Your sister *won* a lot of money but then she was playing red and all Mr. Cobb played was black."

"What," Janes cocked her head, "does that mean?"

"I don't know. You want me to find out? That's why I called you, to find out if you wanted me to find out. Now here you are and here I am and here we are and the question is exactly where are we? Where do we stand, Boss? I'd be happy as a loon to spend the rest of my month in this joint watching after your sister and running up a tab, but I'm going to have to make a report eventually and someone is going to want to know about this Cobb and his, let's say *odd*, gaming system and if your sister's—"

"Where are they now?" Janes cut me off with an earnest look that at least seemed to promise that we were at long last coming to the point.

"They got up early this morning and ate right here, this is my second breakfast, and went out to the fronton to catch the first game."

"They're there now?"

I nodded.

"Let's go there," she said.

"And do what?" I said. "What am I supposed to do? Play bodyguard?"

"If you like."

"Well I don't—"

"You are assigned to me Mr. Bockhorn," Janes reminded me, "That doesn't mean you have to like me. It doesn't even mean you have to like what I ask you to do."

"It does mean I ought to trust you," I said, to get a reaction.

"Don't you?" She reacted almost seductively.

"Sure, Boss," I said, backing down. "But I could probably trust you just as easily and be more helpful if I knew what was going on."

"You will," she said and headed off for the fronton.

When we were closed inside the train I asked her for her plan and she either didn't want to tell me or else she didn't have one. I settled back into the silicaform. I was along for the ride.

The fronton was a little more crowded than it was the day before. The tote at the ticket window ran up 7,934 as we bounded inside, close to capacity. The third game was coming to a close and the eventual finish of the numbers was beginning to take shape, little roars and groans greeted each point, rising in crescendos of gambler's angst. "Ah you bum!" someone called out when one of the players missed an easy shot. "That's why you're being investigated, crook!" To my knowledge the J.A.F. was under no such investigation, but it was always being rumored about that the game was fixed, so everyone always assumed that investigations were underway, drawing to a close or else, at least, on the planning board. Of course it didn't work that way at all. And of course they all kept wagering anyway. "Where are their seats?" T.J. Janes asked. I pointed out two empty red chaises.

"They were there yesterday. If they're ticketed there now they're probably at the betting window getting ready to cash in the third game and pick up for the fourth."

"Can you delay him long enough for me to talk to her?"

I said I'd give it a try. I told her to stay there and keep an eye on the chaises while I went off to find and detain Cobb. "As soon as you see her, go in and get her."

"How will I know you've got the gorilla?"

"You'll have to trust me," I said.

I left her standing by the walkway with her program and her jitters. I headed right for the courtesy booth by the train station, certain Cobb and we had crossed paths on our way in. We hadn't. I got a little nervous. I didn't want him busting up the little *tête-à-tête* my client had planned. It would have made me look bad.

He wasn't at the betting windows either. He

wasn't in the Galleria. I lengthened my stride to go hit the two internationally famous restaurants and suddenly grabbed a door frame and pivoted gracefully, I hoped, into the last in a line of phone booths when I spotted Cobb in a booth in the middle, arguing furiously with someone on the other end. I caught my breath, put an imaginary quarter-mark into the phone, pulled down the privacy screen so no one would be suspicious of my blank vid, and rang up my mother.

I kept one eye on Cobb's phone booth in the middle of the line and with the other eye scanned the crowd for my girls. Fantastic. I could make both at the same time. Lauren and T.J. were too far away for any kind of lip reading but I can read a pair of flailing arms as well as anybody. T.J. was hot.

Cobb twisted around in his booth, still arguing with whoever, I guessed the Arizona number. Then he hung up. Spit.

I left my booth and bounced down the line of phones clumsily enough to bump into the big ape as he left the booth. He was hard, as expected. Maybe a touch more angry, but within reason. "Hiya big guy," I grinned, "Howya makin' out?"

"Excuse me," he started, but I kept after him.

"Lissen I'm ripe for a system," I said.

"I said *excuse me* Mac," he said.

"No really, lissen up," I said, holding onto his arm and sounding just a little squiffed. "Lissen, I'm losing a bundle and if you got something I'll buy it from you. Just level. I tell you what. I'll stake you with whatever, name it."

He looked at me with a coldness I fully expected to break into a grin and say, "Hey Bockhorn!" or something like that, but it didn't. It stayed cold, unrecognizing. If he hadn't wanted Lauren Potter to know there was a MA&P agent nosing around then I could buy the day-before's performance of selective amnesia but we were alone now. The mug really didn't make me. We goddam *trained* together!

Out of the corner of my eye I could see that T.J. and the little sister were still going at it in a big way. I needed to make some noise. He beat me to it.

"Get the goddam hell off my arm!" he bellowed like he'd been wounded.

I caught T.J. watching us. Whatever it was she was flailing about she now speeded up. Lauren shrugged.

"Aw come on, guy," I whined at Cobb. I can be sickening.

This time Cobb didn't shout. He said real low, "If you don't take your fingers off my coat I'm gonna break them off and hand them to you."

Down the slope of the seats T.J. broke away from Lauren Potter. I took my hand off Cobb's coat. He turned and walked away, tippy-toeing menacingly, a combination of the low-G and his anger. T.J. avoided him like a pro. As he walked down the aisle, she slid across

and got lost in the crowd. I waited. She didn't
reappear. I took a guess on the Skybar and a
couple of hours later she finally guessed right
and showed up in the lounge, still shaken.

"Your move," I said, as she steadied herself
on the barstool.

"Bring her in, Bockhorn," she said pulling a
Fatima from my pack. I lit it for her. She
inhaled like a man.

"Bring her in for what?" I asked. "There's
still no law against having a good time. The
way I figure it Lauren Potter has got herself a
boyfriend. The fact that she didn't show up on
Monday means that she took herself a three
day weekend. If you could get arrested for
that we'd all be in leg irons from the first
summer we get our working papers. The fact
that she cleared out most of her clothes and
whatnot means that she's probably thinking
of moving in with the guy. My guess is
Arizona. I had a trace in to some guy the big
ape keeps calling there, a real estate man in
Tucson."

"Well then if she is planning to move back
to Earth then she's in violation of contract.
Pull her in for that."

"Negative. You ever try to *prove* what
someone was thinking? Besides, her contract
isn't with Satcon. She's lend-lease, darling,
even as is your humble servant. Her contract
is with Newsservice on Lunar and as a sender
she comes and goes as she pleases. Maybe
they can do something about her, but as long
as she's turning in work they won't, and for

sure, whatever she's doing, you can't."

"Bockhorn, I have a duty to my sister."

"To meddle?"

"Yes."

"Let's go home Miss Janes. I'm beginning to feel guilty about the tab I'm running up. Aren't you?"

"You know Cobb."

"I thought I did."

"Okay he's got some appeal, some magnetic charm, some butch."

"If you like that type," I said. "What's the point?"

"Well you can see how your sister could be taken in by a man like that."

"I haven't got a sis—"

"Bockhorn! For God's sake!"

"Okay, okay. No I would not like my sister messed up by a yegg like Cobb. Man threatened to give me a manicure. Okay, what do you want me to do?"

"Pull her in."

"I *can't* pull her in."

"Well what *can* you do?"

"Well, maybe we could jawbone her."

"Good, that sounds fine. Let's jawbone her."

"Maybe," I said. "I don't know. Let me nose around this betting system and maybe I can find something lousy, and then you can threaten her with whatever. That'd be up to you. I won't do it."

"That'll be fine. You get me the jawbone and I'll swing it."

I told her to go back to her room and play a movie or whatever. I'd call her as soon as I knew something worth telling.

It was afternoon now and I dragged myself back to the train and settled in for another ride back to the fronton. Lots of things ran through my mind the same time. The face of Lauren Potter, the face of Harry Cobb, the face of T.J. Janes, the face of Perry Oxenhorn. I thought about leaving the force. The doors closed and we whooshed off to the center. As my body grew lighter I brightened a bit. When I went through the gates at Orion I was on the case again, for whatever it was worth.

It was between the fifth and sixth games and I knew the red chaises would be empty. I walked quickly to them, keeping an eye open the while. Two drinks stood half finished on the table. Below the chaises and between them was a pile of losing tickets which I bent down and swept into my pockets. I was about to go into the cracks of the chairs when: "Still after the system?" Lauren Potter's melodic voice froze me in my bent over position. I fashioned my Amos Stargis face and smiled up at her. "Thought I dropped something," I said standing up.

She picked up her drink from the table, sipped and said, "I'm going for a bite at the *Côte d'Azur*. Be careful about Harry. He's more jealous of the system than he is about me. He'll be back to watch the last game any second now. Bye bye."

She whirled off. If Harry was coming back

here and she was going to the *Côte d'Azur*, then that was an invitation; wasn't it? I gave her a decent interval and then headed up to the restaurant.

She was at a table in the rear. "Hello," I said. "Hello Amos," she said, "did you get any public relating done?"

I managed to laugh for her. It was easy. "May I?" I asked, tugging at the back of the chair across from her. She shrugged. I sat. She had silver eyes, or they seemed so in that lighting. "I never saw anybody more determined to lose his money," she said.

"I like to play," I said, looking around.

"Don't worry about Harry," she said, "We never come here. We go to the Galleria. Besides, nothing would tear him away from a game once it starts."

"Doesn't your husband tell you not to talk to strange men?" I asked.

"Yes he does."

"And you don't pay any attention."

"He's not my husband."

"Oh," I said.

"Which doesn't mean he wouldn't knock your block off anyway."

"My block's on pretty solid," I said and then told her about Harry's threat to break off my fingers and she laughed. I laughed. Get to work Bockhorn, I gave myself a mental kick. We went at each other for fifteen minutes over a plate of canapes and a carafe of wine. She said her name was Debbie Greenslade, a twenty five year old divorcée who had caught herself, this morning as it were, in the middle of a similar mistake with Harry Cobb, or Cobbler as she called him. She had met him three weeks ago. "I must be drawn to the type," she said and didn't try to hide the peek she took at my shoulders. She and Cobb had gone on one of those whirlwind Earth-Space affairs. She decided to move in with him. Now she wasn't sure.

"What about him?" I asked.

"He's sure," she said.

I tried her on the system again and she gave me a cock and bull story that was all out of whack. Either she didn't know the system or she did and wouldn't tell. Either way that didn't tell me whether or not it was legal and when I asked her directly she simply didn't answer. Instead: "How long will you be staying at Orion?"

"I'm not sure. Few more days at least," I said.

"Well, maybe I'll see you again," she said.

"You never know," I said, rising as she did.

"I'll walk myself back," she said.

"Right," I said. And she left me with the tab just like it was a hundred years ago. A good sign from Amos Stargis's point of view. I sat down and took out my tickets and began sorting them into games. Then I pulled out my terminal and went to work. Between happy hour and dinner time I must have tried thirty different scams with the tickets and none of them paid off any money. If it was a system, legal or not, it was a loser. I paid and left.

In the lobby of the hotel Mr. and Mrs. Cobbler were leaving for the evening, dressed in the nines, he in a black spandex with string tie, she in white ruffle blouse with matching shorts and diamond skinlays. Another 25immer dropped on my lady friend at the desk got me the following. Mr. Cobbler was spending the evening in the Golden Nova and left word that his Arizona call should be put through there. I thanked her and headed for Cobbler's room. Cobb's I mean.

It was a bigger room than mine, had a full-access multisensorium and a bar. Also, when not opaqued by sunlight, a nice view outside its bay window of Earthrise at even numbered minutes. There was some output on the screen that he hadn't bothered to blank, numbers and such tapped out hastily, but I could make nothing of it. The terminal's inner self yielded more nothing. It hadn't been scrambled; it hadn't even been used except as a calculator. The drawers produced the usual stuff, socks, underwear, hers hardly more exciting than his, devoted as she was to white cotton—expensive taste, that, but it always left me a little limp in the go-motor. The closet was full of clothes. The shoebag was full of shoes. The pillows full of pillow stuffing . . . and one flattish lump, which I removed. It was an envelope, unsealed. I opened the flap and took out a packet of some two dozen photographs, in livid, lurid sensaround. Lauren Potter and her sister T.J. Janes. In one way they were walking through the artifical garden I'd visited on Satcon, holding hands. In another they were sitting on the couch in Lauren Potter's rooms, holding hands. This one appeared to have been taken from the sky-light. So were the rest. My eyes began to bug.

Lauren and T.J. naked, holding hands. Lauren and T.J. naked, kissing. Lauren and T.J. on the floor, sodomizing each other. Lauren and T.J. . . . the progression was hypnotic.

I looked at them again, and then again. My mind was racing in several directions at once. Pieces were starting to fall together. I fumbled the 3-ds back into the envelope and turned to tuck them back under the pillow. But I heard a sound that stopped me and as I turned for the door it was already moving. I glanced at the window—like I was going to leap into space without a hat, but that'll give you an idea of the state of my mind at the moment—I thought about going under the bed or into the closet. Where can you hide in a hotel room that Charlie Chan's #1 son hasn't already thought of? My hand was half way to my Stoner when the door opened up for Harry Cobb, whose darter was already drawn and aimed for my most delicate gear. Next time, I told myself, first pull Stoner, *then* look out window.

"Who *are* you Stargis?"

"Lissen, you're absolutely right. I don't know what came over me. It must be the chem but I got so wrapped up in that system of yours. I . . . I . . . You're absolutely right." I rambled on awhile trying to sound as much as

I could like a compulsive drunk blundering after the betting secret of all time, rather than the stupid careless gumshoe that I was. I hoped like hell he was buying because it was sure as heat-loss that my old pal Cobb was into something a little heavier than cradle robbing. "Put those in the drawer," he said thickly.

"They came from under your pillow," I said, trying to sound the rube.

"In the drawer," he said, and took a step closer. His Stoner was a foot from my middle. I debated going for it and luckily lost the debate. I opened the drawer and put the envelope inside it, and with a fearful lurch Cobb brought up a meaty leg and a black size-sixteen and slammed the drawer shut on me. I exhaled sharply as the fingers of my right hand snapped at the knuckles with a pop I could feel clear down to my toes. "Who are you Stargis?" he repeated, his big foot still pressed against the drawer with all the weight he could muster, which was substantial.

"I'm . . ." I tried to think of something good to tell him but it was hard discussing the problem with myself because of the bell clanging in my head and the fact that most of my circuits were tied up on the other problem. Luckily, I'm not the fainting type. He lifted his foot an inch and slammed it down again. "Who?" The pain from the mashed bones rubbing against each other tore through my arm like a breaker and crashed against my brain.

If he didn't know who I was I wasn't going to tell him, but I decided I'd better come close enough to have it wash. "I'm a private investigator," I said.

"For who!" he bellowed ungrammatically and punctuated it with another kick at the desk drawer.

"I'm . . . with . . . the hotel," I wheezed, hoping he'd noticed *the face* that I'd tumbled to at the fronton and picked up on him the same way. Maybe he'd think we were both house dicks.

"Bull!" he roared and hit the drawer again. It didn't hurt so much this time but I howled like it did—and stuck to my story:

I was a hotel dick working on a complaint of illegal-systems betting. It fit with Amos Sturgis, it fit with *the face*, it fit with the facts, and it seemed to fit with Mr. Cobb. He took his foot down.

"Make you a deal," he said.

"Shoot, I mean, what kind of deal," I said, taking my hand from the drawer. My fingers were swollen up like sausages, and several colors of blue-green-yellow.

"I'll leave. Check out. No more problems. You tell them you rousted me. That's how you hurt your hand."

"Otherwise?"

"Otherwise I'll put your other hand in there."

"Good deal," I said.

"Okay, square," he said, "sorry about your hand."

"Just check out tomorrow morning," I wheezed through the pain, pretending that I was pretending to be tough. "I said okay, square," he said. "Just give me tonight. Okay?"

I left with my right hand in my left and more than I wanted to know rattling around my head.

It was ten o'clock, two hours later when T.J. Janes came down to meet me at the bar in the Skybar lounge. "Did you get anything?"

I lifted my claw and she covered her gasp with a cough. At the station hospital they had strung me up fine. Each finger was bent into a plastic cast and the hand was splayed with a palm pad from which wires spoked out, umbrella fashion to the fingertips. Other, smaller wires fed electricity into the fracture-points. A big white claw.

"Your manicure?"

I nodded.

"So he *must* be hiding something," she said.

"Pull up a chair sister," I said and she did.

Chapter Four

The Skybar was in full swing now. A small guitar combo was playing on the bandstand. Couples danced. Earth was swiftly setting in the mirror behind the bar. That was OK, it would be back in a minute. "Gin," T.J. ordered, "neat." I stayed with my half drained beer, no carbos, and organized what I wanted to say. She was trying not to look at my claw but it wasn't easy for her. I let her struggle awhile. When the gin came she belted half of it down right away.

"You should have leveled with me," I said.

"I did," she lied.

"I'm unshockable lady. I've been on the job for a time. It wouldn't have stopped me for a second. But I gotta know what's what if I'm gonna be of any help to you. Am I clear?"

"Yes," she said, uncertainly.

"Also," I said, "I don't like being played for a sucker. It makes me feel bad. It leaves me in the dark. Things you don't know are there." I threw my claw up onto the bar for emphasis. She looked away. "Let me see your terminal," I said.

"Why?"

"I want to find out how deep we are into Cobb's little blackmail scheme."

"Lauren's being blackmailed?" She nearly leaped off the bar stool in a surprise that looked genuine enough to be real, if over-played. I mean, she didn't knock the rest of her drink over, but only because she was lucky. I decided to lay it right out without being clever.

"Lady, *you're* being blackmailed."

"I'm what?"

"Get out your terminal," I snapped. She removed a tiny, out of character, princess model from her purse.

"Your bank account," I said. "Access it."

"I will n—"

"Punch it up."

She began to unscramble her bank account for me. "How far back?" she asked. I said six months would do. She complied. To my surprise there were no outstandingly significant withdrawals. I mentioned that to her and she looked at me and said, "See?"

I blew up as quietly as I could. For her benefit as well as mine. "Yeah I see." I fire the works at her: "I see that you ring me up and send me on a wild goose chase to find some dame who is supposed to be truant or maybe followed and I find the dame with a yegg holed up in a hotel with a bunch of pictures of said dame and yourself butt-end naked, rolling on the floor of the dame's rooms, and while I'm finding all this stuff out said dame and yegg are running around the fronton and the casinos laundering the money they're getting out of the scam."

"Wait."

"Snow, if you get my drift, lady."

"Please. What do you mean laundering?"

"My first clue so to speak. Lauren and Cobb have a system alright. It's a losing system. But it's meant to be. I toted it up. The way they bet jai alaí, the way they bet the wheel in the casinos, not even by a stroke of *luck* can they win. But they can't *lose* more than twenty, twenty-five per cent. It's a little more expensive than a professional laundry, and a lot more time consuming, but it's more fun I guess, and a hell of a lot quieter. Lady, their scam is to exchange money that may be marked. By the time the stuff gets back Earthside they'll be long gone." Sometimes I wonder why we even *have* money; what's it good for but tax evasion and other criminal activity?

"Ridiculous," Janes said. "First of all, you see I haven't paid a cent. You *see* that. Second of all, we're talking about my sister. Third of all, pictures can be f—"

"Stop, stop, I can't take any more. Go back to second of all. Who's sister?"

"Mine."

"Negative. When you were begging me to

haul her in you said, 'if she's going *back* to Earth;' remember? If you were sisters you'd know she was space-gen, Lunar."

"She went to *college* on Earth," Janes shot back like a pelotero taking off the back wall. "UCLA. She loved it there. She told me so."

"She must have visited there on a football weekend," I said, enjoying myself for the moment, "She went to Stanford." T.J. Janes' face collapsed like someone had popped the air pressure plug. I stayed at her. "Now let's jump ahead to the third of all. The pictures are there, in living sensaround. You can smell the steam. I took a careful look. You and Lauren are not hard to eyeball. And the positions were intriguing. Cobb's got them, no mistake. Now, back to first of all. Where is the money coming from?"

"What money?" she said with feigned weariness. She was stalling for time, thinking hard, but I let her. I had her cold. "Gin, neat, again," she said as the barkeep passed. She waited for him to pour it, took a belt, and turned to face me.

"Do you know what being brought up on homosex would do to my career?" she asked.

"Earthbound for repeat offenders," I said. She nodded. Homosex was frowned on in that age of straightlaced heterosexual backlash.

"Three years ago, when I first came to Satcon, I got in . . . trouble."

I assumed this to be her confession and went right on with the questioning. "So where's the pay off money coming from?"

"Satcon security funds," she said.

"Hmmm. Why'd you call me?"

"When Lauren disappeared I panicked. I thought — I dunno — I thought she was dead, I thought she was being blackmailed too, I thought she was in on it, I dunno what I thought."

"What do you think now?"

She shrugged.

"Well what did Lauren Potter tell you? Down in the fronton. What did she say?"

"To trust her."

"Do you?"

She shrugged again. I told T.J. that I had made, in the guise of a hotel dick, a "deal" with Cobb for him to clear out in the morning. I wasn't likely to find out any more tonight than I knew already and whatever T.J. wanted done she could sleep on it and have me do it in the morning. We went over the options. I could arrest him and try to keep the pictures quiet. She could go on paying. She could fess up. Could she, she wanted to know, employ me to do some freelance undercover work and maybe snatch the pictures back or do something terrible to Cobb? I told her that she and I didn't have the kind of relationship that inspired that kind of thing. She didn't seem unduly distressed. What she cared about most, when you came right down to it, was Lauren Potter.

"Do you . . . love her?" I asked.

She nodded quickly and got up to leave. "See you here for breakfast?" she asked.

"Better make it early," I said.

"Eight?"

"Fine."

She walked out of the Skybar.

I went back up to my room and lay on my bed listening to music. But I couldn't let the problem rest. Was Lauren in with Cobb on this? I couldn't believe that. Why? She'd made contact with me. To find out who I was? Was T.J. safe here tonight with Lauren knowing she was here and Cobb on the loose? I dialed Janes' room and got no answer. I leaped off my bed and started pulling on my clothes.

I knocked on Janes' door still buttoning my shirt. No answer. I pushed inside. No Janes. No signs of struggle. But no Janes. I sat on the bed and called Cobb's room hoping to find him in and therefore, presumably, harmless in the situation. He was not in. I called the desk and asked to speak to him and they suggested leaving a message. I said it referred to his Arizona call and they said they would send a messenger to get him. There was a service stairway just outside my room. I let the phone dangle and headed for the hall, and a hunch.

Two floors down the door of Cobb/Potter room was ajar. I gumshoed my way to the trestle. No noise came from within. I pushed inside. I found T.J. Janes, stretched out on the floor between the bed and the console. I checked the closet, the bed, the porthole, all the places I hadn't hid and then knelt down next to the big girl.

She was breathing. She'd been sapped.

I pressed my thumb against the bridge of her nose and she groaned. She rolled over onto one side so that she faced me and tried to open her eyes.

"Take it easy," I said.

"Bockhorn?" she said. A little rivulet of saliva ran out of the corner of her mouth. She had enough presence of mind to send her tongue out after it.

"Did you find what you were looking for?" I asked.

She nodded and tried to sit up. I helped her into an indian style squat. "Pics . . . still in drawer . . . negs in suit pocket . . ."

"I'll see if they're still there."

"Got 'em all," she said, starting to come around, "garbage."

I looked over at the refuse door on the wall, behind which was the chute that led to the incinerator.

"Should have kept them," I said.

"I couldn't," she said. "Cobb, the gorilla, came in while I was looking at them. Best I could do was dump them. Then he . . ." She knocked herself on the head with her hand.

"Let me take a look at your lump," I said. Actually there were two of them, one on each side of her head, like the beginnings of two little horns. The one that sat behind her right eye was big and blue and ugly. The skin was broken at the crown of the mound. The one on the left was superficial. I took a guess that Cobb made a desperate stab at saving his blackmail negs before they reached the refuse collector, wherever that was. Then, having failed, he roughed her up enough to keep her from following him.

"Got you twice," I said, making gab.

"He did?" she responded absently, "Ouch, that hurts."

"You're cut."

"I think I'm gonna barf," she said, "help me to the bathroom."

I helped her unsteadily to her feet. She stood there for a moment, holding my forearm, closing her eyes against what must have seemed a crazily spinning room. Then she opened them. "Wow!" she said.

The room looked like a bomb had gone off inside it. The bed was torn apart, the vase was shattered, ditto the lamps on the table and the headboard. The ceiling fixture was pulled down. Everything that had been inside something was now outside it. Except for the gray suit out of which T.J. Janes had pulled the negatives.

"You did all this?" I kidded as we staggered off to the john.

"No," she said.

At the bathroom door she propped herself against the wall and I flicked on the light. Her scream was gurgled up with her dinner and exploded out of her face and across the tiny room.

Slumped in the bathtub, his hand still clutching his Stoner, his feet tossed casually over the side of the tub towards us, lay Harry

Cobb, alias H. C. Cobbler, alias etcetera. There was no point in checking his pulse. A Stoner blast had not left much of his chest and lower jaw, and what there was hanging in strips and globules.

T.J. Janes heaved again and brought up some more of Orion's overly renowned cuisine. I tried to turn her in the direction of the toilet bowl but she was rigid. At least she had stopped scream-barfing. After a while she stopped barfing too. I cleaned her up as best I could and got her back to her own room.

There I poured her a glass of water and gave her some pills she had tucked into her bag and asked me to dig out, and suggested she take to bed. She was sitting down on the edge, the blanket pulled across her knees, when I said, "Wait here, I'll be right back, don't do anything; sleep if you can. But first, as soon as I leave, call room service for coffee."

"For two?"

"For one. You need an alibi."

"I guess I'm a suspect huh?" she shivered.

"I guess," I said, "Don't worry about it, yet."

I ran back to my room. I wanted the recodisc of Cobb saying " 'scuse me." I wanted to go back to the murder room and look around, but I wanted the place secured for as long I could arrange it. What I planned to do was call the desk from the room and play " 'scuse me" to open the conversation. Then I'd feign something wrong on the phone and switch to the terminal to print out that I,

H.C. Cobbler, would be staying in the room tomorrow, please send the chambermaid after dinner. That would give me plenty of time before the body was discovered to go through the room the way I wanted to go through it, and still have time to figure out what to do and to call Ox and to make arrangements if we had to fly out, or whatever. I also wanted the recodisc to confuse the issue later. Once the " 'scuse me" was played and identified as Cobb and the hotel desk terminal confirmed his calling at midnite—so being apparently alive during which time certain other parties could have an alibi—because my mind was racing in six directions at once and depending on the direction I wound up in, the killing of Harry Cobb *was* an issue I might want confused. T.J. *was* a client. Cobb *was* a yegg. I *was* an agent. Ours not to question why, ours not to reason why, ours but to do and die. Fine sentiment.

I thumbed my door. It clicked one time too many; I never double-lock my door. Laziness. But my door was double-locked. I drew my Stoner. A light was coming through the bottom of the door. I hadn't noticed it before, careless, but not crucial. As it happened I didn't remember whether or not I'd left a light on anyway. I stepped to the sidewall—plenty heavy enough to stop a Stoner blast—and let the door swing open slowly. No hail of darts came.

I leapt into the doorway Stoner first, held it in two hands, landed in a crouch and hollered

"Freeze!" The room was empty. I looked around. Nothing had been disturbed. The terminal, I flicked it on, then off, hadn't been read. I closed the door and turned the lock to see if it would double itself. Behind me, my toilet flushed. The door opened and Lauren Potter came out. "Sorry," she said. "I'd have let you in but . . ."

"It's alright," I said, trying to read her face. She had her lips pressed together the way people do when they are trying very hard to do something difficult and get it right. "Take your time," I said, not entirely ironically, and not even sure I was still playing Amos Stargis.

"I wanted to report a murder," she said.

"To me?" I smiled. "A what?"

"T.J. told me who you are. I suspected it anyway."

"Who am I?" I ventured.

"Bockhorn of MA&P." she said. "Close enough?"

"Close enough," I said, not playing Stargis anymore.

"*My* real name is Lauren Potter," she said, "But I guess you know that."

I nodded that I did. There came a knock on the door. I stiffened. She didn't.

"That would be coffee. I ordered some from room service. I hope you don't mind." I shook my head no and opened the door. Coffee came in. The boy fussed around with the table, eyeing Lauren the whole time, and spent an eternity leaving. Then I turned to Lauren. "Proceed," I said.

She began to pour. "Cream or sugar?"

"Black," I said.

Her hand shook. It was only a little at first. Then it was a lot. Then she dropped the pot altogether and collapsed in tears on the bed. I don't know what iron will kept me from rising from my chair and crossing over to her, from sitting next to her on the bed and putting a reassuring hand on her, but whatever it is I'm glad I've got it. What I did was straighten out the coffee service, and presently she calmed down, sat up, and began to tell her story.

"Harry is dead. The man I introduced you to as Harry Cobbler. His real name is Cobb and someone shot him. He's in the bathroom in our room . . ." she started to well up again but this time got it under control. "The pistol is in his hand like he shot himself or something."

"But you don't think he did," I said.

"I don't know," she shrugged. "I just thought of that. Maybe he killed himself? Could he have killed himself?"

"How would I know?"

"Oh God," she said. "He's been so crazy lately."

Tell me about it, I thought to myself.

"Like a string tightening, ready to snap. He thought someone was following him."

"Me."

"No not you. He just thought you were a jerk." She was looking around the service cart to see if there was any coffee left. There was some here and there where saucers had

caught it. I emptied it all together into about
half a cup for her. She added cream and sugar
herself, slowly and carefully, and I let her
take her time because I wanted her to put herself together. Finally, she took a sip.

"When did you last see him?" I asked.

"Alive or dead?"

"Last," I said.

"Five minutes ago. I came right here. I'd
have come even if you were Stargis. That's
why I . . . came onto you in the restaurant. I
think I needed someone to put between Harry
and myself. I guess I—oh this sounds
terrible—I guess I picked you. You looked
capable."

"Thank you."

"I came here because I think I may be in .
danger."

"From who?"

"I don't know. Whoever killed Harry."

"T.J. Janes?" I ventured.

"What?" she asked the question like I'd just
drifted in from Mars.

"I saw Harry Cobb about twenty minutes
ago substantially as you described him except
that when I saw him he had company."

"T.J.?"

"Stretched out unconscious in the center of
the room with two contusions, ten o'clock and
two o'clock, like this." I touched my head and
Lauren Potter winced. I returned to the
questions, keeping them gentle but serious.
She had a reasonable but not verifiable alibi
for the moments before Cobb's murder, the

kind of story that didn't help you one way or the other. Certainly not the kind of air-tight alibi you'd expect from the guilty-party type. She was just "out." Walking. Thinking about whether to come here. She'd called she said. I checked. She had. I spoke it all down on my terminal anyway in case she slipped up later on. Then I asked her about the blackmail scheme.

"T.J. is being blackmailed?" she squealed innocently. Two out of two. I rolled my eyes theatrically.

"T.J. was being blackmailed," she said, as if humoring me.

"By you?" I queried.

"No!" she exploded, hurt. Then she calmed down. "No, I wasn't blackmailing her. Actually in the beginning it was me. I was being blackmailed."

"By who?" No point in guessing now. I had finally gotten to story hour.

"Cobb," she said. "But I didn't have any real money. It was only a matter of time until he switched to T.J. She had more to lose anyway. She's way up there you know. Anyway, when T.J. got the first demand we put our heads together and . . . we came up with this."

"What?"

"I was to fall in with Cobb, it was easy, he was nuts about me. God, he was at my skylight every night. I couldn't turn around on Satcon and not find him there. It was awful. So I was to fall in with him, win him over, get the sensarounds, negs was all I needed, prints can be faked too easily, and leave. I was close, I think. He even had my clothes sent to somewhere in Arizona. Then this.''

"Did T.J. know about Cobb all along? All she gave me was a little snatch of his gab. It would have been a lot easier if you both had leveled with me from the start.''

"We did. I think. T.J. probably didn't know anything else. Whatever she gave you was what we knew at the start. We thought it best not to communicate with each other once we were doing the thing because who knew what Cobb was wired into? I didn't know much about him myself until I saw T.J. yesterday and she told me what you knew. We were in bad company, weren't we?''

"Very heavyweight," I said. "Did you get the pictures, any negatives, anything at all?''

"Nothing. Never. I thought tonight maybe, because Harry was really crazy about being watched by whoever.''

"He didn't tell you who?''

"No.''

"And no pictures," I said.

"No.''

"I saw them but I put them back. T.J. says she got them.''

"Thank God.''

"But somebody sacked the room to the seams," I pressed.

"Well that must have been T.J.''

"T.J. was surprised at the mess. Someone sacked it after T.J.''

"Cobb?"

"T.J. said Cobb caught her incinerating the prints and the negatives. If there were more of either, then yes, it was Cobb who was looking for them. But it's unlikely he'd tear the place up unless you had found them and moved them, or *removed* them, and you say no. You're not lying to me are you?"

"No."

"Then it was someone else, the someone who killed Cobb. Someone looking for the same pictures, finding Cobb, killing him. Could Cobb have had a partner? Was he cutting someone out? Was that who was tailing him?"

She shrugged. "That doesn't work anyway."

"Why not?"

"Because then who hit T.J.?"

"Jeesus," I said. The girl was fast. "T.J. says Cobb hit her."

"Wait a minute," Lauren said. "How about this? T.J. comes looking for the pictures and finds them. Cobb catches her, knocked her out. His partner comes in. He wants the pictures. Cobb says they're gone. The partner doesn't believe him. He kills him. He puts the gun in his hand to make it look like a suicide. He tears the place apart looking for the photos and when he can't find them he leaves."

I pulled out a Fatima, offered her another which she declined. I lit up and exhaled. "Did you and T.J. kill Cobb?" I asked. She didn't phase.

"I reported the body! Would I kill some-body and then report to a Fleet Agent?" The answer of course was yes. As a matter of fact about a third of all solved homicides turn out to be the work of the person who first reported the body to the authorities. But I didn't mention it: either Lauren Potter did kill Cobb or else she didn't, and was in danger of being killed herself; either way I couldn't think of a better place to keep her on ice than right by my side.

I asked her what she wanted me to do about her. "Take me away," she said.

"Okay," I said and she looked at me as if I'd just made good on every item on every Christmas list she'd ever got stiffed on. "Do you want to go with T.J.?" I asked.

She thought a minute. "No, I can't. That wouldn't be fair. To her or to me. It's over. I couldn't."

"She says she loves you." It seemed to have an effect on Lauren. She sagged.

"I can't," she whispered. "I can't do that anymore." I didn't try to pretend I understood anything but the pain. But at least that part was clear enough.

"I'd like you to come back to Satcon for a couple of days. I'll set you up in a safe place. If you prove out, I'll arrange for your safe transit."

"I'm under house arrest, is that it?"

"You're safe."

"Okay," she smiled. "Thanks."

"You take the bed, I'll take the couch," I said. "Don't wait up for me."

"Where are you going?"

"To do some errands."

"Aren't you afraid I'll bolt?"

"Nope."

When I left she was cleaning up the coffee service and putting the cart away. I went back to Cobb's room with my recodisc and my turmoiling thoughts.

I ran my little recodisc scam and then rang up T.J. Janes who had fallen asleep which seemed a little nervy to me at the time.

"What is it Bockhorn," she said huskily with the petty annoyance of someone who suspected the caller was informing her about a light left burning.

"I've got Lauren Potter and she spilled all about the blackmail scheme and your silly plan to—"

"Drop it Bockhorn."

"She's in my room. If you want to—" Suddenly the previously dark screen lit up with her tight-faced image.

"Drop it Bockhorn. The case is closed. The pictures are destroyed. Even Harry is destroyed. You are wrapped up. I'm very happy with the job you did. I will file a report to your superiors to that effect."

"Wait a minute!"

"Good night, Bockhorn, and thank you. Off." The screen blanked.

She hung up. That was that. Dismissed. In

mid-stride. What the hell? I walked to the bathroom and looked at the remains of Harry Cobb. Apparently T.J. thought Lauren had done it. Lauren thought some man did it. The USSC, clever as a block, was certainly going to decide that Cobb did it to himself after being run out on by his consort whom no one would be able to find. Officially the case was about closed.

I was only a lawman insofar as MA&P made me so. When they stopped doing so, when I was relieved of duty, I was out. I could have gone to the Command and told them what I knew. And I'd just as well might have dropped my MA&P ID in the trashflash there and kept on going. It was frustrating.

I was in the middle of the biggest case of what I liked to call my career and I was off it. Cobb's remains had stopped dribbling things and now just hung there. I stared at him, enthralled by the thought that fear had killed Harry Cobb. Fear of what? Something had made him crazy, crazy enough not to recognize me when he stared me in the face and broke my hand. Then something, maybe the same something, had killed him. Maybe he was a suicide? But I goddam wanted to find out.

Chapter Five

I went through Cobb's room as hard as I could. I found nothing to implicate either of the girls, or clear them either. And the more I looked the more I figured it would take a mightier man than most to rub old Harry with his own gun. That's when I found the golden tack. A small globe of gold with a spike in it. A clue. I hate clues. Nothing screws up an otherwise good assessment like the misreading of a clue.

The ball headed tack was jammed between Harry's index finger and his middle finger, like he'd swiped at it and gotten it caught there. I rolled it between my thumb and forefinger. I couldn't dismiss it, couldn't spit it out. And the more I tried the further back it slid until I swallowed it altogether. But I'd seen it before. Where? I like assessments. I just had a good one. I hate clues.

Had T.J. really been unconscious when I'd found her on the floor? Was Lauren blowing smoke about her mysterious tail? They both had motive enough to kill old Harry. They both had the opportunity. They both had histories of lying like hell to me. Yet I was turning every which way trying to find some way to clear them. Harry's gun was the only thing I kept coming back to. He was killed with his own gun.

I pocketed the little globe of gold with its tiny spike and took the elevator back to my room. I wanted to go up against Lauren Potter, hard.

I made the series of rights and lefts I'd gotten accustomed to the past day and a half, passed the mirrored courtesy table, the billboard for the Jockey Club Restaurant, and turned up my hall.

There was someone working at my door. He turned to me and all I saw was his face—*the* face—and his Stoner. It was the man from the Gaming Commission. I recognized him from the fronton and I recognized him from the flight out to Orion, that's were I saw him! He was a tail. A hired man. Gaming Commission my tushy. I cursed myself for having fallen for such an open ruse. But I did so quickly; as the pink dot of his laser flirted about me I bent and flattened myself against the wall. A hail of darts whooshed past me, and tinkled against the mirror, spent. He didn't fire again. He turned and ran. I followed him to the end of the hall. Blood was beating in my neck, a warm flush was spreading out all over me. He *was* Lauren's mysterious tail. And I was going to get him or die trying.

The hall he turned up was a long one and I lengthened my stride. I expected at any moment he would dip a shoulder and hurl some darts my way, but he held his piece close to his side. We were coming up on a dead end. He whirled. I dove for the doorway nearest and squeezed myself against the tiniest protection of the frame. He didn't fire. I caught on that his initial burst had been reflex, he didn't want attention called to himself, didn't want the hallway littered with darts. I was willing to play along. I kept my Stoner holstered. He bolted through the service door.

I ran to the door, stood to the side, and punched it open with my elbow. No darts. For a moment footsteps, then nothing. I slid myself into the echoing darkness and waited for the right vision to come. I picked up the minimal lighting and the stairs that seemed to go on forever though I could only see clearly up one and a half flights. I drew my Stoner and started up, expecting *the face* at every dark turn. On the landing eight flights up a door was partially ajar. I kicked it in. Waited. Entered. The whirring of machinery filled my ears and in the semi darkness I could make out the bottom of another short flight of steel steps, and the shadowy shapes of the eco-generators. It was a trap. In here a Stoner's darts wouldn't be noticed by anyone but the recipient. I leaped the steps in one jump and hit the deck in a roll that left me crouching behind a large square steel shape. Now he was trapped too.

I tried to hear into the whirring soundscape. I got nothing. I decided to sit tight. Still nothing. Perhaps he was sitting too. My eyes got adjusted to the dark and, as they did, there came into view row after row of engines and generators and bubbling pots of whatnot that churned out the oxygen and burned up the waste and offered up the power and controlled the atmospherics that made this globe of Constellation habitable. We were in the heart of Orion. The symbolism was not lost on me. I started breathing faster. Was the oxygen a bit thinner in the robotic areas than in the rest of the station? It didn't seem likely, but it felt that way.

There was another noise off to my right, but I made it some solenoid engaging in one of the machines. Then the tinkle of a Stoner blast from off to my left. *The face* had fired at the solenoid.

I tried to force my ears out into the darkness as I pressed myself up against the cool steel skin of the thing that whirred beside me. I heard a footfall. I placed it to be in front of me. That was bad. What diffuse light there was in the machine room was coming from behind me. Likely as not I would be silhouetted for him before he was lit up for me. I moved backwards on my heels until I came to the corner of the big metal box that protected me and pivoted around it.

Now I was staring down a long corridor with big metal boxes whirring and cachunking and humming on either side. I caught another footfall now as my ears accustomed to the background buzz. Of course his were too. I zeroed in on the footfall. It occurred to me that he was on the opposite side of the box I was sneaking around.

I moved down the box wall that formed my side of the corridor until I was in the middle. I heard another footfall, actually an elbow fall; he must have bumped his side of the box. I took another step and listened. We were like the cat and the mouse cartoon running around the tree stump, except that we weren't running, we were creeping. And no one was laughing at our stately and deadly little sarabande. Certainly not I.

On a wall down the corridor a laser's pink dot caught my eye. It fluttered about like a bug a light. Apparently his Stoner's aiming device, which ordinarily flashes on an instant before the trigger blast, had jammed after flirting with my chest. That gave me an advantage, to say the least. But, spit, I *was* due a little luck on this case. Right now it told me he was facing in the same direction I was. If he turned, the Stoner would turn with him and if I could pick up the pink dot again I would know. He couldn't, assuming he had noticed the malfunction, just cover the lens with a finger—flourescent fingers are not good for sneaking up on people. Nor could he drop the Stoner. I sympathized. Sure I did.

Behind me and up the wall off the corridor was a ladder to a catwalk which led, I assumed, out over the machine bay. At first I had disregarded the walkway because it was a place where I could be seen more easily than I could see. Now, with the pink light helping my case, the high ground seemed like a good gamble. There would be no cover, however.

On the other hand, what cover did I have on the ground? If I lost sight of the pink dot for any period of time—and in fact I hadn't seen it for the past ten seconds or so—then the face, if he had the nerve, could come poking around either the corner to my right or to my left and, depending on which way I was looking at the time, it was fifty-fifty I'd be a dart board. I liked the odds better on the ladder.

That solenoid tripped again and this time *the face* didn't fire but I used the opportunity to leap across the corridor and scale the ladder to the catwalk. Misallowing for anti-spinward drift, I landed just a tad wide, and hung, for a moment, like an ape, one handed from the rail. I didn't feel too bad about that; *you* try figuring out which way is spinward in a darkened room at .8-G in a two-minute rotational system. Then I pulled myself up top.

I was looking down onto the box now. It had a grate on top through which I couldn't see but it didn't matter. I made the pink dots movement to mean that my quarry was moving to the far corner of the box on the side that was closest to me. Around it he came.

I was staring into his face now as he inched silently down the wall towards the near corner, maybe ten feet away from me, maybe eight feet below me. I trained my Stoner at his chest against the possibility of his suddenly looking up. I thought of calling out to him. Letting him gander my dart gun. But you never know how dumb a guy is or at what crazy odds-against he'll launch a flachette salvo. I let him come. But he stopped.

He was listening. He was waiting to hear a footfall. Mine. My feet were tucked under me. They weren't going anywhere, yet. I became acutely aware of my own breathing and decided to stop it. I'll bet a thousand immers he was doing the same thing. And there we stood. Two men in the dark holding their breath.

The pink dot of his laser ran quickly up the floor below me as he brought his weapon to his hip. Then he leapt out into the corridor, the Stoner held in two hands. "Stay where you are!" he shouted at me.

But I wasn't there. He leapt a hundred and eighty degrees and prepared to fire in the other direction. I wasn't there either. He flattened himself against the wall of the box across from me. I waited for him to drop his gun to his side so I could jump him. If I was smiling, it was smugly. The jump would knock the Stoner from his hand, more than equalizing the disadvantage of my claw. But first he had to lower the Stoner.

I realized I was still holding my breath, just as *the face* appeared to realize that there was a ladder before him leading up to a catwalk. That it also led to me was something he hadn't tumbled to yet, but, as he was already legging it up the steps, it was only a matter of moments. I didn't want to kill the jerk, but he was making it awfully hard not to. Have I mentioned that I'd never killed anybody? Never did. I'd only fired a Stoner in anger twice.

Now great golf-ball-sized beads of sweat were appearing on my face and running down my neck into my chest, dampening my shirt. I'd either stopped breathing again or else hadn't started back up but whatever, my lungs were banging on the pipes for air. If I retreated across the catwalk it would only put off the inevitable; give him a good shot at me too. But if I crawled to the ladder, we'd be nose to nose, and I would have the element of surprise. On the other hand, crawling across the catwalk might alert him by shaking the whole rig and giving me away.

I had a little time. Whereas I had bounded up the thing in my haste to hit the high ground, *the face* was climbing up step by agonizing step in stroboscopic slomo, eyeballing around in every direction but the one in which he should have been looking.

Having ruled out retreat and doping out the middle of the catwalk as the deadliest of all possible worlds, I decided to meet him halfway. I crawled towards him, matching my step for his. We approached the juncture of the ladder and the catwalk simultaneously; me prone, Stoner pressed forward in both hands; he standing and peering off into the room. When he finally turned to me he was eye level with the top of the catwalk and my stretched out, Stoner-gripping hands. I saw something deep in his eyes, a hesitance that relaxed me, told me I was going to be okay. I smiled. "Howdy."

Wrong again. Crazy! His stoner exploded beneath me, sending a pattern of darts up the catwalk against which I pressed my chest, my belly, my legs and my whatnot. Fortunately the angle of the grating was steep and all the darts but one richocheted off it and tinkled harmlessly on the corridor below. All but one.

One lucky bastard of a dart penetrated the grate where the angle was the *greatest* and slammed into my big toe. It felt like someone had swung a hammer down onto my foot. I nearly pulled the trigger of my Stoner, nearly took his face off, out of pique. But I didn't, or couldn't. Instead, I jammed the thing forward into his face. Teeth crunched and blood exploding from his lips. I jammed again. More teeth crunched. He needed his free hand to hold himself onto the ladder so he brought up his Stoner hand to stop the savage dental work and that's when I had him. I hooked his Stoner with my claw and sent it skittering down the catwalk behind me. Then I let him grab my weapon which he did with both hands and the fear of a vengeful God. I had the bulk of him. I got to my knees and yanked him up onto the catwalk like he was a fish. He landed on his feet.

I put a knee into his groin and he did a graceful sag against the railing. I did it again and he sagged some more. Not so gracefully this time. About here it finally dawned upon him that I wasn't going to dart him up and he let go of my Stoner arm and punched me in the face; a glancing blow as I turned and slipped most of it. He had a small, mean, insinuating little fist. I smacked him back with the fist of my good hand still wrapped around the handle of the Stoner. That about did it for his uppers. "No more," he pleaded.

"You want to talk to me?"

He didn't answer. I put my knee to work again. The pain in my toe made it easy to hurt back, bad. His head rolled back with the impact. "Chat?" I asked.

"Maybe," he squeaked.

I kneed him again.

"I'll make a deal," he said. Everyone wants to negotiate. It was a buyers market so I told him to spit. He told me he'd tell me some things but not other things. Some things, he said, could get him killed if he told me.

"By whom?" I queried.

"That's one of the things," he said.

I kneed him.

"Really!" he mumbled weakly. He was fast approaching the point of no return so I pursued the deal. "Tell me some things," I said.

"Some things, but not everything," he said as if he were getting the terms right so he could give them to his legal steno. "A deal?"

"It depends on the things," I said. "Enlighten me."

"What do you want to know?"

"Start with who you are."

"Marv Throneberry," he said and I cursed myself for asking so stupid a question. It was the kind of thing you ask a guy when you're sitting in an interrogation room and your light is burning in his eyes and you've got all the time in the world. It was not the kind of thing you ask a guy when you're standing on a catwalk above a machine room and your knee is in his groin and if you take it out he may kill you. And it is especially not the kind of question you ask a guy whose made a deal that he'll answer some questions and not others and you can see in his eyes that his question meter started running the minute you opened your mouth. But I had asked him who he was and he did give me the name of an old baseball player and clicked up one question answered. I cut to the heart of the matter. "Who are you working for?"

"Can't tell you."

I gave him the knee.

"The deal, man the deal!" he squealed as he crumbled. I let him.

"What's your job? What are you following me for?"

"I'm not following you," he said and gritted gums and stubs against my knee, but I held up and waited for him to finish. "I was supposed to follow Cobb."

"And?"

"Rub him."

"Did you?" Knee for emphasis.

"Yes." he said.

"What were you doing at my door?"

"I can't . . . Jesus Bockhorn!" he shrieked as I hit him a couple of times where he was bound to be getting sore, but as hard as I had hit him was nothing compared to how hard he'd hit me when he called me by my name. His eyes reflected his mistake.

"Whence the info, Marvin?"

"*No capece*," he lied. I bent him way over backwards across the railing. He was in no position to say no. "Whence the info on my name?" I repeated, pulling my knee way back with a sense of drama of the moment.

"I'll make you a deal," he gasped breathlessly. "I'll tell you something you really want to know. Just let me go."

"Tell me."

"Will you let me go?"

"Try me."

"The piece you're traveling with, the girly?"

"Yeah?"

"She's marked. Stay out of the way. You keep hanging around her and somebody's gonna flatten you."

"Who marked her?"

"I can't."

"Marked for what?" I kneed him. He grunted. "Tell me!" I kneed him twice. "Were you supposed to rub her too?"

"I was supposed to bring her," he was weakening, starting to let go.

"To who?" I spit.

"That's out of line," he bluffed, rallying, feigning an amount of control of the situation that he certainly didn't have. I wasn't getting a lot of fun out of kneeing him in the groin anymore but it was my best shot so I took another. His eyes rolled around in his sockets.

"To whom?" I corrected the question.

"Bockhorn . . ." he said weakly, drooling a bit, "You're killing me."

"Only your progeny. To whom? Who wants the girl! When! What's going on! Tell me! Tell me! I'll goddam mash your—"

"Hey!" came a shout from somewhere in the rooms, somewhere deep off in the darkness. "Hey! . . ."

It said something neither of us could make out and then, as if as a courtesy, repeated itself. We still couldn't make it out. Then:

"I say again, who is in the room?"

I threw a couple of glances around. Marvin, or whoever, did what he could, considering the awkwardness of his position. I pulled him off the balcony, and whipped his arm up behind him and held it as best I could with the claw, and whispered, "Squawk and I'll dart you between the checks." Even I winced at that. But it served the purpose. We pressed ourselves to the catwalk. I tried to mentally disown the toe that was pressed against the grate, throbbing.

A beam of light probed the darkness now. A watchman? "Lay down," I whispered and urged him out in front of me. Where the Stoner was. He went for it. Screw the watchman, I leapt to my one good foot and dove on him before he could swing the nasty thing around.

"Hey!" the watchman called. Quietly we rolled back and forth on the catwalk, four hands on the Stoner—well three hands and a claw. I could feel the muzzle of the thing pressing tight against the inside of my arm, I kept on pointing it outward. He kept trying to point it in, not with real strength but with quick jerky movements. I kept the pressure on it to keep it out but no matter how we tumbled about on our perch I couldn't get the damn thing off my arm. I kept waiting for the explosion, the gentle tug on the trigger that would at the very least tear off my good arm with a series of mini-explosions and then do whatever it damned pleased. After a time it dawned on me that he didn't want to fire. He wanted to get the muzzle on me to subdue me, not kill me. He hadn't wanted clues to his presence. Perhaps he didn't want the inconvenience of a witness, now in the person of the watchman, or whatever, down somewhere on the floor of the room. His reason didn't much matter to me, only the fact of it. Instead of struggling, I yanked in the direction he was pushing, pulling the muzzle of the Stoner *towards* my face! It came right out of his surprised grip. As a matter of fact it came out so easily that it flew out of my hand too and sailed over my head and off the catwalk and into the clattering darkness.

"I know you're here," called our friend somewhere on the floor. The face and I lay entwined like spent lovers, motionless on the sidewalk. Down in the machine room below us I could barely make out the pink dot of the faulty aiming device. Then it gave up and winked out. "Goodby Bockhorn," my companion said and he jumped straight up and ran.

"Hey! Hey! Hey you!" the man on the floor shouted. "I see you!" He started to give *the face* a half hearted chase. "Don't you know this is a restricted area?" he said, to myself I guess; he'd stopped running. The watchman wanted no confrontation with whoever it was he had chased out of the room. He was just happy to have done his job. He closed the door. I stood up. The Stoner was safely out of sight. I swung down the ladder, hopping on my good leg, and scooped up the darts *the face* had thrown at me—I didn't want to leave a curious trail either—and headed for my room. I knew he wouldn't make another attempt at Lauren Potter. Not tonight. Not unarmed. But I felt I should be with her anyway. She had become a kind of client.

Chapter Six

I hobbled down the deserted hallway—as it was 3 A.M., G.M.T.—and stopped by the mirror at the end of the hallway to scoop up the tell tale darts from that first salvo. Sloppy work. He should have thought of this himself but I gave him the benefit of the doubt of having figured out that I would be back this way in one big hurry. When I stood up, the full-length mirror returned to me a shock.

The night had aged me. I looked like I'd lost ten pounds. My cheeks were hollow, which made my nose look long and witchy. My skin was grey. Maybe that was the light in the hall. But I had wrinkles. They were all over my face. Little spidery lines ran here and there. Some big ones near my eyes. Had they happened in a moment? Or had a moment made me realize them? I had never been shot at before, not dead-on, anyway.

I had been in a couple of firefights. There was one at the Anaconda Nodule Dormitory on Delos, when the penal workers had their revolt. I was in that one and there were darts flying everywhere, a steel blizzard. But I kept my head down and after two days the revolt worked itself out and the leaders walked out with their hands above their heads and all the agents but one—poor Isa Aoki who had tried to be a hero—went home to tell the tale in the endless barroom games of can-you-top-this, or else to grandchildren.

I also had been on the team that rescued Pittipat Kennedy from the Safe-cave outside Lunar One when it was discovered that she was being held by the American Independence Brigade. That was a shoot-out. But I was stationed at the MA&P cruiser, where it was pretty safe except for the little counterattack that the AIB launched in the late afternoon, just before the end. A group of them made it to the vehicles and started spraying darts at anything in a mylar space suit (me for instance) but we subdued them almost immediately and then an hour later the action was over and, for me, that was it. Until tonight.

Tonight I had been shot at twice, at close range. And the throb that had subsided to a steady intracranial rumble reminded me; not just shot at, hit. I eyeballed my feet, slowly, deliberately, wincing in anticipation at what I might see.

The outer cloth and plastic upper of my boot showed just a teeny weeny little puncture, but, when I pulled it off, the white sock inside had been satined a woody maroon. Four of my toes I could move. The big one, uh uh. Over the big toe the sock was ripped, but you'd only know it by the ragged edges of the fabric. The toe was the same color as everything else around it, except for a spot right down the middle of the digit that shone back white. I blew out through clenched teeth. It was a tendon or a bone.

I hobbled over to my room with greater difficulty than I had had before my cursory examination. I opened the door. The light was burning at the bedside.

Lauren wasn't in bed! I whirled around, almost fell. She was on the couch, fast asleep. A coffee carafe she had ordered sat on the night table with a bathroom towel wrapped around it to keep it warm. The bedclothes were turned back.

I hobbled to the couch. She was sleeping on her side. The slipcover which she had used for a blanket was pulled up around her chin. Her lips, slightly parted, hissed quietly with her even breathing. I put my hand on the side of her tiny face and moved back the fall of soft shiny brown hair to uncover a delicate, porcelain ear. I let my hand slide down her shoulder and gave it a squeeze. She stirred and I took it away. But she continued to sleep and hiss and, after a moment or two to make sure I hadn't awakened her, I hobbled over to the bed.

I sat down with her pocket book and began to go through it. The usual stuff. A holo of

what looked like her family taken five years
ago at some graduation, not hers. A two-D of
Harry Cobb, unautographed, but dated seven
days ago. Another holo, a dog, Irish setter
type, on an Earthside hilltop, in front of a
house. The cards included her press card, a
B social security card, a Unicharge card, a
Sovexchange card, a spent Laker Spacepass,
probably a souvenir of some Earth Space
camping trip taken as a student. There was a
laundry ticket, an interior decorator's card, a
phone number written on a slip of paper with
the name Duffy on it, an ad clipped out of a
home furnishings section for some kind of
tatami mat, and of course her pocket
terminal—and why hadn't she punched
Duffy's number into that? There was a small
make-up case containing lipstick, blusher,
nose cream, enamel whitener, breath spray,
almost nothing. There was a hairbrush, a key
ring, a pack of bubble gum, and a small
satcon-glass bear. There was a manicure kit
containing nothing but the usual. A sewing kit
with pre-threaded needles ranging from
coarse to practically invisible. I took a toe
clipper from the manicure kit and set to work
on my toe.

I took just a second to wonder why I still
had a big toe. Either *the face* had had the
incredibly bad luck to make his single hit with
a defective round, or his Select had been set
on non-explode. What makes a Stoner the
perfect space weapon for inside work is that if
it hits something hard it goes *tinkle*, while if it

experiences mild resistance followed by warm-wet it goes *pop*! See? Harmless to machines and hull structures, deadly to living things and hot-water bottles.

The dart had gone straight in. If it had exploded the toe would have gone altogether. As it was the little thing had penetrated and severed the tendon, the ends of which were now standing at attention on either side of the penetrating dart, right through the open wound. What I was looking at then, was a wide furrow of toe meat out of which extended two little white human-tissue things and one blue-gray aluminum thing. The blue-gray aluminum thing had to go. What had to be done with the two little white things that had once made my toe go up and down, I hadn't a clue of an idea. I did know that I had no time for a second trip to the sawbones.

I told myself calmly that this was going to hurt a bit and reached down and clamped the toe clipper onto the back of the dart. The exposed nerve ending in the wound shot a lurid message the full length of my body and back. Pain. I bit my lip and pulled. The pain turned purple. I rocked the dart back and forth. The pain turned purple with stripes. Then, with a barely audible tear, the dart popped out with a ripping suddenness that made me gasp and a thrill that made me choke all at the same time. What it was, was a gasping cough and it woke Lauren Potter. She looked around and saw me on the edge of the bed and smiled.

"Did I wake you?" she asked.

I couldn't speak. I could barely shake my head no.

"You're hurt," she said, sitting up, holding the slipcover around herself.

I nodded yes.

She rubbed some sleep from her eyes and said, "Let me help."

I nodded yes again and lay back on the bed. The stripes began to fade. But the purple remained. I pulled myself back to the pillow. Raising the toe to the bed was a big help.

"Let's get something under that," Lauren Potter said as if she knew what she was doing.

"Right," I breathed.

She puttered around the bed and the nighttable and the bathroom and I let her putter. I didn't move. She didn't look like she needed any help anyway. She kept up a steady stream of chatter. Told me she'd once wanted to be a nurse. Went to nursing school. Wound up working on the school paper. Fell in love with the news terminals. California. Boyfriend. Killed in the last Vietnam War. She only seventeen. That was six years ago. Thought of nursing again and went to nursing school, or was that when she first decided to go to nursing school? I think I was passing out.

She continued to trip back and forth from the bathroom, setting things up on a towel at the end of the bed near my foot. She was wearing a pair of black silk man's pajamas. Real silk? Cobb's? Hard to believe that even with his new line of work he could afford something like that, but it moved around on her like silk, clinging to her angular hips and her apple-sized breasts provacatively enough so that it registered on me even through the curtain of purple which lay on my face, suffocating me, enraging me, enlightening me as to why people in hospitals often scream to have limbs removed. And it was just a goddam toe!

"This is going to hurt," she said.

"Oh boy," I managed.

She was sitting over me with a bandage made of the bathroom terry towel, a splint made from a half section of the hygeia stall tubing, and the bottle of spray mouthwash. "Wha—?"

"It's ninety per cent alcohol," she assured me.

"I'll have mine with a splash," I joked.

She sprayed it on my open wound. I saw my sainted Grandma Bockhorn. "How is that?" she asked.

"Fine," I said in a voice not my own.

"Good," she said and sprayed the toe again. *Whoooooof*!

"Cut it out," I said.

"I wish I had. You really butchered yourself, you know? But you'll be alright."

"What about the toe?"

"You will never tango again."

"I never tangoed."

"So I guess you're in the clear."

"I'm serious."

"I'd say you're satisfactory."

"I didn't mean my toe."

"Me either."

She kept this bedside drivel up as she cupped the dangling digit with the half section of silica tubing and wrapped it all tightly with the swath of terry. Then she took two lengths of tie cord and bound up the terry wrap.

"Blink," she said and I did. "Breathe," she said and I tried. "Deeply," she said, "Down here," she patted my stomach. I did. "How do you feel?" she asked.

"Okay," I lied, or at least I thought I was lying. In fact, I did feel okay. The purple was gone. In its place was a dull throb, like I'd stubbed my toe on a bulkhead; it was the way it felt when *the face* first shot it and I was anesthetized by the struggle and its aftermath. "I feel okay," I said. "Really."

"Okay, sit up," she said.

"Oh no," I said, "If I sit up the blood is going to rush to my toe isn't it?"

"Yes it will," she admitted.

"I think I'll lay here a while."

"You're going to have to sit up and you're going to have to put some weight on it and you're going to have to do a little walking. All I did was stop the bleeding and I cleaned and sterilized the wound and immobilized the toe. But that's all. Now they have a very good little hospital here on Constellation—"

"I know," I said and waved my claw.

"Sit up," she replied. I did. The blood rushed to my toe and hit it with a hammer

when it got there. "Just breathe," she said. I
did. The hammer lifted. I tried to flex the toe.
The muscles sent back all the right signals but
the toe did not budge. "Move them all
together," she said. I did. The toe moved.
"When you walk, move all your toes like
that," she said. "Wait here," she said, "I'll get
dressed in the bathroom." She turned to her
luggage which was piled near the head of the
couch.

"Don't bother," I said.

"I'll come with you," she said.

"You're staying right here. I'm staying right
here. Go to sleep. Thanks for the fix."

"Bockhorn, you've got to get attention for
that. It is not fixed. If you want to be a big
hero—"

"I'm not a big hero," I interruped, "and I'm
no dummy either. If I check into the hospital
you check out. I don't want you doing that.
I'm sticking with you, kid."

"You still think I killed your friend Harry."

"He was no friend of mine and no I don't
think you killed him but I think you think I do
so as soon as I'm trapped somewhere, as soon
as you know I'm not coming back any minute,
like tonight, you're going to powder off and I
don't want to have to go finding you again."

"I don't understand something, Bockhorn,"
she said, climbing up onto the bed next to me
and sitting indian fashion sideways to me. "If
you don't think I'm guilty of something, and
T.J. has already dismissed you, why are you
doing this?"

"Because you hired me."

"Me?"

"To conduct you safely off Orion. 'I'm in danger, Mr. Bockhorn, please help me,' I said I would. Remember?" She nodded that she did and smiled.

"I could pay you. I guess I should. That would make it more official wouldn't it?"

"But it wouldn't make you any less likely to skip out. And I couldn't take it anyway. I'm not a private security agent. I work for MA&P. I'm a carrier dick. I pinch stowaways, and bust truants, and check locks, and babysit hand-to-hand stock transfers. That's what I do. I don't pick up big eyed little girls on retainer to smuggle through a galaxy of thieves. Usually."

"Then why me?" she asked. It was a pleasant question asked as if she expected a pleasant answer. I decided not to disappoint her.

"Because you," I said, "are at the center of something."

"What?" she asked, all big eyed.

"I don't know. But so far it has gotten me this," I raised my claw, "and this;" I lifted my bandaged toe, "it has killed off a pretty fair agent who once worked with me, a who was so entranced by whatever it was that when he did this to me," I raised my claw again, "he looked me right in the face and didn't even . . . well, never mind about that. Something's going on. I'd like to find out what it is."

"You're freelancing."

"I'm involved."

"And that's why you're staying with me."

"Yeah that and also I'm staying with you because I think you may be right. You may be in danger. I don't want you to get hurt. I like you."

"Well how long can you afford to keep protecting me? You haven't got many extremities left."

I laughed. "Are you stronger than you look?" I asked.

"Probably," she said.

"Heat up that coffee," I said.

She brought the carafe up to steam and divided up what was left of the coffee. I went at her.

I told her about *the face* and his mission. She seemed to take it pretty well. She pumped me for all I knew about him as would be natural and I told her the answers were still to come.

She still refused to go back to T.J. or deal with her in any way. We settled on an identity of Mrs. Amos Stargis for her and I punched it through my portaterm. I can do that. She agreed to stay under my protection for twenty-four hours, to do as I said, and to help me out with whatever it was I could come up with. I explained I had to come up with something otherwise MA&P would have me back on truant duty by mid-day break the day that they let me out of the infirmary. Either way I'd get her safely on her way back to Lunar or

Earth or whatever she decided.

She asked if wouldn't the discovery of Cobb's corpus raise questions. I told her that Cobb would be pronounced "dead by own hand," within hours of said discovery. It happened all the time. Spouse runs out, usually with cash, remaining spouse terminates.

"What if they find out he wasn't really married?"

"They'll say he killed himself over his girl. Suicide of passion. Here, what do you make of this?" I said and pulled the golden tack out of my pocket. She flinched. "Recognize it?"

"Yes."

"Go on."

"Yes, I recognize it. It was a gift. Cobb, Cobbler, whoever, I gave it to him. Didn't you read it?"

"Eh?"

"Read it."

I looked really closely at the golden ball and what I had taken to be some sort of filigree, some texture, was in fact a rather florid bit of engraving. In wild sweeps and swoops and curlicues it read "I'll love forever L" except that the letter L was real big and placed in the middle of all the sweeps and swoops of words. "It's an old fashioned lapel pin," she said.

"You gave him this?"

"Yes," she said, looking truly self-revolted.

"Sorry," I said.

"Me too," she said.

"Bockhorn, there's one more thing. We're

going to have to do a little more work on that toe."

"Ohmigod."

She went back into the bathroom and returned with an unidentifiable bit of plastic that she proceeded to work on with something from her manicure set. About ten minutes later she said, "If we are very lucky, I am about to perform my first successful tendon splice," and proceeded to undo her bandaging job.

"Ohmigod."

She got out her sewing kit and went to work. I'll spare you the details. Actually it wasn't as bad as Round One.

After we had both rested a bit she said, "As soon as the swelling subsides your big toe will go up and down again when you tell it to. But sometime between tomorrow morning and two weeks from now my little fixit job is going to go *sprong*, and you will be very sorry that you didn't go to the clinic tonight. And Bockhorn. You will never, *ever* tango."

"With my sex-appeal, who needs to tango," I tried weakly, then gave up my Bogart routine.

It was nearing daytime. Tomorrow would be a long day. I argued briefly, ridiculously, with her about taking the bed but she refused. I limped over and made a big show of tucking her into the couch. She smiled and offered up a cheek for a kiss goodnight. I pecked it. "Thanks for everything," she said.

"One last thing," I said. "Who's Duffy?"

She looked at me curiously.

"Duffy. His name and what appears to be his phone number, they're in your pocketbook."

"You went through my bag?"

"When you were a suspect."

"Are you going to call him?"

"Shouldn't I?"

"I'd rather you didn't," she said looking up at me, the bedspread pulled up around her chin.

"I'm an investigator. That means I investigate. I don't have any leads. I don't know what's going on. I'm groping around, you know what I mean? Who is this Duffy? He your real boyfriend?"

She thought very carefully about her answer. "If I lie you're gonna catch me," she said.

"That's right," I said, although I really don't know that. It all depended on how well she did it.

"He's an indie shipper who runs a small Heinlein-class freighter." Heinleins were old, one of the first of the steady-boost commercial boats. "That's his number at the dock on North Port. He's my . . . boyfriend? I don't know. We had a couple of dates. He got really serious. I took the number with me to Orion. I was going to break it off with some story. By the time I'd gotten back I figured he'd be gone on some run. It just seemed the best way to do it. Kinda stinky, huh?"

"You need to carry your boyfriend's number on a slip of paper?"

"I never called him. I never got around to plugging him in. My term you mean, don't you? I don't know, that would have made it more permanent, or something. I told you it was just a couple of dates. I hardly *knew* him, and all of a sudden he's got me down as his crew-of-one. I really wish you wouldn't call him."

"Well, let's see what turns up. Say, would he have known about Cobb? There could be a connectic between *the face* and Duffy. Suppose they're working together, or he's hired the guy. Revenge motive."

Lauren yawned big into my face. "Sorry," she said, struggling to close her mouth. "Okay, call him if you'll feel better about it," she said.

"Alright, go to sleep," I said.

This time she puckered up. I kissed her lips. They were soft and warm. I was embarrassed and quickly kissed her forehead, fatherly like, to cover for the feeling that was crawling through me vigorously enough to compete with my toe.

I laid back on the bed got my foot up as high as I could. The pain ebbed. Closed my eyes but I knew it wouldn't do any good. I have some trouble sleeping in the early hours. Too late for night and not early enough for morning, they seem to be another zone altogether. I assessed instead.

T.J. had gone into the hotel room looking for the pictures. Cobb surprised her in the darkness. Sapped her. Realizing he'd dropped a woman, he went to the bathroom to get a cold compress. In comes *the face*, doesn't see the laid out form of T.J. but heads straight for the light in the bathroom. On the toilet or the shelf or whatever is the Stoner Cobb had drawn. *The face*, knowing a set up when he sees it, shoots Cobb with his own gun, puts it in his hand. Why the lapel pin in Cobb's hand? Why are there two saps on T.J.'s head? For that matter, why did *the face* shoot Cobb?

I assessed again. Cobb is in the bathroom getting dressed. The shower is running so he doesn't hear T.J. rummaging about the room for the pictures. In comes *the face*. He saps T.J. and heads for the bathroom with the Stoner he gets from the night table. In the bathroom . . . wait a minute. Nobody leaves the shower running while they look in the mirror; the mirror fogs.

I assessed again. Since either Cobb or *the face* had to tear up the room after T.J. incinerated the photos then . . . (yawn) . . . I still didn't know why *the face* shot Cobb. That was (yawn) critical, right? Okay . . . *the face* is in . . . the room . . .

I fell asleep. It had been a long day.

Chapter Seven

"Good morning."

It was Lauren Potter, bending over me, dressed in a white blouse and shorts, her hair still wet from her morning shower.

" 'Time is it?" I said thickly.

"Nine, breakfast is up."

I turned my head and saw a big breakfast table had been wheeled into the room. Lauren set about turning over cups and folding napkins and that sort of thing. I watched her bending over, fascinated by the backs of her thighs.

"What would you like?" she asked.

Don't say it Bockhorn, I thought.

"We've got seaweed omelette, real eggs. We've got protose sausages. We've got two kinds of fried potatoes, home and Orion. We've got multi-juice, chopped chicken livers, toasted wheats and—" she lifted the cover off a bowl, "I think this is farina. I had to guess at what you wanted."

"Good guessing," I said and staggered off toward the hygiene stall. "Get me T.J. on the phone will you?"

"I tried."

"You did?"

"She left this morning on the Dawn Launch. She's enroute."

I felt a lot better when I returned from my shower, hungrier too. I spooned myself some omelette and some Orion fries and a little of the sausage. Then, what the hell, a mound of the chicken livers. "Farina?" she asked.

"Please," I said, pushing my bowl towards her. I'd had a very difficult evening. "I thought you didn't want to talk to T.J.?"

"I was calling for you."

"No you weren't. I was asleep."

"Maybe I was going to wake you up."

"Who else did you call?"

"Are you going to check on me?"

"Maybe. Did you call Duffy?"

"Maybe."

"Did he vow to win you back?"

"Several times."

"What did you tell him?"

"I told him there was somebody after me who was trying to kill me."

I laughed, at the incongruity as much as anything else. She frowned. "Well it's true isn't it?"

"I don't think so," I said. "Go get ready. We've got a flight in twenty minutes, Mrs. Stargis."

"Yes dear," she said.

The TraveLounge in Constellation Center was chock full of last-day types, sadfaced at ending their vacations, or flings, or whatever. I juggled all the luggage and checked us through. "Mrs. Stargis doesn't come up on my screen," the desk attendant said and smiled at me. My heart crashed down into my stomach. My toe throbbed anew. "Put it through again," I asked.

The attendant put through the material a second time. "Mrs. Stargis" came up on the screen. "That's fine," the desk attendant said. "You're clear to Satcon Station through gate four on the inner port. MA&P Skytrain 55."

I thanked her just as Lauren, Mrs. Stargis, was returning from the ladies room. She had her term out and tuned to the news.

"See this?" she said. She handed it to me and I played back the tape she'd just made. The second story, after a lead about a guy who hit yesterday's SuperQuadrifecta Royale for a quarter million, was a bit about Harry Cobb, called Cobbler. Suicide said the report. A Mrs. Cobbler was being sought for questioning but, the announcer almost winked, it was suspected that no such Mrs. Cobbler actually existed.

"You've taken precautions," I said, "just in case."

"I've used an interruptor on all my printatures and there are no vocal recordings except one I made as Stargis' wife."

"Good girl," I said.

"Where's my carry-on?" she said.

"I checked it," I said, "there was too much stuff to—" I noticed she had blanched white as a ghost. "You alright?"

"Fine," she lied to me.

"You don't fly well do you?"

"No, not really," she said.

"Strange how people can live in space and even grow up in space and still—"

"Can we get my carry-on back?"

"I don't know. What do you have in it, medication? Maybe we could pick up something at—"

"Just let's see if we can get it back." She had that focused look of the panicky flyer. It was the checking in of the luggage of course. Lots of people have triggers like that. I don't get my Christmas depression until I'm handed that first disposable party-glass.

"Okay," I humored her. But the luggage had already gone into the belly of the big MA&P three-car and an announcement told us that we who were about to board had better get our rears in gear.

We pulled ourselves into seats in the Center tram immediately, Lauren staring straight ahead, me trying to figure out whether I should chat her up or leave her be. Around us were MA&P passengers headed for Satcon, Walt Whitman, and Lunar Central, also Cosmoflot passengers headed for Paris, also some Laker Spacebus people—their homemade lunches and dinners in plastic bags and boxes—headed for New York. Of them all, Lauren looked the miserablest. I put my arm around her. She melted onto me. "I'm okay," she whispered up into my face. I kissed her. She didn't move. So I kissed her again. She made a low sound in her throat and her lips softened and parted slightly. I pulled away with blood rushing in my ears. She leaned her head on my shoulder as the tram pulled away.

"Feeling better?" I asked.

She sighed heavily and squeezed my arm. It was an answer I took for yes. When the atmospherics are just right, and the lighting is just so, I am not an unsexy man. I'm no pretty-boy, and I almost never get my pick of a room. But sometimes . . . well hope springs eternal in the human breast, and elsewhere.

We disembarked at gate four. Lauren asked if I had a girlfriend.

"Dozens."

"Oh."

On the skytrain she asked if one wasn't special. It was a childish question; so direct that it deserved a direct answer.

"I'm sorry. I shouldn't have asked that," she said and giggled nervously. Eternal hope sprang in my elsewhere. You know? You never know. "That's alright, you're entitled," I said and I pulled a Fatima, tapped it a few times on the back of my claw and put it in my mouth as Bogart-like as I could. Mysteries aren't my only vice; I love old movies, too.

"Are you as tough as you look, Bockhorn?" she said.

"Well, I was thinking of eating this armrest

for lunch but I know that MA&P serves their shrimp in lobster sauce on Thursdays and that's not too bad."

She giggled for me. I smiled. "No, I mean with women," she said. "You look like the kind of man who knows what he wants."

"No trick to knowing what you want," I said, opting for the *older but wiser* approach, "the trick is knowing what you need. And getting it."

"And what do you need?" she said, her eyes like teddy-bear lasers, scanning my own crag-shadowed ones.

"Tough guys never tell," I said.

"Good," she said, and squeezed my arm the way she had in the tram. I had stopped thinking about how I was going to keep her alive and started to think about how I was going to keep her, period. As it was, the plan was to hide her somewhere on Satcon for a day or two, satisfy myself that she was no felon, and then send her safely to Earth somewhere. But I was already sure that she was no felon, at least as far as the death of Harry Cobb was concerned. There was nothing really to stop me from accompanying her down, helping her set herself up Earthside. I'd have to think of something to tell Ox. I blurted it out. I said something like let's go right on through. She said it sounded like fun. It did.

You begin to wonder about your motives at times like this. If she wasn't a suspect, what the hell was she?

Was I keeping Lauren Potter around as bait

for *the face*? Was she a way to avenge a smashed toe, a clawed hand—alright, Cobb gave me that but wasn't it because he thought I was in with *the face*? And what about Cobb? Was Lauren a tool to avenge him, no friend but a brother under the badge? Or did I just want to get cuddled? Or was it something more?

I remembered reading a Gogolenko mystery once about a murder in a Soviet concentration camp and how the lovers had covered for each other and how struck I was not by the twists and turns of Gogolenko's clever plot but by the idea that there could be such a thing as love and sex and desire in such a mean setting. But of course there was; there love was not merely a fact of life, but *the* overriding fact, the causer of things, the mover of things. There was, after all, nothing else. So why shouldn't I be in love with Lauren Potter?

The mental utterance of the idea was enough to confirm it, justify it, verify it, and give it life. I was in love with Lauren Potter. All in a day's work, I joked to myself, but I don't think I got the joke. I decided to table until we arrived at Satcon any thought of actually carrying out my plan to take her straight on through. I'd talk guardedly to Ox. Maybe he'd straighten me out.

When we arrived at Satcon the decision began to make itself for me. "I am very sorry," said the luggage attendant as we stood forlornly in the long-since-deserted luggage claim area, "the articles you describe are not on the skytrain nor are they enroute. If you'll register with the baggage desk I'm sure—''

We didn't wait for the rest of the story. At the baggage desk we "sat" and waited in the one-fifth G. And we waited. And we waited. "Satcon," Lauren mumbled. I suggested leaving a note at the desk and nipping across the Mini Ring to Mr. Big's for a drink but she wanted to have her two cents worth first. All of our bags, her two and my two, were lost. Eventually the baggage clerk arrived. He was a tall, thin, flinchy looking man, well suited to the job of absorbing abuse. You just felt good yelling at him.

When Lauren was finished doing just that, he politely told us that our bags had gone on to Lunar and would be returned in several days. Some things just don't change. We thanked him by not yelling at him anymore and lit out for MA&P headquarters.

I wanted to laugh at the face Lauren Potter had on, but I didn't. I looked around. We had no tail. No *face* followed us from corners and doorways. Nor did one await us at our destination.

We used the Stargis ID's at the desk. "I see you have taken a wife," the billeting clerk snickered apathetically. "Keep it quiet," I asked, "and punch yourself a tip. Fifteen."

When we got into the room she kissed me, arms up around me neck. "Later sweetheart," I Bogarted down at her. I left her in the room so I could go out and pick up the toiletries and sundries we'd be needing.

When I got back she was in a state. "Where have you *been*?" she said, leaping off the bed. "You've been gone a whole *hour*!"

"I got us toothpaste and soap and breath spray and nose cream and inhaler and all this, the works." I dumped the bag out on the bed.

"It took you an hour!?"

"It took me ten minutes, tootsie. Then it took me fifty minutes to stand down the hall and watch the door and make sure that no one was making for you." Also that she wasn't going to lam, but I didn't tell her that part. "I feel more secure now," I said.

She said, "Should I order us some dinner or do you want to go out and watch the door for another hour?"

"I'll order," I said, "what do you want?"

I took her order and when she went off to the hygiene stall I called in what I wanted to. Then I collected my messages. There was only one; from Ox. I rolled it on the terminal after unscrambling. Janes, it seemed, had closed the case. I was to report to Lunar HQ immediately on receipt of the message I was reading and await further assignment. I rescrambled the message and did not acknowledge its receipt. (I can do that, too.)

I decided I could not go to Earth with Lauren. But I also decided not to close the case—not to receive my message—until she was safely off.

"I can't go back to Earth with you!" I yelled at the hygiene stall.

"Why not?" she said, peeking out.

"Trouble with HQ. The case is closed."

"It is?"

"Yup."

"Can't you get it re-opened?"

"No."

There was a pause. "Then I'll stay here with you."

I wished. Then said, "Negative! You're going back! First thing tomorrow!"

No answer came back. I sat down on the bed. I wondered why no call from Ox had come in on my portaterm and I pulled the unit from my pocket to see if maybe, in all the excitement, I had missed its pleasant little beep. There was no recorded message. There had been no beep. There couldn't have been. The unit had been hit.

Right in its center, just below the screen, two star-shaped flachette darts nestled slant-wise side by side, only their tips visible through black plastic. I made a mental computation of what part of my anatomy might have been blended had the two darts slanted on through unimpeded by the porta-term. The picture wasn't pretty.

Lauren came out of her shower wrapped in the billets' courtesy bathrobe, a white terry several sizes too large for her. "Feel better?" I asked.

"Hungry," she said.

I told her what I had on order from the local Ho-Jo's and talked her into the whole bunch of garbage: fried protose clams, french fries, seaweed slaw and of course the wonderful strawberry ice cream shortcake. Satcon grew wonderful strawberries. And the fact that some of the other stuff was not real didn't make it bad. It tasted fine. Ordinary, but fine. And when you came to think of it, even the "fake" stuff *was* real. It was real seaweed. Funny that on Earth it is cheaper to go straight from elemental chemicals to synthetic foods while in space the organic methods are still more efficient. I was sure that in another fifty years or so the better part of North America would be fully returned to forest and prairie again.

"What are you talking about?" Lauren said and I realized that I had been going on a bit about one of my favorite subjects.

"Smoke?" I said and pulled out the pack of Fatimas. She declined. She sat down on the room's one chair and pulled her slender, sculptured little legs up under her. The robe buckled at her breast just enough for me to catch a glimpse of softly rising curve. "I'll take the chair tonight," I said.

"I'll take it," she said, "You're too big." I laughed. I called to check in on our order and the woman on the other end apologized that the delivery would take two hours. Their number two boy hadn't shown up for work. Whoever it was I had on the phone went on for a bit about truancy and third-world quotas and the paperwork involved in getting a replacement for a tru. I grunted in agreement. But that only encouraged her. She kept at it long enough for Lauren to walk over for a peek. She looked at the screen and shrugged and sat down beside me on the bed. Out of range of the pick-up I pantomimed yak-yak-yak with my hand which she took in hers as if consoling me in my hour of trial. The woman droned on. Lauren held on, my big paw clutched in her small ones laying in the moist warmth of her lap. I was beginning to get a message I hoped I wasn't garbling. "Yes, yes," I told the woman on the phone, "absolutely, something should be done. Yes, must be done. You did say two hours?"

"I can push it," the woman assured me.

"Please," I said and hung up before she could start again. I turned to Lauren and sighed theatrically. She sighed bigger than mine. Her thigh was resting against my own. I was aware of that. I was aware of everything. That the MA&P insignia on the blanket was upside down. That we were sitting there like adolescents on a porch. A moment passed, awkwardly. Then she got up, released my hand, and straightened her robe. Something inside me slammed its fist against its palm.

I relit the Fatima that had burned half out in the ashtray.

"You smoke too much," she said.

"Everyone's got a vice," I said. I had seen her with T.J. Janes. I had seen the pictures. I wanted to change her. I wanted to turn her around. I wanted.

"Bock?" she began, sitting back down again in the chair and pulling up her legs.

"What is it?"

"Oh . . . never mind."

"Never mind what?"

"Never mind that I'm acting like a jerk. I swear to God I am acting like a schoolgirl locked in the bathhouse with the lifeguard."

I laughed. "Me too, the lifeguard part."

"Well, that's different. You *are* a lifeguard."

"I suppose," I said, Bogarting a mite.

"Thank you for it," she said.

"You don't have to thank me, I'm doing what I want to do."

"Me too," she said.

"Snow again, I'm not getting the drift," I lied.

She didn't say anything for a minute. Just picked at the terry cloth. Then, "This is our last night together," she said. Considering that the previous night had been our first night together it seemed a somewhat strange thing to say, but I knew what she was getting at. "Do you . . ." I stumbled, "do you want to ah—"

She nodded, then stood up.

"Me too," I said, standing up too.

She untied the front of her robe with a flourish, but it was so big and she was so small that instead of falling open to reveal her in all her miniature magnificence, it just hung there. She looked sweet. "Don't be afraid to ask for what you want," she said.

"Okay," I said.

I wanted everything. I asked for most of it. I got all I asked for. She was sweet, she was sexy, and she was marked. Marked! What in the hell had *the face* meant? As I lay sated in the hollow aftershock of the big event, pulling at a Fatima, staring self-satisfiedly at the plastiform beams of the ceiling, my brains, which had been working on love-drive overload for the past 36 hours, started working like a Fleet Agent's again. I figured I had maybe an hour or two before my hormonal clock summoned the desire that would scramble my circuits again, and I had until the first flight out tomorrow morning before the object of said desire would be removed from me altogether so that she could pursue the rest of her life Earthside, or elsewhere, against a future that I knew was, at best, uncertain.

The food arrived. We went at it. Then we went at each other again. And, in the quiet darkness again, I thought some more. This Lauren Potter snoring lightly beside me, her back to me, her small butt offered out as something for me to hug around should I feel the need, was in danger. Thought number one. She knew it, and was letting on less than she knew. Thought number two. In the absence of any other thoughts I kept at these two, turning them over and over. I decided I was going to help her in spite of herself. I woke her up and told her that. "Okay," she purred and cuddled up. "Get some sleep."

At about seven A.M. we got a phone call that our baggage had been intercepted and would be returned to North Port at ten A.M. I had a notion.

Ascertaining that the room next to us was vacant, I moved Lauren Potter into it, tucked her into bed, and told her I was going out. She wanted to know where. I told her only that I would be back before nine and would take her to get her luggage and see her off. "Stay awhile," she said. She kissed me and her eyes begged for a little more of everything. I stopped. I started. I nearly popped a hern deciding whether I was coming or going. But I went.

Chapter Eight

It was artificial morning on Satcon. Bird tapes were singing in the plastic trees of the green area. A lone sanitman was slowly going about the never ending process of picking up after others. A mutty looking guy slept beneath a bench, perhaps he was a long-term truant. If I wanted to know something about Lauren Potter's problem I had to pick up a thread somewhere. I had only two names to run down and a vague desire to chat up O'Doul at USSC. The names were T.J. and Duffy. Knowing she ran a seven thirty office I headed for T.J. first. I got there ten minutes early. She wasn't in.

"Can I borrow your term?" I asked the boy at the console.

"For a minute," he said but he didn't look at all happy about having it tied up. He swiveled it around to face me on a slant.

"Less than that," I said as I punched up

Duffy's telephone number and received back
the information that it was a special listing,
North Port transient, belonging to an independent contract vessel named the
"Naughty Schoolgirl," North Port slip six. I
craned my neck to read it off the boy's mirror.

"Thank you," I said.

"You're welcome," he said grabbing the
swivelling input board like I'd borrowed his
oxygen line.

"I'll wait outside," I said, sparing us the
effort of having to look at each other across
the narrow space. I felt better than he looked,
a night with Lauren Potter having taken
inches off my hips and years off the weight of
my winters. I walked out into the hallway and
lit up. Then I saw them. Up the walk, a
hundred yards or so up the endless hill, came
T.J. Janes, her long legs scissoring in her
thoroughbred gait, and next to her, *the face.*

They strolled up the path chatting away.
Once she touched his arm. Once he shrugged.
But that was all I got. Then they passed me
and went into the Security Suite. To T.J.
Janes' office I presumed. I let them clear the
reception area and then went back in.

"Oh you just missed her," the boy squealed.
"She just went up. But I can't ring her just
yet, she's with someone."

"Oh, who?"

"With Mr. . . . Miss Janes' meeting are not
for public scrutiny you know. What is this in
reference to?"

"Doesn't matter. Did you tell her I was here?"

"How could I? You didn't give me your name."

"I gave you my name two days ago."

"I've seen a lot of people since two days ago. We are very busy here." Without thinking too hard about it, I slipped my claw behind me and out of sight.

I was satisfied that T.J. didn't know it was me. So there was no sense tipping myself trying to get a handle for *the face*. "It doesn't matter. Tell her I'll be back," I said and left.

"Tell her whom?" the boy screamed at my back.

"Whoever you like!" I answered and slipped back into my doorway. The boy came out. He looked up the slope to his left, then up the slope to his right. Then he shrugged. Five minutes later *the face* came out, whistling like the artificial birds. I followed him.

Tailing a man in a hallway is like hiding a blueberry in a saucer of milk. Possible, but you have to be pretty clever about keeping your thumb over the blueberry. I went fifty yards or so, ducking into doorways like in an old Peter Lorre 2-D flick, and then managed to pick up a buffer: two gents out upon their own business. I fell in behind and the four of us strolled for about a quarter of a mile.

Here *the face* hung a left into an elevator headed toward North Port Mini Ring and I lost my "thumbs." But another car arrived in

short order and as I started to lighten up as I
was eased in toward the mini, I took note that
North Port was built rather like a 20th
century shopping mall, with two center aisles
that ran the circumference of the ring and
with transverse aisles intersecting to the
walls every several yards. If I could make him
before he got out of sight of the elevators, I
figured I'd be able to parallel him, peaking at
him at each corner. It worked like a top. As
the doors of my car opened I caught him and
never lost him, and he never tumbled, though
it got a little touchy when we made the
transfer to the counter-rotating dock area.

We had been skipping, grabbing the side
rails every few yards to convert upward into
forward motion. In the zero-G of the docks we
began to straight-arm it past a row of indie
ships and sky train modules, their noses
thrust inward, their tails jutting out into
vacuum. At this pace it was getting hard to be
discreet. I did my best to stay behind the
ship's chandlers and loading ramps and
dockways that were set off from the dock
wall.

Fortunately at the other end of the line of
indies *the face* hung a right and started back
to the mini. I didn't bother to keep a tight tail
now, since I was almost certain I would catch
him at the transfer elevators, if not before.
Worked like a top.

The doors closed behind me and I fell in
behind *the face* in the Mini Ring hallway
again. I made that he was carrying a package,

a small envelope. Probably something handed to him as he went by one of the ships at the dock. By some appointment, perhaps. I eased a little closer; risky, but if he had any more appointments to keep I wanted to see with whom they were kept. But he had no further appointments. We followed the circle nearly fully back to the other side of the Ring. He went past the gift shop, past the hardware store, across the square to "Mr. Bigs." Into "Mr. Bigs."

I stopped, half expecting him to emerge with another envelope, or emerge without the envelope he had been carrying. Or emerge with someone in tow. But, he didn't emerge. I gave him five minutes; that was all I could afford if I wanted to keep a schedule that would have me back in time to get Lauren's luggage and see her off and maybe hug and kiss a little. Damn. I'd also wnated to drop in on Duffy. Damn again!

Duffy! My dim bulb flickered. Duffy Warren. The denizens of Mr. Big's had been discussing one Duffy Warren the day before last. Duffy Warren, they had said, was a man they admired but wouldn't stand up with. He was bucking the system too hard. He was heading for trouble. They were talking something like that. Weren't they? The more I thought, the surer I got. There was a connection here. I bounded across the square and I went into Mr. Big's.

Chapter Nine

It was nearing eight A.M. Greenwich Mean, but in the 24-hour worklife of Satcon that didn't mean much, at least not at Mr. Big's. The bar was pretty busy. A few shifters were just getting off and having their happy hour complete with a tray of canapes at the end of the bar and the half-price drinks. The rest of the clientele were having breakfast. Two teenagers played "Dragonslayer" at the hologame in the back and everyone else seemed to be trying to ignore the image of the dragon that swooped around, occasionally over their heads, or else trying to speak above its electronic roar; or else both. The dragon was winning. The bumper-pool table was crowded and a few people stood by watching or waiting to take on the winners. Money was being wagered in cash and on portaterms. The table that had been full of engineers and skippers the other night was filled with different faces this morning. Too bad. I sat down at the bar. Mr. Big turned, eased his bulk around from the antique cash register. He laughed. It was not a laugh of humor but of recognition. "So," he said, "how did you make out?"

I cocked an eye at him, and tossed my claw noisily to the bar. He affected not to notice.

"Your class reunion, how is it coming?" he asked.

"Fine. Beer, no carbos."

"Try this," he said and poured some pinkish fluid that made a small white head. "Just came in. Proto-beer. Sample it. Let me know what you think."

I picked up the glass and rolled the oily pink stuff around in it. I sniffed. It smelled like number six lube. I put some on my tongue. I put the glass down. "Beer, no carbos."

"Hmmm," Mr. Big laughed as he took the glass, spilled the contents into the sink and rinsed it out. Then he drew my beer. "Did you find your girl?" he asked.

"No," I lied. The bathroom door opened; past the man who came out I could see it was empty. *The face* was either not here, or in the office, or else he'd slipped in and slipped out to give me, ah, the slip. Asking would tip my hand. But maybe I wanted it tipped.

"There another way out of this place?" I asked. Sometimes the only way to find what you want in a pot of stew is to stir it up.

Mr. Big laughed again. "That's a felon's question my good man, a felon's question indeed. Is someone following you?"

"What if there was?"

"I should like to know if the USSC were about to stage a raid in my café, that's all. Otherwise it would be entirely your business."

"You've got something to hide?" I asked returning to my beer.

"Everyone's got something to hide, Mr. Stargis," he laughed. It was starting to get on my nerves, his laugh.

"I'm looking for a guy," I said.

"This reunion grows like the armies of China," he laughed.

"He looks a bit standard; this high, dark hair." I went on a bit, but describing *the face*, I told him, was like describing a bad smell. You had to be there.

"I know what—I mean who—you mean," Mr. Big said, to my great surprise. "He was here a few minutes ago. Hmm," He laughed, "A bad smell, indeed. He's not here now. He left; yes through the other door in my office."

"You know him?"

"No."

"Then why would you—"

"He drinks here. He pays money. He doesn't cause a fuss, minds his manners. He came in a minute ago and said someone was following him, could he please duck out the door. I said of course. I didn't know he was part of your reunion."

"I'd like to talk to him."

"Leave a number," Mr. Big said, "I'll ask him to get in touch with you." He laughed real big now. That laugh. "Such a reunion. I only wish I could attend."

I left the number of my hundred-year-old friend, Tarbox.

He picked it up and looked at it. "That's the Centenary," he said musingly as he eyed the screen after punching the number I gave him. "The rooms are cheap," I covered weakly. "I'll tell them I'm in remarkable shape." Bigelow laughed.

"Oh yeah," I said. "One other thing."

"Remarkable shape indeed," Bigelow said, still all a-chuckle from my little joke. "Sorry . . . one other thing?"

"What can you tell me about Duffy Warren?" I asked.

He didn't pretend not to recognize the name. "Indie shipper, good man." Sobering, "I can tell you that. Also that someone's looking for him."

"Yeah? Who is?"

"You are!" he guffawed and collapsed with the hilarity of his own joke. I waited for the rolls of waving flab to subside. "You . . . want . . . him . . . for your re . . . re . . .re-union!" He went on like this for awhile. When he quieted down I asked him a few more silly questions and got a few more silly answers and then I split for North Port.

The doors opened. I bounced out. At the first wall phone I bounded over and called Tarbox. He was tickled pink to hear from me.

"Are we having dinner?" he asked.

"Soon I hope," I said.

"Bring something to smoke, I can't get anything to smoke, they take everything away—"

"Tarbox," I cut him off, "Listen up," I filled him in on what I was doing and that he was to expect a man to call. The man would ask for Bockhorn or for Stargis, probably the latter. Tarbox was to call me on another line and together we would work out a way for me to meet the man. Under no circumstances was Tarbox to give any information about me to the man directly.

"Okay, pally," Tarbox said, "not a word shall pass my lips."

I thought for a moment. "We're dealing with rough customers. Don't be a hero."

"I'm not a hero," Tarbox said, "I'm your friend. And I'm as tough as anyone. I didn't get to be a centenarian by not being as tough as anyone."

"Okay, let's get this guy, whoever he is," I said and Tarbox said, "Right," and rang off. I felt good about the call. My thinking went this way. If *the face* still wanted Lauren and couldn't find her, he might work through me the same way I'd worked through Cobb. It was worth a shot. I wanted another go at *the face*. I also wanted another go at T.J. Janes. But first, Duffy Warren's "Naughty Schoolgirl." Luckily I was running a little ahead of schedule.

When I reached her nose I pressed the button on the deck monitor. There was no answer. The hatch was open so I walked in.

On a Heinlein-class freighter you enter the cockpit first. Duffy's was neat as a pin. He was the kind of guy whose pencils all pointed the same way and were lined up flush to the eraser side. The rest of the place followed suit. Above the pilots chair I hit the general klaxon. A horn sounded throughout the ship. I hit it again. And again. I glanced at the time. Then at the open cockpit cabin door. I let myself float to it, gripping the railings as I went.

"Duffy Warren!" I shouted through the door. "Ahoy!" I stepped into the sleep quarters behind the cockpit. Heinleins used a crew of four when they had their original controls. Now they could be single handed. But Warren had all four pivot beds made up just the same. I'd assumed by the chatter at Big's that he was here alone. I smacked the bunks. All but one, his, brought up a cloud of dust. He was alone. The spines of stripped pivot beds must have been offensive to him. He'd arranged it so they all looked tip top. I began to look forward to meeting him. "Duffy Warren! Ahoy!"

There was no one in the tiny galley, no one in the crew storage-room. There was no one in the engine bay, no one in the life-support bay. "Duffy Warren! Ahoy! Ahoy!"

I lowered myself down into the tube-transit to enter the outer servo pod. Since then they were designed to work isolated claims in the Belt, all Heinlein class ships carried their own cranes in a pod on the shell of the ship.

You had to pass through a narrow tube-transit to get there. I pulled myself through the tube to the closed iris at the other end. The button above the door had no effect when I punched it. No horn sounded. The door stayed closed. I banged it.

"Duffy Warren! Where the hell are you?" He wasn't in the servo pod. I turned around in the tube by pulling my legs high up into my chest and ducking my head to meet my knees. I was still a tight fit. When I got myself righted I looked up at the other end of the tube, just as the door irised shut. "Hey!" I panicked—hand-over-handed back up the tube so fast that built-up inertia banged me hard into the closed iris. I bounced a few feet and clambered back yelling, "Hey open up! Open up! Open that door!" I pounded away at the tight little pucker of closed steel sphincter. "Open up goddammit!" Cool it, Bockhorn, I said to myself. Right.

I backed up and looked around the perimeter of the door. Perhaps some automatic system had triggered it. No buttons or levers were immediately apparent. I banged again. "Open up!" The force pushed me back down the tube again.

I was growing short of breath. I'm out of shape, I thought. But I wasn't *that* out of shape. The oxygen was already starting to thin. The access tube's other end was sometimes open to vacuum; there must have been some automatic shut off that engaged whenever the inner iris was closed. Like the rest of Satcon, the dock's counter rotation wasn't quite right; when I let go of the rail I floated ever so slowly back to the outer iris, twisting imperceptibly and landing, feather like, feet first, looking back in the direction I suddenly took to be up. I tried to draw a deep breath and couldn't. The first panic of a drowning man; the inability to flood the lungs with surplus O_2. Breathe shallow, I told myself and I started to. I considered the options: either spend what oxygen I had trying to pry the steel door open, or conserve and hope for a miraculous rescue. Nature solved my problem. I passed out from lack of oxygen. My life, I'll note, did not pass before my eyes.

When I came to I was on one of the dusty pivot bunks in the sleep quarters. The hammer that had been banging in my toe was now playing counterpoint to two more that were banging away behind my eyes. My mouth was dry. My ears rang. My lungs were full. But not full enough. I breathed in as hard as I could, arched my back, expanded my chest and flooded my little bronchiols with all the clear, sweet life-gas I could draw into myself. Ahh.

Then I got up. Ooh. My head. My ears. My client! I checked the time. I was late by half an hour. Had I missed her? Had she waited? The door to the rear of the sleep quarter was locked which saved me the decision of whether or not to go looking for Duffy Warren again. I pushed myself gingerly into the cockpit; it too was empty.

I let myself out onto the dock.

I'd been out for a long time. Quickly, I checked myself for brain damage. My name was Bockhorn. 66 and 66 are 132, not 136. The Red Sox had just won the pennant in six over the Metro Yankees. I was okay. No better or worse than usual. I lit out for my quarters not knowing whether to hope that Lauren was safely gone, or safely still there.

The desk clerk smiled at me. I had no messages. I opened the door and it bumped half way through its arc, against something on the floor. Brain damage you *schmuck*, I screamed silently at myself, you were brain damaged to begin with! What if Lauren called T.J.?? T.J. was in with *the face*—if Lauren told T.J. she was with me at MA&P billeting, then T.J. could have told *the face* and, omigod! I snaked in around the jammed door. It wasn't Lauren on the floor. It was everything else.

My room had been hit by the same trash bomb that had gone off in Cobb's room the other night. I went through the wreckage frantically, praying that I wouldn't find what I was looking for. Finally, I sagged down on the bed. Lauren's corpsed form wasn't among the detritus. But that didn't mean she wasn't dead.

"Bockhorn?" came her voice from the door. "Shoo," I exhaled at myself. *That* meant she wasn't dead. I sat up.

"Come here, toots," I whispered, unable to summon the energy to rise. She worked her way around the door and into the room the same way I had, and tippy toed through the debris. She took my hand and I pulled her into my lap. "I thought—" I said, and she covered my lips with hers. I pulled her to me and buried my face in her neck. "Thank God," I said.

We lay back on the bed, side by side. "I thought I'd lost you," I said.

"What happened here?" she said.

As relief sank in I began to get angry.

"Where the hell where you?"

"I went to the space port."

"You went to the space port. Why did you go to the space port? I'm trying to keep you under wraps. I'm trying to protect you." I looked around at the shambles made of the room. "Thank God you went to the space port. But why?"

She began to cry. "I wanted to get out of here, that's why. It was your idea," she sniffed. "You told me to go. We were supposed to pick up our stuff at ten and I was supposed to leave and oh . . . Bockhorn . . . you *told* me to."

"Yeah but I didn't want you to."

"I didn't want to either," she smiled, her small chest heaving.

"I'm glad you came back," I said, "We'll work it out." She grabbed my arm and squeezed it. I wanted to ask her about T.J. and her connection with *the face*, and maybe Duffy, and maybe Mr. Bigelow. I kissed her forehead instead. Goddammit she was involved in something heavy and she needed help and she wasn't helping me help her. I had to get through to her some way.

"Are you okay?" she asked me.

I wasn't sure. I was, after all, a truant buster, a stow pincher. Alright I had a good head—I always figure out the Christies and the Nero Wolfes—but this was the real thing and it was confusing as hell. For two days now I had been turning things over and over, each flip of the file pushing every thing a little further beyond my reach. It was like repeating a word, like banana, over and over again until it doesn't make sense any more. That's how my so-called assessments were sounding to me. They didn't connect. The facts didn't link up.

I tried putting different sets of people into the scam with one another; T.J. and Lauren, T.J. and Lauren with *the face*, T.J. and *the face* and no Lauren, Lauren and Duffy, *all of them*. Each assessment made sense but only for a little way and then pffnGH. Imperfect mazes. False anagrams. One thing was just not leading to another. Whatever was going on, it wasn't *neat*, it wasn't Christie, it wasn't Wolfe. It was real. And a depressing realization was beginning to sink in; whether Lauren talked to me square or not, I wasn't all that sure that I *could* help her. I wasn't all that sure that this case wasn't beyond me altogether.

"I'm alright," I lied to put us both at ease. My hand found her tiny breast and she shifted her weight against me. We made love.

Afterwards, as I lit the post-act Fatima, the intercom rang. It was the desk. It seemed someone couldn't get a message to me over my term. Someone named Ox. They also told me that I had a call on the line right now. My term was indeed flashing. It was Tarbox.

Chapter Ten

"Bockhorn," he said. Blank screen.

"Go Tarbox, what's what? Why no visuals?"

"Uhh . . . it broke. Come to the Centenary, my room. Your man is here. He says he wants to talk."

Was he alone? Was it a trap? "Is everything okay?"

There was a short pause on the other end and then: "I'm okay."

"Good," I said, "I'll be right over." I had a bad feeling.

I hung up. Lauren's questions were phrased in a single look. I answered the look with a torrent of pent up words. "Okay toots, I'm off. My guess is that whoever sacked this place is pretty well satisfied and that makes it a pretty fair place to hide. Stay put. And use the time. I want you to think hard for me, real hard. I want to know everything that you know, whatever it is. Everything."

I checked the Stoner and the Magnum. "It means something to me, Lauren. It means more than a case. It means I want to know you're on my side, that you're with me." I packed the heat. "Do you get my drift? I want to know that we're still a team when we're out of bed and on our feet. I want to know you trust me. When I come back I expect to know something or two, so don't snow. I've had enough of that. Figure out what you want to tell me and let me have it. Maybe we can stay together. Maybe we can skip out with our skins intact and maybe, you and I, I don't know, maybe who knows what. Okay?"

"Okay," she said and kissed me lightly on the lips the way women do when they send their men off to work on the 8:45.

"I'll pick up our bags on the way back," I answered in the very same way. Didn't feel too bad either. I kind of liked it.

I ate up the rubberized turf of Satcon hallway with hungry boots. The pain in my toe was nearly gone. I supposed I could forget about it until it went *sprong*. The oxy-dep headache had subsided to a sinus attack. Background was what I needed, background.

"You *see* things, Watson," Holmes said to his biographer in "The Red Headed League, "But you do not *observe* them." I could not work that way. Few could, or can. Nobody could really look at a boot and determine that the clay comes from a certain hillock in Wales and that therefore the receipt in the pocket must come from the nearby inn and that since the price of amontillado goes up a shilling at eight then the man must have been at the inn at the time of the murder and blah, blah, blah. Nobody. Well, maybe a few guys who have certain powers of mind or ways of thinking or whatever. Maybe a Sherlock. Certainly a Mycroft, if such a thing could be, a *deus in machina*. But not me. Not the regular guy. For the regular guy the smartest advice I ever heard came from the introduction to the Santa Fe, New Mexico Police Department Manual of Detective Procedure. It went something like:

". . . the working detective, part of a group of detectives working as a team, is not responsible for, nor can he rely on, moments of sheer genius. He can rely only on his ability to accumulate the facts that make a background to the case. Once a sufficient background of evidence is collected, a case takes on the nature of a pattern hidden within a spray of dots. It is like a child's game of a rainy afternoon. The unimportant, unrelated dots begin to fall away, leaving those that fit together in a picture plain for all to see—a clear, readable, understandable pattern thrust up from the background."

Something like that. And somewhere along my way, somewhere between finding out that it wasn't a simple truant case, and wallowing into blackmail, and discovering a murder, and being called off the case, and forcing a confession to the murder, and finding a connection between client and confessor—somewhere along that way I had forgotten the admonition of that introduction which is taped to the inside of my medicine chest back home on Luna. Okay, I was alright now. I was back on the case. I was sketching in background. Tarbox had a mess of dots, or at least a way to get same.

The lady at the desk at the Centenary remembered me and waved me through to Tarbox's room. It was on the second level. Impatiently I hand-over-handed up the escaladder. I flew down the narrow second level hallway. I stopped in front of Tarbox's door and pulled the Stoner. I hadn't had much luck with doors this case. I wasn't taking any chances. I rang the bell.

"Bockhorn?" came the voice from inside, weaker and paler than I remembered it. I pushed open the door. Tarbox was on the bed, tied. I whirled around to avert my head from the line of the expected hail of flachettes. But no one was there. "He's gone," Tarbox whispered.

The centenarian was tied to the bed spread-eagle, naked to the waist. There was blood.

"What happened?" I said.

"I didn't tell him where you were," said Tarbox. "How's that for tough? I didn't get to be a centenarian not being tough."

"I know," I said and tried a smile for him as I undid his bonds.

"He hurt me," said Tarbox.

That was putting it mild. Large clumps of the old man's white hair had been pulled from his scalp. His mouth was a mass of red swollen tissue. His nose looked broken. There were cigarette burns all over his chest. Lots of them. "He said," Tarbox wheezed, "he said to tell you that if you didn't turn over the girl this would happen to you. I told him you weren't scared."

"Good man," I said. I got Tarbox down to the infirmary where the on-duty nurse gasped. We gave her a cockamamie story about a break-in and I left. God, I wasn't doing anybody any good, was I? There had to be a better way to handle this.

At North Port I checked the time of the next flight out and the one after that in case we missed the first one. Then I went over to collect the luggage. The same wimpy clerk was there.

He went into his flinch as I approached. "Stargis," I said and slapped the plastic square down on his desk. "Four bags."

"Oh I told you that they wouldn't be ready," he said as if that made everything alright again.

"You said ten A.M.! That's two hours ago."

"Oh but I told you ten P.M."

"You said *this morning* at ten."

"That was when I called at seven," he said, "I said ten A.M. when I called at seven A.M."

"That's right."

"Well there's been a change. You see we had gotten an intercept notice on your bags—"

"All four of them?"

"All four, as I told you, and they were to be

here at ten A.M. but it seems they weren't off-loaded and so that's when we had to change the delivery to tonite, same flight, ten P.M. I told you that."

"You didn't tell me spit."

"Well I told your wife."

"You did?"

"This morning at nine thirty. She called to ask if she could come by and pick up the shipment and I—"

"See you tonight," I said.

"Pleasure to serve you," he said.

Lauren had the room pretty well neatened up when I got back. I collapsed heavily onto the bed, a tremendous weight growing in my chest. "What is it?" she said.

I wanted to tell her that I didn't think I could handle it. That just this minute I had had another of those primal moments of fright. That, at the door, it had occurred to me, what if the call to Tarbox's was a decoy? It hadn't been, but spit. Dammit I couldn't think of everything; and I had to! And on top of that, I had another message from Ox. Unscrambled it said: "Close case . . . T. J. Janes—Satcon Station. Urgent you report on compliance. If no response . . . 24 hours . . . will assume foul play. Ox."

"I think we should both go now, right now," I said, "Earthside. Let's go for it." I tried to read her face. She didn't look as pleased as I wanted her to look. As a matter of fact she didn't look very pleased at all. She tried to hide it but you could see the wheels turning. I rolled onto my back and stared at the ceiling.

"Let's wait for our bags," she said.

"Let's screw the bags and get the goddam hell out of here before I cause any more damage. Listen, my boss is after to me to close the case. I think he's about to send someone to find me. I haven't done you any good, or anybody else for that matter. I'm gonna at least get you out of here. Maybe me too."

"You'd go truant?"

"It's not exactly truanting when you don't plan to come back. But yeah, why not? I'm an expert at it. Let's *go*. We'll forward the bags to wherever. They've got as good a chance of getting there as they they've got of getting here."

"Don't say that, Bock."

"Why not?" I said rubbing my eyes, "Why the goddamn hell not?" I knew why not. Because there was a job to be done. Because I had a duty. To her. To the Fleet. To myself. Because it was bad for business that a tough mug like Cobb could get rubbed without a blink. Because it stunk about Tarbox. Because it stunk even worse about T.J. and *the face*. Because I was running scared. Because I was giving up a dusty old battered dream. I couldn't bear that most of all.

"Because," she was saying, "there's something in those bags that I need badly."

"Don't worry about it, tootsie," I spoke like Bogart into the back of my hand; "Bockhorn's still on the case."

"I can't leave without the bags, Bockhorn. I

can not leave without my red bag." She hadn't
heard a word I was thinking. "I *will* not leave
without that bag."

There was something in her voice that made
me sit up. She was standing against the
room's desk now, arms folded across her
chest, hips tilted, like a miniature T.J. Janes,
no teddy bear.

"You asked me to tell you what I knew.
Okay I've thought about it. I've thought about
it a lot. You're wrong about it meaning anything, I mean it meaning anything about us.
Its got nothing to do with that. I could love
you even if you were a spy."

"A what?"

"But that doesn't mean I'd want to keep you
on the level."

"A what?"

"I'm going to tell you what I know. I'm
going to tell you the truth. I've been getting to
it for a couple of days now, I swear it. I just
want you to know that I'm not doing it to
prove I trust you, or I love you." She looked
down. "I do both."

I breathed in deeply.

"But I'm scared Bock. No, I'm okay. I'm
going to tell you this now simply because I
have no other choice. I hope you are on our
side."

"Tell me and I'll let you know."

She told me. It went something like this.
While working on a story about corruption in
the purchasing department of the Centenary,
she had stumbled onto a link to an organized

crime cell working out of Titusville, Florida, Space Center territory. She'd spent the next year quietly following it up. She began working with T.J., who became a kind of double agent and together they were collecting the goods, waiting to put together a story that would rocket them to the top of their respective careers. They had assembled a lot of material in physical memory chips, the old fashioned kind, bulky, unbreakable, and decodable, since each was unwilling to commit the stuff to the communal data-base's priable memory.

"How good is the stuff?" I asked, titillated to my marrow.

"Not very," she admitted, "but you could make a tax case with it. But a month ago we got three people to swear out depositions. They were encoded and included in the package. That's when Cobb began shadowing me. He was working for them, the Mob. He told me and T.J. that he'd use those sensarounds against us if we didn't pipe down." She stopped, as if I could figure out the rest. I could.

"It doesn't wash," I said.

"It's the truth!"

"It doesn't wash!" I shouted back. "Where does the money come in. There was money. You were laundering it up on Orion. What was the money?" I shouldn't make myself out so dumb. I'm really not, sometimes.

"But that was our scheme, T.J. and I," she said. "When I fell in with Cobb—I told you all about that already and it was true—I was supposed to convince him that there was a lot of money to be made by splitting from the mob and using the photos to pry Satcon funds out of T.J."

"Dangerous business, splitting from a crime family, and the blackmail money couldn't have been all that great," I said as if I didn't believe her, which maybe I didn't. She shrugged and turned the big blues on me. I got the picture.

"Cobb was so crazy in love with me that he bought it."

"Gotcha."

"So there we were, collecting money from T.J. and laundering it, sending it to Arizona, making plans, and me hanging around for a chance to grab the photos and split to the nearest Earthside D.A. with our bag of evidence. That's when Cobb started getting the feeling he was being followed by some guy he called *face*."

Curious, I thought, how we'd all been trained to think alike.

"And then you showed up," she continued.

"Correction, we showed up together, *the face* and I."

"That's right! Harry couldn't figure you out at all. I think he was so crazy with love and fear and whatever that he may have actually bought Stargis."

"People in full command of their senses have been known to buy Stargis."

"Sorry."

"I'm not sensitive," I said while I collected what passed for my thoughts. "Why me? Why did you come to me if you didn't want to tell me what was going on? Why did T.J.? Why—"

"Slow down," she said. "I'm not sure why T.J. went to you; maybe she'd gotten nervous. I don't know. Maybe she thought I needed a hand."

"Okay, why did *you* come to me?"

"I don't know. I was scared. You were big. You'd stood up to Harry. So I checked you out, remember? The restaurant?"

"I remember."

"I didn't know what to do. I didn't have a plan or anything. But you were there. Cobb was crazy. Unpredictable. I needed someone. You seemed nice."

"And big."

"Very. Then when I saw T.J. and found out who you were I didn't know *what* to do."

"Until Harry got rubbed by *the face*, and then you came straight to me."

"Not straight. I went after T.J. but I couldn't find her. Then I went to you. I figured either I'd be a suspect or I'd be a material witness or something and either way, if there was someone out from the mob to get us and get the incriminating material we had, then the safest place I could be would be with you."

"Well then either you're dumb, or you think I am, and guess what? I'm not buying either."

"Snow again," she Bockhorned, "I'm not getting your drift."

I had to laugh, but I couldn't. "Sweetheart, if you thought I was a spy for them then running to me had to be the dumbest—"

"Not a spy for *them*!" She appeared truly shocked. "Not a mobster. I thought you were a spy for MA&P!"

"Snow again, I'm not . . . say again, Toots."

"A spy for MA&P!" she said again, like I was thick headed. "The first thing I thought was, boy, isn't that the way. MA&P gets wind of my story and sends an agent to track it down and what's the windup? MA&P gets all the credit for my year's hard investigation. I didn't know what you knew. I didn't know what you needed to know. I didn't know why T.J. had sicced you on me. I didn't know anything! So when you got all heated up about the 'blackmail' thing I thought, if that's all he's after let him believe it until I could find out a little more about you. About your intentions."

"I intended to save your pretty little ass."

"I know. But I didn't then. I saw the story slipping away from me. I had happened before to me. I—"

"I know all about it," I said, cutting her off. Her *true* story was a little strange. Maybe a lot. Then again, what we had here was a bunch of amateurs playing at detective and, after twenty years of truant work, I wasn't sure I wasn't one of them. I wanted to believe Lauren. Who could make up such a bizarre story, I asked myself? T.J. Janes and Lauren Potter, I answered myself.

There was, of course, one way to check it

out. Talk to T.J. and talk to some of the people involved in the investigation. I asked Lauren for some names. She proffered three.

Artemis Squigg was a manager of the hydroponic farm on "D" Ring. B.T. Hannigan was a laborer whose quarters were on "B." And the ever popular Duffy Warren was an indie shipper, you will recall, whose Heinlein-class freighter "Naughty Schoolgirl," was moored in the North Port.

"Better see Duffy last," Lauren said. "I'm gonna have to really work on him if he's gonna talk to you."

I agreed, taking a reflexive deep breath.

"Are we a couple again?" she asked. "How did I do on the Bockhorn veracity/love-chart?"

"pffnnGH!" I said. If she was on the level, I had myself one hell of a case, and one hell of a doll. Too good to be true? Whatsamatta? You don't read detective stories?

I was a bit uneasy about leaving her in the room alone again but I was even less easy about trying to move her around the station with who-knows-who-and-how-many mob operatives looking for her. So, after extracting from her a promise that she would lock the door and hop into bed, "and stay there!" till I knocked, I gave her a low-tech, five minute block of instruction on the care, feeding and firing of my monstrous .357 Magnum and, placing the cannon in her tender mitt, I took off for the outer limits of what had become *our* case.

For my immediate part, I had some interviews to run. Like I said, I'm good at that kind of thing, a real gumshoe that way. I felt comfortable for the first time in hours. Interviews are background, and background as we all know, is my meat. I shifted into tru-buster overdrive. Or at least part of me did.

Chapter Eleven

Alone with my thoughts in an elevator headed for "A" Ring, I was uncomfortably aware that I was increasingly becoming of two minds about this case. One mind was screaming this is it, The Big One! It couldn't wait to get back and report. Holy goddam spit, I was about to uncover the first mob operation in Space. Okay it was only Satcon. But it was Space. And what more logical a place for the mob to start than on the oldest, most neglected dock facility in the sky? The other mind couldn't have given two spits less.

The other mind was thinking about the American Southwest and yellow print short sleeve shirts and white shorts; and a nice little place to share with Lauren Potter. The other mind was thinking about the beatings given and taken in the pursuit of the hapless runaways of space. It was thinking about the grind. It was thinking that the idea of going back to that after all this was just too terrible to contemplate. The other mind wanted out.

Maybe I'd take a job as a bank dick watching over mega-plus physical document transfers. Hell, I had savings; maybe I'd open up a little bar. Bockhorn's first case would be his *last* case! Two minds, see?

"I'll see if she can see you now," said T.J.'s boy. "Where'd you run off to?"

"Oh, busy, busy, busy," I said.

T.J. buzzed me up. But I never actually got into her office. She met me in the outer space, standing, looking exactly as she had when I first met her. "Where's Lauren?" she said.

"I thought I'd ask you," I said.

"Don't play games Bockhorn. You're in deep trouble. Your boss Oxenhorn has been all over my console trying to find you. You're falling in a shallow orbit my friend, you're touching atmosphere."

"I am?" I could afford to play cute. I knew that as soon as I walked in with the stuff I was walking in with, the data, all my minor indiscretions would be forgotten and I would either accept kudos, or quit, or both, with the greatest aplomb. "I have the memory chips," I said, testing.

"So what?" she said. It was a satisfying enough response. She could lie about their importance to her but she had enough sense not to pretend they didn't exist and that was good enough proof of their existence for me. She grabbed me by the arm. "Stay out of this," she said. "I'm warning you partly for your own good. There is more to this than you know."

I knew enough. I wanted to burn her like the picture of T.J. and Lauren still burned in my mind. And double agents could get burned. Especially ones who continued to play both sides so far into the game. I wanted some T.J. bad, even just a little piece. I never much cared for hitting women, but I wasn't all that sure my aversion extended to T.J.'s category. "How did you do it, Janes? How did you get a girl like Lauren to . . . what was it, your power? Your position? Information? Blackmail? How did you *get* to a girl like Lauren?"

"I just whistled," she said. That was all I wanted. I whipped her arm off mine and up hard behind her back. She gasped and rose up on her tip-toes. She didn't whimper even though I knew I was hurting her plenty. After awhile you get to be an expert at just how much twist a given arm can take before a tendon pops or a ligament tears or a bone breaks. Arm twisting is a science unto itself and I hated my own self for having learned it so well. But I had. I could measure out the pain in millimeter doses and I gave Janes all any man could expect to handle without tissue damage. Not a whimper. The monster.

I bent her forwards over the outer space desk and leaned hard against the backs of her thighs, my claw up around her neck for leverage. I felt her muscles stretch tight against the pressure.

"Who is the man you met with this

morning? The man you walked to your office with? The man with *the face*, who was he?"

"I don't know what you mean," she hissed and I pushed a milimeter deeper into the limits of sinew. "Bockhorn," she whispered, "Please."

"How are you connected?" I whispered back, a co-conspirator in her pain.

"I thought you had the documents?" She laughed through my arm lock. It infuriated me. Not her laughing but that I had made such a stupid mistake. I picked up my knee and placed it into the small of her back, softly, just to let her know it was there. She knew.

Her body convulsed as she brought up a heel that exploded between my legs like a grenade. I let loose her arm and staggered backwards, holding myself together. She was on me in an instant.

She grabbed me by my ears and heaved me down and the prettiest knee you ever saw grew and grew and exploded just north of my nose. Sparks flew behind my eyes as I landed on the desk. She reached for me again. Vaguely I put a hand up to ward her off and she grabbed it and yanked; now *I* was over the desk.

She pressed herself against my back and forced me over the way I'd forced her. I tried to wrench free a shoulder and in my shock a shard of light caught my eye as I craned, twinkling off a globe of gold, a small filigree ball on T.J.'s earlobe. Meanwhile the broad had pinned me!

"What shall I do with you Bockhorn?" she cooed.

Nothing, as it turned out. There was a clanking of the escaladder and her boy came up. She let me go just as his head was popping up through the ladder latch. "Is everything alright up here?" he asked.

"Mr. Bockhorn just took a nasty fall," T.J. told him.

I took the opportunity to clear out of the room. "It's the spin-G," the boy asssured me as I put myself back together downstairs. "It can get to you if you're not careful." I thanked him for the information and left.

I was still walking a little bent over when I reached the hydroponic farm on "D" Ring.

Squigg wasn't around his office when I got there which was just as well because I had some time and wanted to take a look and have a think. The hydroponic gardens of Satcon weren't bad for either. Slowly, I began to recuperate. Me, the great Bockhorn, taken by a dyke! Like I was *candy*. She took me by surprise, I told myself. Spit! She took me, period. S'okay, I can take it. *Spit*!

The gardens of "D" Ring stretched as far as you could see, each way up the endless hill. Satcon's hallways rarely looked so good. Long troughs of cabbage, vine apples, peas, beans, tobaccos of one kind or another. Satcon had once been a low-volume, *very* high priced tobacco exporter. "Satcon Havana" was primo, even in Havana. But in those days, all the fruits of Satcon were choice.

Now, as I walked between rows of vinelemon and vine orange, as I took the closer look, the fruit seemed as tired as the station itself, almost like the genes were unsplicing. I pulled a Fatima and contemplated the withered citrus, the disrepair, the empty troughs, now unnecessary to feed the diminished population. At the least, the air here was still fresh, and the gurgling waters of the troughs and the hoses and the pumps, though no babbling brook of Scotland, were poetry enough for the plastic and steel landscape in which they ran. A worker came walking up the citrus ramp. He was one of the few I had seen. He was dressed in a sleeveless white t-shirt, white work pants and rubber shoes. He didn't have the hands of a hydroponic worker. More like a welder, full of scars and nicks. I noticed because they were waved in my face. "Hey, you got business here?"

"Squigg around?" I asked.

"No. Not around. Go home." It was an accent I could not place. Callisto? Certainly one of the far asteroids. Real heavy duty space-gen, that.

"I'll wait," I said.

He took me at my word and moved off down the ramp. After a very short while another man approached. This one wore a business suit but the same kind of rubber shoes.

"Squigg," he said, extending a hand. He had a pencil mustache, trimmed so neatly it looked penciled onto his hawkish face.

Actually, hawkish flattered him. Rodentoid. I shook his hand without telling him who I was. Instead I said, "Lauren Potter sent me to ask a few questions."

"How is Lauren Potter?" Squigg asked.

"She's fine and sends her love," I said.

"I'm understaffed. I'm busy. I have no time for sarcasm. Lauren Potter is missing. If you know enough to drop the name then you know enough to know that. I tell you the truth? I don't know who Lauren Potter is anyway."

"You sound scared Squigg."

"Of what?"

"Of what happened to Lauren Potter?"

"Forget it," he said and made to go up the ramp.

I put a hand on his arm. "Your man, the one who told you I was here. Where's he from?"

"Callisto."

"He's no hydroponist."

"You can do better?"

"He's a welder and he's part timing. Is your whole crew part timing?"

"Some. Most maybe. Lissen what the hell do you want? I fill out my reports. I comply with Racial and National Quota; I comply with Safety Factor: my average pollutant composite is a minus-5 profile, pollution-wise I'm a plus; I've got all the proper filings for Comp, for Commo, for Health and Recreation, for Food and Drug, for Product Packaging, for everything. For every one hour we spend making a peach we spend six hours filling out reports on that peach. I got one lousy loophole here that says I can use part time help on an as-needed basis in any way I see fit, you bet your life I'm gonna use all the part time I can get to get product out."

The creep had the arguments down pat. I'd heard them from better men than him when I was in military. Looking forward to a life of enforcing stupid beaureaucratic U.N. regs for the U.S. Space Command was a big reason I was a private-carrier dick now. But damn! Space is raining soup; they should get out of the way and let ordinary people make some buckets! To hell with it. I ignored his yak.

"Down Earthside," I said, "when the mob moves in on a dock, one of the ways it does so is it sets up work gangs of disadvantaged workers, third-worlders, illegals, cons, and then it moves in on the legit businesses and 'persuades' them to use their gangs. Cheap labor at high prices. Up here, part timers fit that profile. Especially the second generation ethnics; guys from Sabros, Pushkin or Callisto. Snow if you get my drift?"

"You're looking for trouble buster. You're gonna find it."

"Lauren Potter says I might find some here. Any idea what she's talking about, Squigg?"

"Ask her. If you can find her," he said, and walked away. I didn't stop him. I had heard enough.

I left with a tidy assessment. Squigg thought Lauren Potter had been rubbed. He may have known who I was—I still wasn't clear about the connection between T.J. and *the face* and Cobb and the rest or how well they were concerting their efforts, if at all—and then again, maybe he didn't. He knew who Lauren Potter was, and what she'd been up to, and had taken a guess as to where she was now. That he was wrong about the last didn't matter. Talking to me must have seemed a sure ticket to get there himself. Two out of two. Lauren seemed on the level.

I finally picked up the expected tail as I was leaving the farm. Not a very good one. He was a big guy, dressed in a green worksuit. He had a big shock of bushy, unruly hair. I made him to be about thirty, about six-foot-five and a few pounds heavier than me. I decided not to go up against him. I had plenty of time till the ten o'clock baggage pickup and only Duffy Warren still to talk to, so I led my man a merry chase.

For two hours we walked around Satcon. We stopped for lunch. We bought a tie. I did. He bought a spaceball paddle at the next counter. We watched the stockmarket ticker. He never moved more than twenty yards from me and every time I turned to him he turned away. The fellow had an IQ of six, top. I guessed that the operation I was up against was tiny, perhaps a pilot program, with a lot of hang-around guys who were pressed into service on gangs, like the hydroponic farmer, or as, what, tails? It was time to see Hannigan.

I walked to an elevator and pressed the

button. My tail stood behind me. A car
arrived. The doors opened. I made to enter
and then stopped. My tail nearly ran me over.
We smiled apologies and as the doors closed I
bolted for them. My tail dove in front of me. I
slammed on the brakes. He was already
inside, the doors closing. Frantically he
jabbed at the "door open" button. Too late.
"Bye Bye." I waved.

As my erstwhile tail whooshed off to the
next ring I strolled to Hannigan's quarters.
They were in the "A" Ring "Village," a
complex of simple, cell-like living quarters
from the early days.

Here Satcon was more than anywhere else a
museum, a relic, a theme park of the way
space used to be. The Village was no more
inviting than a jail, and its denizens lived little
better than cons.

It was constructed of honeycomb composite, painted grey. The living-cubicles
were four-by-seven-by six cells that contained a bed, a term and an open locker.
The Village contained nothing but cells and
narrow hallways now. Once it had held
dreams. With the decline of the dreams had
come a little elbow room, and the more enter-
prising of the Villagers had broken through
neighboring walls to set themselves up in
little suites of two or three and even four
cubicles. But for the most part it was one web
bed, one honeycomb-aluminum stool, one
term. Jail.

It was in one of those simple unadorned

cells that I found Hannigan the laborer. He lay on his stomach interacting with a pornographic display. It was a fifth level cell—no escaladders here—and by the time I had climbed up to it I was a little out of breath. Hannigan rolled his head to face me when he saw that I was stopping at his cell and apparently wanted to talk. His eyes were burned by the chem. They were deep red and very far away. Again I introduced myself as being sent by Lauren Potter. There was no reaction for a moment, and then "Oh."

"I'll give you a 'guess what' I've come to talk to you about?" I said.

"I give up."

"Try."

"Lauren dead?"

Word had certainly gotten around about Lauren Potter, and the fact that the data was incorrect in detail did nothing to diminish my respect for the speed of the grapevine.

Hanningan was not from Callisto. I made him Earth-gen, maybe an ex-con, which would have made him eligible for government mothering and private entertaining. I asked him what he did for a living and he told me: "Bilge."

"Bilge is part time," I said. Bilging hasn't been a full time job on Satcon for years. "What is your assigned specialization?"

"Maintenance, electro," he said, this time not taking his eyes from the screen.

"Where do you work?" I asked.

"On the dock." He meant bilge.

"Where's your maintenance shed?" I corrected myself.

"Don't do no maintenance," he said, "only do bilge."

"What do you do when you're not doing bilge?" I replied, mildly trying to keep it simple.

"This," He said, miming masturbation . . . no, not miming.

He didn't remember talking to Lauren Potter. I left him and his terminal to their dreams. Like Squigg, he'd told me enough. Stonewalling indicates something behind the wall right? There was something here, right? A simple truant case, right?

Hannigan was apparently part of the bilge team that the skippers had been complaining about the day before yesterday in Mr. Big's. It was one of at least two teams, the other being hydroponic, that somebody on Satcon had put together to do some business. Legal enough. But something about these teams had driven the competion out of business, or into other lines of work, or off Satcon altogether (who'd notice?), and judging from the bar chatter about the high prices of the bilge unit, I knew it was not their rates. I had a feeling it wasn't excellent work habits either. I took a breath and headed for Duffy Warren's ship. Unless he blew my theory completely out of the water, I was headed home with the start of something big.

I wasn't sure that Lauren had talked to Duffy Warren or what his response had been to my second visit but I didn't want to risk a call to Lauren at the MA&P billets so when I'd crossed the dock to the nose of the "Naughty Schoolgirl," I just braced my feet in the rings, put my hand on the Stoner and leaned on the klaxon with my claw.

"Come on in," Warren yelled from inside as the door slid open. I pulled myself into the cockpit. Warren was velcroed into the co-pilot's chair, playing with a gauge and something that looked like a screwdriver but probably wasn't. "Are you handy?" he asked, looking up at me.

"No," I said.

"Okay," he answered and he threw the gauge into the snap drawer receptacle and closed it. "You sit around and sit around," he said as he slid the screwdriver-thing into a packet with several others and slipped the packet into his pocket, "you start looking for things to do to keep busy." He was pretty chatty for a guy who'd tried to kill me earlier in the day. I said as much.

"Saved you too," he reminded me.

"Thanks."

"Don't mention it. Glad to do it," he said. He was one of those sincere, up-beat guys.

Duffy Warren was more Lauren's age than mine and I was surprised at how much that seemed to bother me. I rarely envy people younger than myself. But not never. I envied Warren and couldn't dope out why Lauren had turned off to him except for *say-la-vee* and all that.

The kid was good looking, big as me and a whole lot better shaped, obviously from a good school, with the kind of upbringing that shows itself in little things. Ivy League. Smart. I wanted to drive his *gunyones* up behind his eyes.

"Come on back," he said.

In the captain's quarters, a small room with a pivot harness, a real bed—the one I'd woken up in—two genuine teak chairs and a desk to match, he "poured" some excellently brewed coffee into a squeeze bulb. "High mountain," he said, "last of the cache. Enjoy."

He spoke freely. He had been in port for a couple of months. He didn't see much reason to stay. Rules prohibited him from off-loading until he was bilged. He had rebelled at the ridiculous bilge prices. Despite the fact that it was hot, nasty, dangerous work, and entirely too radex for my tastes, he had spent a full month bilging by himself. Now he was waiting for his certificate, the piece of paper that said he had satisfied all Port Authority requirements, including bilge, and could proceed with off-loading. Waiting.

"How long now?" I asked.

"Two weeks."

I whistled. He nodded. "What do you think the hold-up is all about?" I asked.

"I'm bucking the system."

"What system?"

He told me. Basically it was the Bockhorn theory; the old Twelfth Avenue freeze-out. Duffy had been warned about it by a skipper he'd docked near on Walt Whitman. But what he'd been warned about, he said, was only a pale image of the real truth. What Duffy Warren had heard was that someone had taken over bilge and several other ships' services, and by offering absurdly low fees had driven the competition out. Okay, that was fair. But the resulting price increases once the other guys were out of business weren't.

Duffy Warren was an independent sort of fellow. He didn't tell me that but he didn't have to. He did tell me that after two years of running his own indie and just now beginning to see the profit in it, he wasn't about to knuckle under. He contacted Port Authority Security, a Ms. T.J. Janes, and complained about it. She "was very sympathetic" and put Duffy Warren in touch with a reporter named Lauren Potter who was compiling data on the subject.

"I didn't want to talk to a reporter; I wanted to unload at a fair price and get my tail out of here. But I talked to her. Well, you know Lauren."

Yeah.

"We started seeing a lot of each other. She showed me her data. I helped her out with as much stuff as I could get from the other skippers and from the guys who were trying to gouge me. It was fun. We became . . . more than friends. Although, I don't know, I was always a little suspiscious she was more interested in my data than she was in my . . . anyway, we managed to put something together."

"You drew up a case."

"Well not really. You see, T.J. had all the real stuff."

"What real stuff?"

" 'The nature of the the change,' that's what the skippers slang it. T.J. had the lowdown on the nature of the change." He read my blank stare and added, "It's a term from entropic physics; you came across it in fusion drive engineering: in a closed system, any attempt to change the system becomes part of the system. You don't know about the nature of Satcon's change?"

I didn't think it was a great analogy, but who knows why engineers' minds work the way they do. I just said, "Tell me and we'll see."

Here's what came out. Sometime before his arrival on Satcon, six months before, he estimated for me, the offical response to all these dockside shenanigans suddenly changed.

The Port Authority simply stopped fighting it. "These guys, the syndicate or whatever they are, they got right through all the red tape. You see what happened, don't you? The original Space Treaty of '99 put up the U.N. Authority, with all its regulations, requirements, licensing fees, excise taxes and you name it, as a way of controlling the space enterprise—to keep it free of 'robber barons,' and to see that everybody on Earth profited.

For a while it even worked, or at least it seemed to; Space is so full of wealth it's hard to keep people from making money. So at first the Authority just seemed to hold everybody's natural rapaciousness in check.

"The people in favor of it said events were proving them correct, that 'uncontrollable growth' would have been a disaster, and that the Space Treaty had prevented that. But after a time there was so much red tape, and it was so tangled, that it became worse than the Sargasso it was intended to protect us from. It *became* the jungle it was meant to prevent. Crooks, robber barons or commissars, thrive in jungles. Bullies love chaos, any way they find it."

He paused in his lecture. That would have been fine by me except that I think he was getting to the point. "I'm not sure I follow," I said.

"These guys got things done. It was a little more expensive, but it was worth it; they got you in and out quickly. Ships and crews are expensive; time is money in space even more than planetside. The port liked it because shippers liked it. As word got around Satcon, became more and more competitive as a way-station. The rest of the place may still be a pest-hole, but look at the current North Port traffic records. Bigelow says the rise started right away, too, all part of the 'nature of the change.' "

"Bigelow? Mr. Big?"

"His tavern was the meeting hall for all

this. That's where all the deals were made and where your clearance came from, all your permits and certifications and things. Bigelow was connected to some people in the Authority. You see, all the permits and papers were still necessary but only for form. The appearance of red tape—to satisfy the powers that be—without the annoying reality of it."

He was on a roll now and he kept at it, going over and over the same territory. I didn't stop him. If you want a guy to tell you what he knows, you're smart to let him tell you what he thinks, too. Anyway, this went on for awhile, until Duffy Warren said, "and so that was the first part of 'the nature of the change,' the co-opting by the system of the anti-system."

"Gotcha," I said.

"The second part was the logical consequence."

"What's that?"

"The warranted assumption, the thing you'd naturally expect to happen next."

"Which was?"

"The application of the golden rule."

"Do unto others?" I asked.

"He that has the gold makes the rules. The big indies moved in. With the port alive again, the big boys started getting eyes for a bigger slice of the growing pie. Besides, all of a sudden there were too damn many competitive little guys around. So the big guys raised the ante so that only they could afford it. The small operators couldn't. You had to be a certain size, be turning over a certain volume for the tribute—and that's what it is—to be cost-effective. If you were too small you couldn't pay."

"Sort of an 'unnatural selection,'" I quipped.

"Well, *you* could say that," Warren said. Cute kid. "And you could say that because if you couldn't pay, you didn't get a certificate. And if you didn't get a certificate you didn't off-load."

"Yeah, but that couldn't happen," I said, "unless Port Authority officials in charge of the certification process were in bed with the people laying the service rates."

Duffy Warren smiled grimly.

"Oh," I said.

"That's when the payoffs started. Not just the inflated rates for services, but real bribes. Big ones. From the larger indies. To keep the whole lousy system running."

"You know that?"

"The payoffs go to the mob through the Authority which siphons off its portion. The small indies are curtailed. The mob makes money. The port thrives. And the only guys hurt are the little guys."

"The Twelfth Avenue freeze out," I said.

"What's that?"

"Before your time," I said. It was so simple it was practically piss elegant. All the mob wanted to do was score some cash by eliminating dockside competition. All the big indies wanted to do was drive out the little indies. All Satcon wanted was some business. So they all hopped into bed together and screwed the little indies. Neat.

I reached for a Fatima and came up empty. "Sorry," Duffy Warren said, "Don't smoke." I went down again. My brain was turmoiling. Duffy Warren went on. He said that at least a dozen of the bigger indies were involved in this war of economic attrition and that in the end, "you know who'll reap the most? The Six Sisters. Them that has, gets. They'll be the big winners because they can sit back smug and safe while the shippers knock each other out of the box, narrow down the field, narrow down this port—and who knows how many others tomorrow—to fewer and fewer operators."

This was *his* "nature of the change." The big guys gobbling up the little, paying off a mob to do its dirty work and a port authority to certify it clean. And T.J. had all the information; T.J. and Lauren.

"Hard data?" I asked.

"Well Lauren did, yeah, but like I said, not the real heavy stuff. T.J. had come up with that. It was killing Lauren too. T.J. kept holding it back and holding it back."

"Why?"

Duffy Warren shrugged. "I guess she wasn't ready to go public."

"Change of subject, Duffy," I said, my wheels turning, spinning.

"Sure."

"What did Lauren Potter say when she

called you?"

"Which time? First, the other day, she said 'let's split to Earth.'"

"She did?"

"Yeah, she was calling from Orion Fronton."

"And then?"

"And then next day she calls up to tell me she's changed her mind."

"Did she say why?"

"No."

"How about today? She called today?"

"Twice. First, real early this morning. Said you were coming and that if I valued anything we had shared—and so on—I should detain you. I'm sorry about the air-seal. Careless of me."

"Go on."

"Then she calls back maybe an hour later and says let you go. That's when she told me she'd decided against going back to Earth with me. God. For you, Bockhorn? Sorry, I didn't mean it quite that way."

I shrugged.

"For you. I could tell it in her voice."

"When she called this afternoon?"

"Yeah! This afternoon she calls and says you'll be over and that if I valued anything we had shared—and so on—I should tell you everything I know. I didn't know what to do. I called T.J. She said spill. So I'm gonna. You recording?"

"There's more?"

"Pull up a chair."

I should have felt like I'd won a major battle with my life, but I didn't. Something else was on my mind. And I had a crushing need for a smoke. I asked him if he wanted anything from the store. He didn't.

"Right," I said, dumbly. A danger buzzer was ringing in my brain. I needed a minute to track down what it was that had tripped it. I checked my watch. The bags would be in by now.

"Right," I said again, to check, and stepped through the hatch and walked out into the rest of my life. The hatch door hadn't been closed behind me for a full second when I heard a shudder and a rumble inside the belly of the "Naughty Schoolgirl." The shock wave ran up through my feet to the small of my back and made all the little hairs stand on end along the way.

Stupidly, I grabbed at the hatch but my luck held; it had frozen itself shut. Bells and lights started going off all over the dock. Automatic systems kicked on. The central computer was very calmly and very loudly ordering all personnel to clear the area. A second explosion. A third. The nose of the "Schoolgirl" twisted inside its bay. Another explosion. She was pulling herself apart.

"Anybody in there?" someone shouted at me. It was a volunteer, the first on the scene. He was running and donning his fire gear all at the same time. Two more volunteers were bounding along the other walkway. With them was T.J. Janes.

There was another explosion inside the freighter and the two volunteers began debating whether or not to pry the hatch, or just rig a wall and expel *The Naughty Schoolgirl*. Volunteers were arriving in waves now. T.J. was seeing to their deployment. She looked over at me. I couldn't read the look. But I didn't have to. I split as soon as she was occupied elsewhere.

Chapter Twelve

As I made my way through the halls I found myself swimming upstream against a current of gapers, gawkers and official emergency personnel bouncing off one another as they bounded along to the accident sight. Behind me they were prying the hatch, looking for survivors, finding the remains of Duffy Warren, scraping him up with a spoon, God knows. I moved along as best I could, rebounding off people, sidesliding around equipment, fighting as in a nightmare. I made the elevator to "A" Ring. Blessed weight took hold. I stepped out into the square and I pounded away until I came to the MA&P billet. I put my fingers to the lock and poked my number. The door opened. Lauren screamed.

She was standing on the bed, trying to close the red suitcase. The rest of the bags lay around the room. The red suitcase snapped closed under her collapsing weight. I ran to her and held her up. She sagged into my arms. "You scared the life out of me," she said. I wanted to kiss her; I wanted to slap her. She needed slapping more. I whammed her along-side the head. She flew out of my arms and up against the side of the bed. "Child!" I roared.

"Bockhorn." she whined grabbing me by the leg. I kicked her off. She rolled over and got to her knees. "Bockhorn, *please*," she whined again. I let her have it again, across the top of her head, like a schoolgirl gets hit. She collapsed onto the floor in tears, her head cradled in her arms. I spoke loud enough to be heard above her sobbing.

"You child! You thief! How goddam important can a news story be! You stole T.J.'s investigation! You lied, you cheated, you stole! *Didn't you*! People are dying for these stupid lies! You lied to me!" I slapped her head again. "You lied to me and you nearly got me killed." I slapped her again. "Every delay, everything you did, everything you said to me in the past two days has been to safeguard your papers, your documents, your goddam story." I hit her again. "Admit it!"

"No!" she squealed, covering herself from the blows that I was now indiscriminately raining on the back of her head and shoulders, punctuating my tirade.

"Admit it! 'Stay Bockhorn!', 'Go Bock-horn!', 'Come with me Bockhorn!', 'I love you Bockhorn.' It was all to buy time. To

safeguard your goddam story. So I wouldn't
be able to 'steal' it. So T.J. wouldn't 'steal' it
back! And what am I a schmuck? To believe
everything you say! To go off on your wild
goose chase? Spend a day 'interviewing'
people so you have time to collect the goddam
suitcase." I went to hit her again but I had got
control of myself. I walked over to the red
suitcase, picked it up and heaved it against a
wall.

She looked up. Her eyes were red and her
lips trembled. "You think what you want,"
she said. "I *do* love you. And it *is* my goddam
investigation!"

I walked over to her and pulled her up by
the front of her tunic. She hung from my fist
like a rag doll.

"What am I hearing that Duffy Warren
didn't hear? Or T.J. Janes? 'I do love you.' You
don't know what it means, Teddy Bear."

"But I do!" she squealed, "I do, I do, I do."

"You were skipping out on me with the
story, a story I couldn't give two spits about!
You sent me to Duffy Warren because you
knew he would bend my ear off long enough
for you to collect your bags and blow without
me. For a goddam news story you *stole* from
T.J. Janes."

"I didn't—"

"Child!" I slapped her face, "Did you ever
stop to think that T.J. may not have wanted
that data for the same reason you wanted it?
Did you ever think that T.J. may not have had
any notion of ever publishing the stuff? Did

you ever think that T.J. had gone over to the other side?"

She stopped whimpering and stared at me for a minute. The possibility of my assessment had stunned her into silence. "Okay," she whispered, "if you want to beat me up, go ahead."

"I already did," I said and threw her down on the bed.

"Bockhorn?" she sniffed, "It *occurred* to me. About that."

"Primo."

"But I didn't steal the investigation. It was ours. And I didn't run out on you. You're right about the stall and you're right about the lies and you're right about how I . . . seduced you. I was confused. I wanted you. I was afraid of you. You're right. But you're wrong about one thing. I don't expect you to believe me but, listen, you might just ask yourself why, after I got the luggage, why I came back to wait for you?"

"So you left something behind."

"Who's the child, Bockhorn? Who's the child?" and before I had time to answer there was a knock on the door, a very perfunctory one that was followed immediately by a mighty whomp and the whole door blew into the room. It was T.J. and with her was a USSC man, not O'Doul, so I surmised he was Lt. Obermeir. "That's them." T.J. said.

"Hands up Bockhorn," Obermeir said.

"Wha—"

"You have a right to remain silent."

"What's the charge?"

"Arson. Unlawful imprisonment," Obermeir said; apparently O'Doul's clipped speech had rubbed off on him too.

"Where are the documents?" T.J. asked Lauren.

"What documents?" Lauren said.

"Never mind," T.J. said. "Obermeir, you take our friend Bockhorn. I'll take Lauren. The documents are in the bags somewhere."

"T.J. what in the hell are you trying to pull?" I said.

"Obermeir knows all about the investigation Bockhorn. I filled him in so don't try to snow him. I don't know what your part was in trying to silence it but if you've hurt this girl so help me—" She held Lauren by the chin and saw the tears and the red welts where I'd slapped her. "It's gonna be your ass Bockhorn." The very efficient Lt. Obermeir snapped the cuffs on me and led me away.

"You're making a big mistake," I said.

"That's what they all say," he answered.

On the way to the station I begged and pleaded and cajoled and threatened and otherwise acted like a common yegg. I stopped before I got in so deep I couldn't get back out. I hadn't endeared myself to Obermeir.

At the station I got pretty much what I expected, which was roughly the stuff I'd been dishing out for twenty years or so. Obermeir put me in a chair, same one I'd sat in when O'Doul had run the Cobb voice snatch through the USSC computer, and ran the treatment on me. He told me if I cooperated it would go easy. Then he hooked me up to the equipment and began asking questions. Problem was, the answers I was giving him, although they rang true on his charts and meters, didn't make much sense to him. Didn't make much sense to me either. I told him about Cobb. I told him about the blackmail. I told him how I covered up in case my client was suspected of murder. He told me that Cobb was definitely a suicide. I was too polite to laugh. He told me he thought I torched the freighter to silence Duffy and was about to do the same to Lauren Potter. I was too polite to spit. I hung in there. All through I kept hammering back at him. "You're holding an innocent man here while a girl is in mortal danger."

"Tell me another."

"Does my story check out on your goddamn machine or not?"

"Yeah but it doesn't make any sense."

"What am I doing here, writing a book? I don't have to make sense. To you or to me. I'm telling you things that check and you're sitting on me. Why don't you go out and find Lauren Potter, that's what you ought to be doing."

"Says you; tell me about the girls' investigation." I was deciding how much to let on when he tipped his hand and decided it for me. "Where are the gaming houses?"

"Wha—?"

"Where do they gamble; where do the games take place?"

Oh brother. I would have done the best I could at fleshing out the details of whatever lies T.J. Janes must have told him to convince him that the investation was into illegal gambling on Satcon, hoping it would win him to my side, but I was hooked up to a damn truth machine. Fortunately, that's when O'Doul walked in. His eyes popped open when he saw me. I must have been in a state. I'd been Obermeir's machine for six hours, breakfast, and another six.

Obermeir started going through the motions of turning over to O'Doul the station business, part of which was me. "I got nothing to hold him," Obermeir said.

"So let the man go," said O'Doul and gave me a see-what-I-meant-about-Obermeir look.

When the lieutenant left I told O'Doul the story as near as I could figure it and I laid out some suggestions. Cover all space stations and colonies, although that might be too late; cover all Earth ports at least. Alert all liner and skytrain operatives. Put a man in Mr. Big's for a listen. O'Doul sat busily at the term rapping things in as quickly as I could spit them out.

We figured out which space stations they could have split to and landed on before our net would be in place. Came out to six. Ditto Earth; came to two. Lunar was out. I stood to go.

"What'll you do?" O'Doul said.

"I'm going to find them."

"Where?"

"I don't know but I did it once before, didn't I?"

He wished me luck. I thanked him. I left him at his terminal, banging out more questions for which I hoped he'd soon have answers. I stepped out into the hall and latched the door. The "O" of a Stoner's nose tapped me in the small of my back.

"How's your toe, Bockhorn?" the man said.

"Hello Marvin," I said, "Are you breathing regular yet?"

The Stoner pressed itself into my back. I decided not to do anything foolish. I moved off in the direction it was urging. "Where to?" I asked.

"That's for me to know and you to find out," said *the face*, who certainly hadn't gotten any zippier in the lip. I resigned myself to my fate. I had a feeling that, at the least, I was about to get some answers. Throneberry took my Stoner and I felt stupid for having given up the Magnum.

I was not totally surprised to be taken back to the North Port Mini Ring, across the square, and into Mr. Big's. The place was empty, maybe shooed out. At any rate, it was unoccupied and a sign on the door flashed "closed." "Sit," my friend said to me and I did, at a table against the wall. He sat at the next table, the Stoner placed theatrically before him on a napkin. I contemplated my options. None looked promising. Then the curtains moved, and from behind them stepped Bigelow, Mr. Big. He walked behind the bar, poured himself a glass of red wine, then looked up at me. "Beer, no carbos?" he asked and smiled.

"Thanks," I said.

He poured the beer and carried both glasses to the table, slid a coaster under each, and eased himself into the chair across from me. "Prosit," he said, raising his glass to me. I nodded to him and sloshed some of the suds my way. "You have," he said, "proven to be a most worthy and tenacious and competent adversary and I am humble in your presence."

"Thanks again," I said unsure what his game was, whether I wanted to play it, or for that matter, whether I had a choice.

"Too bad it has to end this way," Mr. Big said. His eyes twinkled but without mirth.

"Too bad it has to end what way?"

"It is too bad you have to be terminated."

"Well, its gonna be harder on me than on you," I managed. He's bluffing, I told myself, stay calm. Termination, the word had come as a little surprise. I knew that I was in over my head. For two days I had been blundering around hoping for the best. I was about to get the *other* thing. A bluff, I told myself again, but it didn't comfort. I began looking around for an out at the same time stalling against the possibility that there was one. If worse came to worst, and I could see it coming, I preferred to be remembered by the fat man, and even by so mean and meaningless a creature as his humble servant, Marv Throneberry, as a class act.

"And you were so very close," Mr. Big said. "*I* was so very close. *We* were so very close," he laughed. "We almost had her, you and I, in our turns. Didn't we?" He raised a glass and toasted me again. "To better days, Mr. Bockhorn, even if we never live to see them."

"That's easy for you to say," I said and laughed. Tried to read him. Couldn't.

"You are entitled, at the very least, to an explanation," he said, enjoying his moment. I wondered just how far I had gotten under his skin, and why.

"I would terminate myself," I said, "and bleed slowly to death in your garbage can, if only I could hear my adversary, most worthy of worthy foes, explain to me what in the goddam hell has been going on these last few days of my miserable gumshoe's existence."

Mr. Big laughed out loud, twice, tickled pink I'd decided to play. "Marvin Throneberry! Another round!" he called and *the face* got up, handed his boss the Stoner and went behind the bar to pour the two drinks. His name really was Marv Throneberry!

"Bockhorn," Mr. Big said, "bane of my fiefdom, tracker of my horde, shame of all shamuses, thief of girls' hearts," he was going overboard now, "tell me what you know of the whereabouts of Lauren Potter?"

"You guess is as good as mine."

"Better maybe. Ah well. Explanation. Termination, and for me, rededication."

"At your pleasure," I said as Marv Throne-berry delivered my beer, no carbos, and Mr. Big's wine. The fatman quaffed, smacked his lips, sat back, played the little red dot of his Stoner on my chest, talked.

"I'm in love with Lauren Potter," he said. "Does that sound ridiculous to you? That a fat old man should be in love with so sylphy a womanchild? No it would not sound ridiculous to you, would it Bockhorn? You are eldering. You are, shall we say, girthing. In ten years or so you would look quite a bit like me."

"I should live so long," I said.

"Quite," he laughed. There was no humor in it. And no stopping him. He was on a roll. Snake-eyes if my luck kept running true to form, but they were his dice, and I couldn't leave the table.

"She came to me a year ago. Here in the bar. She was doing a story on organized crime in space. Organized crime in space? I told her there was no such thing. She told me she'd traced a connection through Mr. Big's. Very clever young girl. We went around and around each other. After a while," he laughed now, remembering, "it finally occurred to me that like the dry old spinster who monitors other people's sex because she's really fascinated by it, Lauren Potter was fascinated by . . . me. I seduced her. Don't be shocked. I was not the first. The girl was deflowered by birthright it seems. But that doesn't matter anymore. We were lovers. I was young again. We planned to marry. I told her some things about the operation, not much, just things I thought she'd need to know if she was to be my wife. Things she would have to know in order to handle herself properly in certain situations. Not everything. But some things."

"Trusting, weren't you?"

"Testing . . . wasn't I?"

"Touché."

"She was a perfect *gangster's moll*," he rolled the words around clownishly. Then his face hardened. "But she was loose Bockhorn. But I guess you know that."

I was still trying to dope out Lauren plighting her troth with the fat man, and with Duffy Warren, and with Harry Cobb, and with T.J. Janes, and with me. I drifted away from Bigelow's monolog. It *had* to be me. Lauren *had* come back with the luggage, maybe she *had* forgotten something. Couldn't be, not at that stage of the game. Maybe . . . Oh, knock it off Bockhorn!

"I had a new man up here," Bigelow was saying, "name of Cobb. I sent him to follow Lauren Potter. Find out who she was seeing. Who was beating my time! Get some photographs. Anything. I was going out of my mind. Next thing I know Cobb's disappeared altogether. Her too. Then you show up. Who's he connected to, I say? Why does he want my girl, I say? I send Mr. Throneberry to follow you. You look competent enough—far more so than our Marvin, anyway—maybe you'll find her."

"And Marvin then finds Lauren and rubs Cobb."

"You've been paying attention," Big said. "So he does the deed. Not a great job of it but good enough for a start. Then I find out that Lauren has been intimate with the statuesque, stunning T.J. Janes, my *bag lady*," he rolled that second archaism around like *gangster's moll*.

"And that Lauren's got the goods to blow your operation out of the sky," I said, feeling just peachy that I'd finally fingered T.J. as the Port contact for all this and hoping like hell I'd get a chance to do something with the info. "Goods!?"

Bigelow laughed so loudly that he started to cough, violent wracking coughs. The Stoner waved around wildly, banged against the table top. Bigelow kept laughing and coughing and laughing and coughing. I focused in on the Stoner. Timed it. Zeroed it, It banged the table top again, the Laimer dot jigging crazily across my chest. Bigelow continued to rock the Stoner. I grabbed for it. Bigelow pulled it back, didn't even stop laughing. Slowly he got himself under control. "Goods?" he said, disregarding my pathetic attempt at the gun, "To blow me out of the sky? I've gone *public* Bockhorn! *Evidence* can't hurt me. She had *the money*!"

My hairs prickled. Money? Of course.

Money made it all make sense. Well, love and money made it all make sense. I supposed I could figure it out from there but Bigelow had a lot more yarn left so I let him spin it out and as it spun it got easier and easier.

"So, you came back to Satcon," he was saying, "and when Throneberry recovers I send him back out after you and he turns your room and finds no trace of my money or my Lauren."

I didn't bother to remind the fat man that Lauren didn't smoke, didn't drink, didn't chem, nor did I tell him that, courtesy of our friends at MA&P luggage handling, she had no clothes to leave lying around. But I silently thanked the billets' desk clerk for being so "discreet" about my "dalliance" when Throneberry came to call.

"Aaaargh!" from Bigelow. "I was almost ready to give up, throw in the proverbial terry, walk away. Lauren gone. With my money as well as my foolish heart. Then, aha! There is a call from T.J. who informs me that you are about to talk with Duffy Warren who is about to spill to you his estimable guts. I decided to blow you up. You *and* Duffy Warren. Neatly. By remote control, a device so excellently rendered by my associate Mr. Throneberry."

"I thought that 'the goods' couldn't touch you?" I said.

"They can't. I was angry. You see Duffy Warren too had been . . . sleeping . . . with my little girl."

"T.J. told you that?" I interrupted.

He grunted in the affirmative. "T.J. did," said Throneberry. He smiled at me that ragged, tired smile. I saw it again. Something deep in his eyes, I don't know what, it's indefinable, but it was there, just like it was there the other night on the catwalk, the night he confessed. Mentally I smacked myself in the head. I don't know how many mistakes I had made so far in the case; two dozen, three? They all paled now to insignificance besides my misjudgement of Marvin Throneberry. Admitting that was like lifting a veil. All of a sudden I know everything, even down to the clue that turned the lock that closed the case.

The illicit love affair, the double cross, the blackmail scheme, Cobb's murder, Duffy Warren's, the attempt on yours truly, all of a sudden I knew how and I knew why and I knew who. Good God, I thought, let them please be bluffing.

"But you!" Bigelow suddenly roared, "You don't blow up so easily. Do you, my master detective?"

"I'm just lucky," I said, hoping it was true.

"And now T.J. too is gone," Bigelow said. "They're all gone," he sighed. "One way or another, they are all gone. I have no one left to take it out on Bockhorn, no one but you. Pity. Throneberry?"

"Yessir," said the gunsel, with the slightest hint of a whistle.

"Bring him back to me in a bag."

"Yessir," said Throneberry.

If it was a bluff it was working goddam well. A thin film of scared sweat was crawling all over my body and into the damndest places. I struggled for control as I played my trump. "Bigelow," I said, "T.J. has run out with Lauren. They're together now and my guess is that they have the money. T.J. set me up with USSC. She used you to blow the "Naughty Schoolgirl" and then convinced Obermeir it was me. She brought him to my room, hunching Lauren was there. See, she knew that if I knew enough to talk to Warren then Lauren must still have been with me. It was a good hunch," I rattled on. I'm not sure what my play was to have been. I could have asked to join forces, to look for Lauren as a team. I could have invoked USSC. I could have given it all a rest because the minute I was out of words and reaching for a breath Bigelow curled his lip and said, "In a bag, Marvin. Thank you, Bockhorn. That will be all."

My legs were sodden wood as I rose on them to take my last walk. Spit. I finally knew what happened. I finally had an assessment that worked, even in the room, even for the killing of Cobb. For the past 48 hours I'd been carrying the clue in my pocket. The tie tack. I had read it wrong. Now I knew how to read it right. All I needed was the chance. And to survive. Marv and I strolled like old friends to the back door. My heart pounding in my ears. At the door I braced a leg against the jam and whirled on the creep. He stepped back smartly, leaving me clutching air, and waiting for my feet to touch in the one-fifth G. "Once more and you get it between the cheeks," he said. Turnabout is fair play and all that; still, I thought it had sounded better when I said it. We exited the rear portal of Mr. Big's.

There was no one in the area of the port within hailing distance, no one to question our peregrinations or even stop to beg a light or the time of Satcon's artificial day. I began to wonder how much it was going to hurt. Death, whatever it was to be, didn't bother me so much. In a way, I was sort of curious about it. But the pain. I wondered about the pain.

I saw myself on a porch in Santa Fe. I was wearing a white short sleeve shirt and a pair of tan khaki shorts. I was drinking beer, real beer. I was a little fatter than I am now but not much. The house behind me was a simple four room adobe decorated with rugs and Indian stuff. Cheap. Out front was a Fiat aircycle. Also cheap. Lounging on the porch beside me in a white dressing gown was Lauren Potter. She lay back, one arm thrown across her eyes against the morning sun, one knee drawn up throwing the hem of the flimsy gown back far enough to show off the curve of her thigh. She was barefoot. I was pulling on a Fatima. Prol heaven. A life of semi-impoverished leisure. I reckon that when you face awfulness in some meaningful way, daydreams take on a less grandiose sweep than they used to. I'd never faced real awfulness before, at least not in the way that gave me this much time to think about it. "Alright," Marv Throneberry said, "Get in." I looked around. We had arrived at Mini-Ring North's eco-section. We were standing in front of the trash shredder. My bowels heaved but I held them in. This was gonna hurt like hell.

Chapter Thirteen

To my right was the garbage machine, a mean, squat, square affair six inches taller than myself and painted green. It would squeeze me, crush me, compact me until I was separated from my juices and liquids, which would be drained off and fed into the fluid system for reprocessing. The dry material remaining would be shredded, divided into organic and non-organic, and fed where the stuff was needed. I would be a permanent part of the space enterprise, like the rest of the garbage generated by my fellow man.

To the left was the muzzle of the Stoner, a small, black hole on the other side of which resided my entire life up to this instant. I knew what the Stoner would do to me. Just lately I'd seen what a close range blast had done to Cobb. It was, in the end, my choice. Force Throneberry into serving as a one-man firing squad, or take a seat in the big

green eternity machine. I chose to die trying
to live. A quick spring; I'd close my eyes;
Throneberry would hit or miss. But the gunsel
read it in my face. He took a step back. "Get
in," he said, "Just trust me and you'll be
alright."

I couldn't figure out his play. But I couldn't
get to him either. Double crossing had
become a virus in this affair, maybe
Throneberry had the bug. Maybe he was
grateful I hadn't skinned him on Orion.
Maybe those were his standard last words to
compactees. Lotsa luck, Bockhorn. I stepped
into the compactor.

There was gooey sludge on the bottom,
black and inky darkness. It smelled like the
sinkhole of the devil. With a lurch and a clang
the machinery whined and the walls began to
move. Large metal arms with six-inch turn-
knuckles flexed on the walls and brought the
ceiling down on me. Below me the ooze
drained through the grate that I was kneeling
on. Suddenly, hysterically, I remembered a
scene from an antique space movie. The
ceiling touched my head and forced it down. I
got lower. It kept coming. Fans, blades,
grinding rollers began to whir beneath the
grate. The machine was a cacophony of
destruction. It pressed me down on my side
and kept coming, juggernaut, Shiva, shatterer
of worlds, garbage machine. My bowels
heaved again at the thought that I had guessed
wrong, been suckered one last time. I was flat
on my back now, the blades slicing beneath

me, the ceiling coming down, touching my
nose. I turned my head to the side. I was
determined not to call out Throneberry's
name. A scream fought its way up my
windpipe but I stifled it as the cold steel of the
crusher touched my cheek, bruised it, be-gan-
to-crush . . . there was a handle: "auto-stop." I
reached for it, sinusus bursting, skull about
to, and got it with my claw and tried to . . . it
caught the edge of the handle and slid off. I
tried again. The machine pounded in my
ears—quite literally—and the claw grabbed
hold.

WHreeeeeeoosscreeeeeee-clunk. It stopped.
The ceiling sprang back to its original
position. The blades stopped below me. I
wasted no time climbing out. Throneberry
was gone. Either he'd counted on me to find
the auto-stop, or he was lying to get me to go
quietly. I guessed the latter. I didn't care.

In half an hour I was on a Laker flight back
to Orion Fronton. In three hours I was in the
tram of the Jai Alai stadium. A half hour later,
after a brisk cleaning and laundering in the
men's room, I was touring the seats. Lauren
Potter saw me before I saw her.

She was a blur, rushing down the aisle at
me, leaping into my arms. "Bockhorn," she
shouted it and whispered it at the same time,
"I thought you were dead. T.J. said that you
were—"

"I can imagine what T.J. said," I said. We
kissed. She was shaking and vibrating like a
little motor, her skin hot with flush. "Are you

being held?"

"No," she said.

"Honestly," I said and she nodded.

"When I thought you were dead I . . ."

"Went back to T.J." I finished for her.

"Oh Bock, let's get out of here."

"First things first," I said. "Where's the money?"

She didn't say, "what money." Then again she didn't say, "I was going to tell you. I was trying to protect you. I was blah blah blah blah," either. She told me where it was and that was enough.

"Are you sure?" I asked her.

"Yes!"

"About me?"

"Yes!"

She admitted that she hadn't been, that at first she'd wanted me and then didn't want me, and then wanted me again. "But I'm sure now," she said. "When T.J. told me you were—" And she began to shake again.

"Okay, Okay," I said, starting to get embarrassed. I still wasn't sure about her. But I was pretty confident that she'd finally narrowed down her field of suitors to T.J. Janes and myself, good enough odds against which to place a bet and I was betting that once she saw what I was planning on coming up with in T.J.'s room, well, let's say I was betting to win. I hugged her. She was still vibrating. I was too. Were we ever out of our element? Were we ever two onions in the

petunia patch? I started to think about Santa
Fe again, hard.

T.J. was at the betting windows which left
us a clear field for the moment. Lauren led me
to the tramway station where there was a
bank of safe-deposit boxes. She produced a
key for one. The red bag was in it. "This is it?"
I asked.

"This is it," she said.

I checked it just in case. It was *it* alright, at
least it was enough of *it* to be very, very
impressive. It even smelled impressive. I was
impressed. The bag suddenly felt very massy
in my hands. "Let's go," I said.

"Where?" she said.

"Your room," I said, "get going."

We kissed each other goodbye and she
stepped into a glass tramcar. I waited till it
left, then I went into action.

I carried the cash with self-conscious
casualness, like a bag of laundry; all behind-
eyeballs darting in every direction, keeping
lookout for heaven knows what. A million
immers makes a man protective. At the port I
handed it over to a baggage clerk.

"Where to?" He asked. "Sir? Where to?"

"Huh?" I said, "Oh, wait, give it back to
me."

He slid it across the counter at me. I
touched it. I had had the bag only five minutes
and yet it was hard to let it go. My understanding of the case deepened a little more.

I made arrangements for the bag of bucks

to be sent back to Satcon and then cabled ahead instructions on what to do with the bag when it arrived. Then I cabled O'Doul the ticket number and the authorization for pick up. With that off my mind I turned to my other problem.

I knew what to do about T.J. Janes and the murders. I was of two minds about what to do with Mr. Bigelow. The same two minds I'd been lugging around since yesterday morning. One mind said, "pretend to want to split the money with Mr. Big, as a finders fee. Tell him your plan is to break from the command, set yourself up with Lauren Potter in Florida, maybe with some Titusville mob connection that he could make. Half-and-half on the money." That'd wash. And if it did, I'd walk out with the marked money, whatever tapes I could make of our conversation, and the names of the Titusville people that connect with the space operation. The other mind said, "screw the tapes and the names." Take the money and run. Go to Santa Fe and set yourself up with Lauren Potter for real.

"I'd like to take back the pick-up authorization," I said to the clerk, deciding to keep my options open.

"I'm sorry," he said, "It's already gone out; I can cancel it though."

"Please," I said. I left instructions to be called at Lauren Potter's room when the bag arrived. If Ox was sending someone then staying at the billet would certainly curtail my options. Then I made for Lauren and T.J.'s hotel room.

"Hiya," Lauren said, letting me in.

"Hiya," I mimicked and got right to work. "Get T.J.'s bag on the bed," I said as I went through the chest of drawers. The girls were traveling light. Not too light I hoped. I was looking for something that I suspected T.J. Janes had brought along. But it wasn't in the chest. It wasn't in the suitcase either. It wasn't anywhere.

"What are you looking for?" asked Lauren.

"A tie tack," I answered, enjoying a very private joke.

The lock to the door *clicked*. I went for my Stoner which, of course, was in the property office of USSC-Satcon. The door opened. It was T.J. Janes, and she was wearing my tie tack, my golden clue, just where I wanted it. But, again, I was just a tad too late. Behind her were Marv Throneberry and Mr. Big. They had the pink dots of two Stoner Laimer Devices dancing all over her broad back.

"One big happy family at last," twinkled Bigelow. He twinkled less after I began talking. I told him I had the money and before he could tut-tut the deal I cut him right off. "A sixth sense and a tingling in my fingers whenever I touch the stuff tells me that the bag of immers is not quite as unimportant as you make it out."

He laughed, grunted, both. "A million units coin of the realm can never be too unimportant," he agreed. "I intend to have it."

"How about half of it?" I caught Lauren out of the corner of my eye. She didn't flinch. T.J. just stared off into space, a condemned woman. Marvin just watched.

"You're in no position to deal," Bigelow said.

"I'm in a very good position to deal," I said. "I know where the money is."

"Thief," T.J. whispered under her breath and I couldn't figure out whether she meant me or Lauren and it didn't matter.

"Shut up," Throneberry said.

"Bockhorn," Bigelow implored theatrically, "Steadfast gumshoe, stout-hearted sleuth, indefatigable stalker of felonious enterprise, don't throw your life away on anything so base as love or money. Tell me what I want to hear and you walk out of the room a free man with a future."

"Half."

"You can't deal."

"Tell me why not."

"Because you have nothing to offer in exchange but information, and information is now a buyer's market. You see, if I cannot get the information out of you nicely, than I will just have to get it out of you *not*-nicely. And either way, it's cheap at twice the price. Marv Throneberry?"

"Yes sir."

"Will you please feel free to light up one of your foul smelling natural-Havanas?"

"Yes sir," Throneberry said and began the

ritual-selecting, unwrapping, tonguing, and end-clipping of the cigar smoker. He looked ludicrous, but dangerous. I thought of poor Tarbox and the skin started to crawl between my legs. "Heh, Heh," I laughed as convincingly as I could.

"What's humorous," Bigelow said: not a question. "You think I like this?" This was a question but one that didn't demand an answer.

"You know it won't work," I said.

"Because you're too tough? Throneberry is clever. He'll find a way—"

"It won't work for the same reason it didn't work on Tarbox. It hasn't got a threat of death behind it. Torture is just pain if it hasn't got the threat of death behind it. It is the thought, see, of enduring all the pain for nothing that makes a guy talk. Its the thought that he's gonna be in pain and then die and nothing good will ever come of the suffering that makes him throw up his hands and say what-the-hell. But you have to have the threat of death behind it. You have to hold the final sanction. That's why Tarbox didn't squawk. He's a hundred and eleven years old; death wasn't all that meaningful to him, see? Me? I know you can't kill me because if you kill me the whereabouts of the money dies with me. See?"

Throneberry took a puff on the cigar and let a big blue cloud out into the room. "Shall I take out an eye, Mr. Bigelow?"

"Egh," Bigelow said, waving it away. "Dis-

gusting. Bockhorn? I give you one more
chance at acting like a sane man."

"Where do you want to start?" I bragga-
doccioed, reaching for my collar.

"Keep your shirt on, Bockhorn," Bigelow
said. "Throneberry? Tie Ms. Potter's arms to
the chair. Behind her. Tight, so her breasts
stick out." It had not occured to me. It was too
low.

"Not even you, Bigelow," I said. "Even you
couldn't."

"Why not my friend? You hardly even know
me."

When Throneberry finished tying Lauren
her arms were stretched tightly enough behind her to arch her back mock-proudly. "God,
Bigelow," T.J. said as Throneberry guided her
across the room by the elbow to sit on the bed,
with the rest of us to watch the show.

"Don't tell," Lauren said, "Don't tell anything."

"She'll need a gag," Bigelow said and took
his handkerchief from his pocket. "Open your
mouth," he said.

"No."

He smacked her. It was like he smacked me.
I didn't do the hero bit. Getting myself killed
would solve no one's problems. Bigelow
smacked her a second time and this time she
opened her mouth. He shoved the handkerchief. Then he put his hands at the collar of
her eggshell tunic and ripped down. The
fabric parted and Lauren Potter's apple-firm
breasts were exposed for us. Bigelow rucked

back the fabric around her shoulders so that we would have a better view. Marv Throneberry drew absently on the Havana and its tip glowed a red coal. They were breasts I have touched, kissed. T.J. closed her eyes.

"For your edification Mr. Bockhorn, the girl will be tortured, mutilated and ultimately killed for your very particular satisfaction. Unless of course you care to stop the proceedings."

Throneberry stepped to Lauren's side, took a drag, blew the smoke in her face. The bulge in his pants implied he wouldn't be holding back. He brought the glowing tip of the cigar down to Lauren's breasts, circled them slowly, then poised it over a pink nipple.

"Don't do it Throneberry," I said.

Lauren started shaking her head no. Throneberry looked at Bigelow. Big looked over at me. "I'll tell you what you want to hear," I said.

"Thanks, Bockhorn," T.J. muttered.

"Quiet you," Bigelow said, "You are *persona non grata* and soon enough you shall be *persona non* altogether." He had held a brief conference with himself and come up with the following. We were all to go back to Satcon together and after Bigelow took delivery of the payoff money we were to be compacted in that big green eternity machine. "Perhaps this time," Bigelow said, "I will handle it myself." Discussion at that point, ended.

We sat aboard the Cosmoflot Gulushin-28

that was taking us back to Satcon like a
family sullen about going off on a vacation to
a place that only daddy wanted to go to.
Lauren sat with Throneberry. T.J. sat with
me. Bigelow sat by himself, ordering cock-
tails and chem for all, flicking around
impatiently on his entertainment console,
waiting.

Space sat quietly by out the window off my
shoulder. The moon was in quarter phase and
lights dotted the dark part. We rolled past
Sunstar, the dead powersat that got holed
during the first days of the Satellite War. We
overshot a MA&P Skytrain silently boosting
its way to Lunar Central. "Please extinguish
all smoking implements and insure that your
seat is in swing mode," said the accentless
Russian computer in various languages. We
were approaching Satcon.

Phony papers were handed out and
stamped and signed, interrupters were used
on printatures, no one spoke. The meeting
reconvened in Lauren's rooms. We spread
out. Sat down. Waited.

On Bigelow's order I called the port and
ascertained that the cargo flight was on
schedule, had two more stops, and would
arrive within the hour. "We wait," said
Bigelow.

I pulled out a Fatima. Throneberry relit
that same Havana. T.J. looked at him in what I
think was real horror. He shrugged. Bigelow
paced. Lauren winked at me. I winked back.
She was sitting on her couch, her handbag

tucked beside her against the cushion. It was the way she sat down when she'd first come into the room and like all the rest of us except for Mr. Big, she hadn't moved, She winked again. So did I.

Bigelow adjusted the lighting to get the full benefit of the skylight. "Nice place," he said. "Thank you," Lauren said and winked at me again. Her bravery was laudable but she was beginning to get on my nerves.

"What time is it?" T.J. asked.

"It's later than you think," Throneberry said.

"Please Marvin," Big sighed, "get a new writer."

I looked at Lauren and shrugged. She winked. I frowned. She winked again. Slowly it began to register on me that she was trying to send me a message.

I raised one eyebrow slightly to signal I was getting her drift. She looked down into her bag. That was good enough for me. I stood up. Bigelow and Throneberry looked at me, hands going to holsters. "I want to sit with Lauren."

"Is that a last request?" Bigelow smiled.

"No, but it'll have to do," I said. As I sat down on the couch she moved quickly to the center as if to accomodate me but effectively putting her handbag between us. I looked down into it and staring back up at me was the handle of my very own .357 Magnum. This time I winked at her.

"Loaded?" I asked cheerfully, right out loud.

"Yes," she smiled, silly-wise.

"With what?" Throneberry asked. He rifled through Lauren's cleaned out cabinets and found nothing to eat, drink, chew or sniff.

"With this," I said and reached down into the bag and pulled out the Magnum.

"Jeesus Goddam Christmas!" Bigelow bellowed, "Throneberry!!"

"Sit down, Marvin," I said, standing up. The Magnum felt big and hefty and hard. So did I. "What are you doing?" T.J. said. It took a minute for all the wheels to stop turning and the blood to stop racing and the minds to clear, as each player tried to deal, each in his own way, with how swiftly the rules of the game had changed. But they got around to it. Then they all started talking at once.

"Quiet!" I shouted at them. I didn't want to hear any deals until, at least, I had figured out what my own was going to be. I finally had my chance to make my split-up-the-money play and I still wasn't sure which way I wanted it to go.

"C'mon, Bockhorn," Lauren said, rising.

"You be quiet too," I said. She sat back down. All decisions, no matter how long mulled over, are invariably arrived at in an instant. All subsequent explanations are good-intentioned rationalizations, worked upon in leisure, to justify actions you couldn't have defended for a second when you took them. I had wondered how I was going to defend this one. "I want half the money," I said.

"Preposterous," Bigelow said, "a finder's

fee is ten percent, tops."

"I'm not the finder, I'm the goddam owner," I said. I told him my plan about retiring to Florida and all. He bit down hard on it. Lauren took my hand and squeezed.

"In that case," Bigelow said, "perhaps a larger share might be in order." He offered a third. "Take it," Lauren said. I held out for half. He offered me forty per cent plus some kind of consultancy position that would give me a steady income wherever it was I decided to "hole up." His word; *hole up*. Someway or other it didn't jibe with my own vision of Santa Fe and all that, and it made me mad the way he put it. Besides, I hadn't decided yet that I wasn't going straight to the MA&P with everything and would have told him so just to see the expression on his fat face, but that would have loused up my play. Which was to be what? Make up your mind Bockhorn! Time's a glimmering! There was a banging on the door and Sgt. O'Doul's voice. Glimmer, glimmer, gone. The best decisions, say the people in the know of such things, are the ones you never have to make. "Come on in, O'Doul," I said, thumbing the door. I guess I was relieved. And as a consolation I had the room set up picture-perfect for my detective-novel style final summation.

O'Doul came in waving his Stoner. "Everything's under control," I said, "I got them all. All we've got to do is sort them out. Wait'll you hear the story."

The arrival of USSC had sort of decided

things for me. I'd play it straight. Of course it decided nothing of the kind for O'Doul who as soon as I turned back to the assembled masses stuck his Stoner into the small of my back and demanded the Magnum.

For a minute it was I who couldn't deal with how the rules had changed. But I got around to it when Bigelow said, "Nice work, O'Doul."

Of course O'Doul had been in on it. That's why T.J. had called Obermeir when she wanted me pried loose from Lauren; she knew about O'Doul. And that's why the good sergeant had seen fit to spring me when he found me at the USSC. So that Bigelow could have me. I had misjudged badly again. But this time, so had my fat adversary. O'Doul may have been in on it from the start, but he wasn't in on it anymore. The look at his eyes told you that in a minute.

Too much money had been introduced into the game, and too much love. Either one thing or the other had eaten away at everyone in the case. Love had consumed Bigelow, destroyed Duffy Warren. Love and money had twisted up Lauren and T.J., and killed Harry Cobb. And plain old lucre, all by its sweet self, was this instant munching away on the brains of Sergeant O'Doul, USSC Military Police, NCOIC, Satcon. Chomp chomp.

"Don't be a fool," Bigelow said.

"Hah-hah," O'Doul laughed, as if that's what his cue card said. "You made first mistake canceling ticket, Bockhorn. Big One. Much thanks."

"Don't mention it," I said. Keeping him talking seemed much preferable to having him stop and get on with whatever he planned on getting on with.

"Figure why be schmuck," he said. Why indeed? "Watching T.J. cut self in. Ditto Cobb. Then Bockhorn makes play. A regular sweepstakes, I make it. Take a ticket myself. Good a chance as anyone, eh Bockhorn?"

"It's a pretty fast track O'Doul," I said, "Be careful."

"Hah-hah," he said again. "Knew you were in. Canceled ticket to me key. Knew you were holing up somewhere. Pretty easy figure where. Bit of a cock-up on the old hidey-hole game, eh Bockhorn?"

"Okay, a gold star for you O'Doul. What you plan. . . what do you plan to do with us now?"

Well you see, he hadn't actually thought of that and now his dimbulb began to flicker six ways at once. He said he wanted to accompany me to the pick-up point, to get the dough, see? He wanted the rest eliminated. He also wanted protection from MA&P. He also wanted the rest as hostages. "Dead or alive?" I queried and while he pondered that Lauren bent down, casual like, picking flowers like, and flicked the switch that plunged the room into total darkness. And I mean total. There are moments in Satcon's rotation when there is nothing but nothing and more nothing out Lauren Potter's skylight, and this was it. Well, maybe a twinkle or two, but the room was ink. (Not that I had such thoughts at the time; I didn't even remember the skylight.) Well I know what happens next so I dove right to the floor.

I couldn't tell from the whoosh of the Stoner blast how nearly I'd come to being scratched from the running but, as no one screamed, and there was no ghastly pop-pop-pop I assumed that the shot had had no effect. Bigelow began bellowing for Marvin, who was quiet as a tomb; else the risk of taking up residence in one. T.J., to my surprise, was whimpering and seemed to be sneaking her way across the floor looking for something to hide under. Given Satcon's thirty-second rotation, as I remembered it, the moon would rise outside Lauren's window in some time between *now* and fifteen seconds. That's the amount of time I had to find O'Doul in the dark. *Good luck*, I thought.

"Put that damn fool gun away," I yelled and rolled out of the way of the whoosh of darts that hailed down on the spot I yelled from. The pink light of the Laimer afterglowed just long enough for me to get a bead. I leaped. Just short of the expected impact someone hit me broadside in the air and I fell down to the floor in a heap. "Spit," he said. It was Throne-berry who'd been trying to same play.

"Move it!" I bellowed and shoved him in the chest. We rolled away from each other as a pattern of darts struck the floor between us, splattering all over my back, spent. I found a leg in my hand. T.J.'s by the footgear. She pulled away. I tried to get under whatever she was under, but she kicked me in the face. Then someone grabbed my leg and began pulling me across the floor.

"I got him," Bigelow whispered loud enough for everyone to hear.

I braced for the *whooosh*-pop-pop-pop that would herald my dismal death at the multiple impact of darts, but none came. In its stead was a scream such as a man makes when a swift object has made contact with a pair of *guyones*; O'Doul's I assumed, then the clatter of a Stoner to the floor. The grip was released from my leg and I scrambled to my feet just as the moon flooded into the room, stopping us like a strobe, an Attic frieze of space-age mayhem.

T.J. had curled herself into a fetal position beneath the coffee table. Lauren was standing in the corner next to O'Doul trying to fit herself into the crack. Bigelow lay sprawled across the dart-littered floor like a bear-skin rug. Throneberry was over him on one knee staring up at O'Doul who was pointing to the Magnum, which he'd held on to.

"Don't do it," Bigelow said. "If you miss you'll put a hole right through the wall. We're in a hull room."

You could see the dimbulb flicker as the pale, unsteady light of an idea lit gloomily behind O'Doul's Irish eyes. He looked at the skylight, and then down at us and around the room. Then back to the skylight. Then at me. It wasn't hard to figure what was crossing his screen.

He needed us eliminated. He didn't have a plan. He was standing by the bulkhead door. If he shot out the skylight we would all die of asphyxiation. An all-but-inexplicable accident. He'd be free to collect the baggage and lam without a clue. That is, if he could make it to the safety of the door and slam it on us before it autolocked from the pressure drop and he joined us in our fate. It was a long shot. It was a thousand to one shot. But Satcon was old and its circuits were tired; the light in his eyes was now a neon sign saying he was going to take the shot, you should pardon the expression. He raised the Magnum and pointed it at the skylight. "No!" Bigelow shouted from the floor and from nowhere and everywhere came the sigh of a Stoner that stopped whatever came next and rendered it irrelevant regardless.

The blast caught O'Doul in a tight pattern on the neck and part of his lower jaw. For an instant all you could see between the USSC sergeant's head and his broad shoulders was about four inches of rattan-patterned wallpaper behind him. The head pitched over on the body and the body pitched over to the floor. We all turned to see who'd delivered the *coup de grace*.

Stoner's don't make smoke; they hiss quietly. O'Doul's Stoner was hissing in Lauren Potter's hand. She had a strange faraway look in her eyes. I stepped toward her and gently took the gun. "Good girl," I whispered and she nodded to me, and the

phone rang. It was port. My baggage was
ready now, coming in on a MA&P. Starfreighter
scheduled to dock in ten minutes. I had the
gun hand again. I had my summation ready
again. It was my show again.

I began reopening negotiations on my split-
the-money plan. "Fifty-fifty," was all I had to
say. Lauren stepped beside me and squeezed
my arm. I patted her murderous little hand.
"What about it Bigelow? Fifty-fifty and a
Florida set-up. Can do?"

"Supposing I said yes," Bigelow said
dragging himself up from the floor, brushing
off the few darts that clung to his clothes.
"What would we do with Ms. Janes here?"

I knew what to do with her alright, but I had
to go about it delicately. I could already read
the concern in Lauren's face. I wasn't
completely rid of my rival suitor yet, but I
was on my way there. I changed the subject to
go into my act. "You've got another problem
to deal with first," I said.

"What's that?" asked Bigelow.

"The instructions I left at port cargo were
to notify me and USSC when the baggage
arrived, so that a USSC man would meet me
at the port. Presumably, that's been done."

"You're lying," Bigelow said.

I shook my head sadly. I was not lying.
Leaving word for the USSC was the bright
idea of the part of me that wanted to play
straight. "It is going to be Obermeir," I said,
"and Obermeir is on the level. We're going to
have a body to explain. Sergeant O'Doul's.

Someone is going to have to take the fall."

"Well," Bigelow smiled, "T.J. of course."

"Pigs!" T.J. spat.

"No you *can't*!" Lauren wailed. "T.J. has to be let go. That's part of the deal, isn't it Bockhorn?"

I didn't answer her directly. What I said was, "How about Marv Throneberry?"

"Jeeze, Bockhorn," he squealed. Really, he did.

"It fits like a glove. We work him up as a sneak thief. Couple of days he's working Orion when a john name Cobb surprises him and Throneberry offs said john. Today he's working Satcon when a dick surprises him; he offs said dick. All Obermeir's going to want is something neat. This is neat. Especially if the gunsel's dead. See we will the gunsel with O'Doul's gun and it looks like they rubbed each other."

Marv Throneberry squeaked again. His eyeballs were darting back and forth between me and his boss like he was watching a ping-pong game that would decide his fate. He was.

"It's got possibilities," Bigelow said.

"It's got everything," I countered, "even justice in a screwball sort of way. I mean what the hell, the gunsel did gun down Cobb so it's not like were setting up on an innocent man. Is it Marvin?"

The kid didn't have a breath left to squeal with. He looked imploringly at Bigelow who had begun to chuckle, "I'm afraid my man

Marvin has not killed anyone and he is a very good boy for not mentioning it. Thank you Marvin, you are most loyal and your loyalty will now be rewarded by my own. Impossible, Mr. Bockhorn, that Marvin should take the fall. I will not permit it. He never murdered Cobb. He was supposed to but he didn't. He admitted as much to me. I suspect he would have admitted as much to you but I forbade it. No, not Marvin."

"Then who killed Cobb?" Lauren asked. Bigelow looked at me. I smiled. I had set it up perfectly. "The same person who set me up to die with Duffy Warren," I said slowly, savoring it, "It was—"

"T.J. Janes!" Marv Throneberry blurted out, stepping on my triumphant curtain line. "It was T.J. Janes!"

Lauren went white. "I'm sorry," I said and squeezed her to me. "I knew you wouldn't buy it if I just out and told you, so I had to set up something. You alright?"

She nodded.

"You see, O'Doul was only doing what just about everybody else in this mess of a case had been doing. Grabbing. And when too many people grab at the same thing at the same time they get tangled up."

"But I didn't do anything," T.J. said evenly.

"Shut up doll, this is my moment." I glanced at my watch. I had not much time to spare if I wanted to get to the port before Obermeir. I began to pace, like Hercule Poirot, like Maigret, like Philip Marlowe, like Holmes. I had somehow contrived by luck and last-second design to get me a room full of people, I had forced the confession—well, in this case a confession of innocence but don't be picky—that I needed. And now I would slowly, deliberately, and with all due pleasure, unravel the case.

I found that I didn't know quite where to begin. But that didn't stop me. "You people really threw me," I said, "You really had me going." I pilled a Fatima and lit it. "Anybody wanna smoke?" They all remained silent, staring up at me from where they sat. "All my life or all my career anyway, I'd told myself if I ever had a case, a real case, then I'd show my spit. Well this was a real case." I turned over my claw once or twice. "A real case. A dart in my toe. A trip into a garbage machine. I've been shot at, a lot. But that didn't bother me. Tru's have done worse. What bothered me was that I was in the middle of a real case and what was I showing? Spit! I couldn't figure it out. I said to myself, Bockhorn you are obviously up against some mastermind, some wondrous criminal with a scheme so incredibly clever that in no way can you ever conceive it. I thought that. I thought, all those years of being passed over for detective sergeant; they weren't for the blotch on my record, and they weren't for whatever, friendship, who knows what? They were for *this*!" I banged myself on the skull with my fist. "I said to myself, maybe I don't have this! Maybe

I'm just a lousy tru-buster after all? And I panicked a little, you know? I wanted to quit. But I didn't. I couldn't. I couldn't get off the case; I was involved with one of the subjects. We'll talk about that. But I couldn't *stay* on the case because I couldn't compete with the mastermind. And I had this time limit because my own people wanted me the hell of it anyway and they were getting testy."

I drew on the Fatima. Exhaled, "Then slowly it began to dawn on me that I wasn't up against a big mind at all. I was up against the random complexities of a lot of little minds, you know what I mean? A crooked civil servant. A small time mobster. A sneak thief. A greenhorn gunsel. A rogue cop. All in there tangling and tangling things until nothing made sense at all."

I went back to the Fatima again and hit it hard. After 72 hours of struggling through the case I was now struggling equally clumsily through my summation. I tried to keep it all together. I knew it was all there; it was just a question of laying it out in the correct sequence. "Lookit, let's review," I said.

I took them through the case step by step. A summons for a tru bust. Finding out about Cobb. Cobb and Lauren on Orion. The lurid photos. T.J.'s admission they were lovers, not sisters. Cobb's craziness, Cobb's betting system, Cobb's murder. Throneberry's confession. Lauren's arrival and the "truth" about the blackmail scheme. My losing the luggage—very important. Squirreling away on Satcon Station with Lauren and her "real truth" about mob story. My interviewing the principals in the mob investigation. Duffy Warren. Duffy Warren's murder. My capture by Bigelow. Bigelow's confession about Lauren, about the money, about T.J. triggering the hit on the Naughty Schoolgirl. My escape. I laid that one on pretty thick. My finding the girls again on Orion and Lauren's "real *true* truth" about stealing the money. The arrival of Bigelow and Throneberry. The arrival of O'Doul who had finally put two and two together and come up with a million. A ticket to an impossible dream that Lauren Potter had canceled with a Stoner.

I stubbed out the Fatima and lit another. "Anybody wanna smoke?" No answer. "Sure?" No answer. "You see, from here it lays out pretty logical," I said and loosed a cloud of blue smoke. "Finding out about the money was the key. You see that's how I cracked this case, you bastards. I hung in there. And I kept hanging in there. I took all your snow and I caught the drift. Just like a regular old tru bust. I outlasted you sonsabitches. When I found out about the money I knew I was home free. Lookit, here's what happened. First of all there was no blackmail. That was my first mistake, not a fatal one but it cost me a lot of wasted time. You see Lauren *had* been working on a news story about the mob's efforts in space. She'd been sleeping with Duffy Warren, a victim, for info, and also sleeping with T.J. Janes, a security official, likewise for info, and also sleeping with Mr. Big, a mobster, also for info." I breathed in. "Am I right?"

Lauren nodded. The truth was painful, but it was also past tense.

"Bigelow gets curious about whether Lauren is being 'faithful' and so he detailed a new man, Cobb, to find out something about her. In the meantime T.J. who must have been walking a very thin line between her love of Lauren and her ties with the mob Lauren was investigating, takes possession of a very big bag of bribe money. Why? Because she is Mr. Big's bag lady, the lady in charge of the *payoff and certification* operation.

"She decides to skip out with the loot, using Lauren as *her* bag lady. She has correctly intuited that the million IM would be more interesting to Lauren than the investigation, which has bogged down—T.J.'s doing— anyway, but what she has failed to intuit is that the million is also more interest- ing to Lauren than *she* is. Lauren grabs the whole bag and starts ad-libbing her way home. By now she has become intimate with Cobb, the mobster sent to spy on her. Am I right?"

Lauren nodded. I sighed. The correct answers were killing me. But I kept at it. "So she uses Cobb who is a whiz kid at false certification, and a man with a strong arm, as a way of getting safely clear of the Bigelow operation and T.J. Janes. T.J. is panicky over what might happen when the money is discovered gone. No longer in a position to lam herself, she is forced to try to get the money back. In desperation she calls for me and makes up the truant story. In the meantime, Lauren and Cobb are on Orion laundering the mob's money through the betting windows in case it is marked up in some way. By the way, Lauren, I figured out that at the rate you two were laundering the stuff it would have taken you about a year. How much did you tell Cobb you'd stolen?"

"Fifty thousand," Lauren said, proud and embarrassed at the same time. Bigelow guffawed.

"So Cobb was in it crazy for love," I continued, "and he gets a little crazier when he tumbles to the fact that the gunsel is tailing him, also tailing me I suspect because Bigelow, who I talked to in the bar, surely had some interest in my interest in the case. Anyway I find the dirty pictures which, of course were pictures Cobb took when he was still working for Bigelow, to bring back as evidence. But I don't know that. I just see skin. When I confront T.J. with them she admits everything, including the blackmail thing! Why not? She'd a long shot rather have me think that than what's *really* going on! Blackmail is a good cover. Spit! It's a great cover! I invented it myself, dumbheadedly. T.J. went to the Cobb room to find money, not dirty pictures. But the gunsel has also arrived to rub Cobb. The gunsel snaps T.J., probably a case of mistaken identity, but later when he runs into T.J. they realize. Now T.J. turns the whole case over to the mob, tells them Lauren stole the money with Cobb, and dismisses me from the case, saying she found and destroyed the blackmail negatives. Case closed. Except that Lauren now comes to *me*. What do I know? I'm still trying to figure out the blackmail! I run that through Lauren and she does the same thing T.J. did; she admits it! I pull the wool a little tighter. I buy her screwball story partly because I believe it, partly because I don't, and because Lauren has got her love pumps working on overdrive and we've all seen what that can do to an otherwise healthy person. I go back on the case. And almost the first thing I do is manage to lose the suitcase with the money. I gotta laugh. But of course I don't know this and I don't realize that Lauren is trying to shift me around this way and that way until she can retrieve the bag. But it is not that easy. For one thing we've got the monumental incompetence of MA&P baggage handling to deal with. For another, it turns out that Lauren and I am . . . *simpatico*. Am I right?"

Lauren nodded.

"It's not all that easy for her to get rid of me. Then again, it is going to be very expensive to keep me and so Lauren is waffling back and forth about what she wants to do with me and to buy time she gives me this cockanbull story about her mob investigation which happens to be the truth but wildly irrelevant to what's going on. On the other hand, I'm picking up some pretty good stuff for my report to Lunar HQ. Until I get to Duffy Warren's. Now as near as I can figure, when Duffy called T.J. to ask about talking to me, T.J. decided to get me back in the game. She figures if I know enough to talk to Duffy than I must be with Lauren. She sets it up for Duffy and me to get the final sanction, something which Bigelow must have had in mind already, and then finds out that I've somehow muddled through again. She thinks fast, gets Obermeir who is on duty, tells him about the investigation and how I am trying to squelch it by killing off the principals. Obermeir grabs me and T.J. grabs Lauren, telling her that I am as good as dead, which for a while was true enough goodness knows. You know the rest."

For a moment no one spoke. Then Lauren said, "I thought you said the gunsel didn't kill Cobb?" The word *gunsel* on her lips would have made everybody laugh in almost any other situation. It got a smile from Bigelow anyway who then said, "So it is not a very good assessment?"

"Well," I said, "It is and it isn't. You see, for me, this has for a long time been a case of really two detections, not one. One detection had to do only with Ms. Potter and me. It was a highly personal detection and, yeah as far as that particular detection went the assessment was pretty darn good. The girl had grabbed and gamboled, improvising all the way. Knowing that seemed to clear up a lot of confusion for me, explained a lot of her lies, satisfied a lot of things for me. Yeah I'd say that part of the assessment was okay. Now the other part, the whole ball of wax part, looked even clearer. I mean everything fit together so nicely. I had Throneberry's confession for Cobb's murder, a third party testimony for the torching of the "Naughty Schoolgirl," and a nice, consistent little package. You know its always been my experience, in mystery books that is; I never actually had a case like this before but in the better mystery books if there are two murders or more than two murders, look for one guy to have done them both or at least had a part. The fact is that there are murderous people and people who are not murderous and they don't flip back and forth too much. So it fit that Cobb was killed by Throneberry, who I knew torched the "Naughty Schoolgirl." And that was my second big mistake, believing the gunsel's confession. Because the more I tumbled it around in my mind, the more I was sure he *hadn't* killed Harry Cobb. He'd been in the murder room that night. For sure. That's how he knew Cobb was dead. But that didn't mean much, there'd been some pretty heavy traffic in the room that night. No matter how I ran out the assessment, no matter where I put him in the room or when—behind the curtains as T.J. rummaged, or in the bathroom while Cobb rummaged, or whatever—I could not square the gunsel with the room." And there was something more than that. There was something I had seen in the boy's eyes that night up on the catwalk and again outside the garbage machine.

I looked over at Marvin and that look was still there. I smiled at him. "The kid simply doesn't have it for the final sanction; no offense Marvin. You're just not murderous. Oh sure he can torture an old man or take a cigar to a little girl's breasts. He's no choir boy is our Marvin Throneberry. He can rig a freighter to blow by remote control. But face to face . . . he's not murderous. So why would he fake a confession?" I smacked myself on the head for effect. "Why would he confess to a crime he hadn't committed? To impress an over-the-hill space agent? Maybe he thought I was going to tell his boss on him. No." I paced for a second, silently. "Listen I'm not gonna tell a big old lie that I figured out that the gunsel did this and that on the basis of clues and deduction. Sometimes you just have to guess, move things around so that they fit other things. I needed some answers. Some background. See, in my pocket I was carrying a third mistake. My tie tack. My clue. Something Harry Cobb had in his hand at the moment of the murder. I had to be reading it wrong. It had to mean something. It had to in some way prove my hunch that it wasn't the gunsel, that it was someone else. Or maybe it didn't, I don't know, but I took a guess anyway, actually a couple of guesses. I guessed that Throneberry lied to protect someone. Who?

"Then I guessed again, that all the figuring and mumbling and refiguring that I had watched Cobb pound away into his term at Orion was a symptom of what had really driven him bats. He tumbled to the real money. That was good too; it explained his hysteria. He was torn between Lauren and the haul. That's what had brought him into the room that night, carelessly sacking like the rest of them. That stirred me up. Better, I thought, better. I put all of this into the grey matter and let it boil down, boil down. And all of a sudden, in Mr. Big's, with Bigelow spilling his guts about T.J. and Duffy Warren, all of a sudden I knew how to read the clue and it was a neon sign pointing the way to the murderer. You see, I had the pleasure, late in this case, of *wrestling* with Ms. T.J. Janes!"

"I kicked his ass," T.J. said.

"Yes you did. You kicked my ass! And it was exactly what I needed most because sometimes that is precisely where I keep my grey matter! You see the two murders *were* consistent, but they didn't connect the murderer of Cobb and the *detonator* of Duffy Warren; they connected the murderer of Cobb and the person who *triggered* that detonation. Guess what happened in the murder room!?"

"Wha—" Lauren said, open mouthed.

"T.J. shot Harry Cobb," Bigelow said.

"But you said you found T.J. unconscious," Lauren said.

"Bingo," I said, "Don't you see? T.J. is in the room rummaging away for the money. Cobb comes in with blood in his eyes looking for the dough. He saps T.J. who he doesn't know from anywhere, lightly. Now this T.J. is a horse, right? She comes to while Cobb is taking a whiz in the tiled room. They struggle. She gets his gun. She can do that, believe me. She gets his gun and drills him at close range. Then she goes back out and continues tearing up the joint but who comes in now?"

"The gunsel," Lauren says, catching on.

"He saps T.J. hard because, well he's Throneberry. Okay? The two saps. That bothered me those two saps. Now I know where they came from. And why T.J. was unconscious when I saw her. And why later in the evening, after T.J. and Throneberry have doped each other out, the gunsel 'confesses' to protect his prime operative, his Satcon connection. Nothing changes from my assessment . . . except that I got the murderer backwards. It is clear. It is complicated as hell—but that's your own fault and not mine—and if you're gonna tell me it's full of guesses and speculations and all that you're absolutely right but that don't matter at all because they all helped to lead me up to the correct reading of the clue and the clue tells all. Anybody want to see it?" I smiled and practically strutted in place. I can be insufferable. Throneberry looked at Bigelow. Bigelow shrugged.

"I would be happy to see it Mr. Bockhorn,"

Bigelow said smiling, "because your, *assessment*, is so neatly muddle headed."

"Don't make me mad Bigelow. I've got the money and the badge and the gun. We're playing my rules now."

"My dear friend. I believe you're right that whoever murdered Cobb also marked you. But please some facts first. One, you never escaped the compactor. You were let go. I had more faith in your tracking prowess than Marvin's and I wanted *you* searching for Lauren while Marvin followed you as you cleverly turned the trick on your departed colleague Cobb earlier in the game. And of course we had to tell you that it was T.J. who called to warn me of your meeting with Duffy Warren because we wanted your sympathies with Ms. Potter. I didn't want you to harm her. *I* wanted to harm her. In fact my main interest in the game, from the very first, has been to harm Lauren Potter. I am the lover wronged Bockhorn. I wanted my blood revenge."

"And you don't care about the million intermarks," I said.

"Oh on a professional basis of course, but shipments have been lost before and either recovered or reshipped. I dare say each company would, when pressed, ante up again. No, my interest was in meting out a lover's justice to the little hussy. Surely you understand, Bockhorn? You are a man of passions. To contemplate leaving the service with stolen money so that you can rabbit away in some beach shack with a slut like Lauren Potter—'' actually, it was beginning to sound okay again "'—who has *honked the horn* of nearly every player in the game save for Marvin, *and*," he looked at T.J., "those who are hornless, certainly that is the absolute height of lunacy. She has made you at least as insane as she made Cobb. Maybe worse. I am now quite content to mete out my justice by watching you dispatch the little whore when I tell you it was *she* who *offed* our friend Cobb as per your *whoever-did-the-one-did-the-other* theory, because it was Lauren Potter who tipped me off to your meeting with Duffy Warren and she who urged *your* rubbing out. A request with which at the time, I was only too happy to comply."

"Liar!" I shouted. "I told you I had proof!" I fumbled wildly in my pocket for the little ball of gold and brought it out, holding it up like a sword *en garde*. "Proof that you're a liar!" I screamed at Bigelow.

"A tie tack?" he said.

"An earring!" I shouted back. "Read it. No I'll read it for you. It says, 'I'll love L forever.' I thought it was a tie tack too. It looks like a tie tack but it's an earring. See? This is the gold stalk. A little thing goes on this end when you stick it through your ear. And I was reading it wrong too. Because Lauren, I don't know why, told me it was a gift she gave to Cobb. 'I'll love L forever!' Get it?''

"I was confused," she said, "I was stalling.

What's the difference. Let's get the bags and go."

I hardly heard her. "It was absolutely a gift she'd given to T.J. and it, whenever you read it right, says, 'I'll love forever, L.' "

"So what?" said Marv Throneberry, getting right down to the point.

"When Cobb got hit he reached out to smack his murderer, and this spike here got stuck between his fingers. See? He slapped her this way." I made a broad slow slap at T.J. who ducked, all elbows because now she was taking off one earring. The one that had flashed at me during our wrestling match.

"That's it, take it off," I said. "I went through all her stuff and I couldn't find the other earring," I was talking to Lauren now, showing off. "I knew she'd save it. It had to mean a lot to her. Then she comes walking in and she's wearing the damn thing all by itself. She's wearing the other damn earring!"

"Silly man," she said to me. Then she tossed the earring at me. I caught it in my palm. The ball end looked the same; same size, same filigree, same lustre, but the stem was different. It was U shaped. "Read it," T.J. said.

In the same script I read, "I'll love forever, T.J."

"That's 'I'll love T.J. Forever!' " T.J. said.

Small hairs started to crawl all over my body.

"I'll love T.J. Forever," she said. "We bought them for each other, Bockhorn. *One* set of earrings. We had them hand-engraved and altered. An earring for each of us. One from Lauren to me that said 'I'll love T.J. forever, and I always wear it. One from me to Lauren that said "I'll love L forever', and she always wears it. At least she did until Cobb's murder. Look at them Bockhorn. One is for pierced ears and the other is not. I do not have pierced ears."

"Lauren," Bigelow said, "has pierced ears. And you my friend have a pierced *assessment*. Although I must admit that no one concerned seems to have had much success in getting a good assessment of Lauren Potter. At least Harry Cobb had the good fortune to slap her once before he died."

Lauren had killed Cobb? My gray matter smoked. When T.J. arrived to look for the money Cobb surprises her, saps her, gently as in the prior assessment. Cobb had found out how much money there really is. He now bags Lauren, threatens her, tries to win her any way he can. She gets his gun, shoots him. Then T.J. stirs. Lauren, afraid of what T.J. might see saps her *hard*. Two saps. It fit.

Everything else fell into place. Lauren had been in it alone as long she could. When things got tough she latched on. When she could, she jettisoned. She was in it alone, and that included me.

"You set me up?" I said.

I didn't have to hear the actual words she uttered to know that they meant I had been a prize chump. She claimed confusion again,

professed love again, begged and pleaded and
threatened as Cobb must have, she promised
the world as T.J. must have, then called me
every epithet and slimy word in the lexicon,
her face twisted into smiles and grimaces and
leers and tears and sneers and there wasn't a
person in the room who did not want to put a
boot into it. Eventually she folded to her
knees, sobbing, the image of the supplicant.

"Shoot her Bockhorn," Bigelow said, "and
you've got your deal."

I raised the gun.

"How could you," she wailed looking up
into my eyes.

Actually it wasn't hard at all. I aimed at her
tiny chest. She thrust it out in a last gesture of
defiance. And then the phone rang.

Chapter Fourteen

The flight was in. "Come on, let's go," I said, "all of you, move it."

"What about her?" Bigelow said, nodding at Lauren.

"I'll think of something," I said.

At the baggage counter we were met by our old friend the flincher. "Mr. Stargis," he smiled.

I flashed my badge. "Asher H. Bockhorn," I barked, "MexAmerican and Pacific Security."

"Oh," the flincher said. "Well your baggage will be right along. Your Lieutant Obermeir will be right along too. He said eight and that would be ten minutes by my clock."

"I'll want the area clear," I said. The flincher picked up the phone and arranged for all other baggage than ours to be diverted to another area. My colleagues sat quietly in their silicaform chairs as if so directed: Bigelow to the left, next to him T.J. Janes, then Marv Throneberry, and then Lauren.

Size places. I read in their eyes that they were all wondering what I was going to do. I wondered if they read the same puzzlement in my own.

The public address system blared, "Flying Tiger Aerodynamic Module 88 now departing for Great Lakes Metro, non stop. This is the last call. FTI Skytrain M-88. Last call." It was that alright.

I could grab the bag and pull out on the Great Lakes Metro and let my "friends" shift for themselves. Who'd squeal? And to whom? Then again, I could put all my friends on the 88 and use their air time to pick out a flight more to my suiting and take that; whatever. A million intermarks was a lot of money. I could bust truants for several lifetimes and never come near it.

"Fifty-fifty," Bigelow mumbled out loud, "and a personal guarantee against any syndicate-type coming after you. That's my final offer. Take it or leave it."

Then again, I thought, it would be nice to see Bigelow take the fall. My investigation had turned into quite a considerable coup. "Line security officer uncovers mob operation on space plot." Sounded good. A promotion out of the humdrum office? At my age? Who was I kidding. Me.

"Mr. Bockhorn," the flincher called from the desk, and he now had on his most flinchy looking face. I walked over to the counter. He whispered in my ear. After a long moment, I chuckled.

"Bigelow," I said, "front and center." Then I turned to the flincher. "Tell it to him," I said. The flincher leaned over to whisper to him what he had just whispered to me.

Bigelow listened and turned red, then veins started standing out on his head, then his lips started fluttering about. "The bag has gone to where!?" he screamed.

"Callisto," the clerk finished, "I'm afraid they're bound for Callisto and unless there's an intercept—"

"It'll take months for them to come back from Callisto!"

"Well four years actually," the clerk said, "you see the ship is of course a Hohman orbit robotic freighter, and—"

Bigelow reached across the counter to throttle the clerk but I grabbed him just in time. "Let me kill him!" Bigelow hissed at me. "For God's sake Bockhorn, let me kill him!" Then, to the clerk; "Where's Obermeir!"

"Well, he said he'd be here at—"

"Get him! Get him!" Bigelow shouted, and my warning buzzer started banging away again.

"Punch me up two tickets on the 88," I said to the clerk. "Hurry."

"Well, it's irregular. You should really see the lady at—"

"Do it!"

"You'll never get away with it," Bigelow said, "whatever you're doing. She'll cut you up and leave you drained dry." He meant Lauren of course. He had me figured. Which was more than I had. It would be nice to see him fall.

"I'm not going anywhere with anyone, yet." I motioned Throneberry to his feet, T.J. and Lauren too; then I took the two tickets and said, "Alright everyone, march."

We bounded along the Z-G to Bay 5 where the "Pride of Peoria" was tied not a hundred yards from the twisted wreckage of Duffy Warren's freighter, which we all pretended not to notice.

I marched Bigelow and Throneberry onto the Skytrain, handcuffed them to their seats, deputized the conductor, and said goodbye.

"And just what do you think you're doing?" Bigelow said.

"Still don't know," I answered, "but I'm taking no chances. I'm betting you've gotten to Obermeir, so I'll arrange for you to be picked up when you land in GIM. Bon voyage."

The klaxon blared. I got off with the girls. We cleared back to the departure observation area where I called the cargo desk and got Obermeir on the horn.

"I got the girl who killed O'Doul," I said and I told him where to meet me.

Then I turned to the sisters of Satcon. They had settled into stay harnesses with a view of the departure. I looked from one to the other, deciding.

T.J. said, "What are you scheming about, Bockhorn?"

"Shut up," I said. I had one last play, one

last run of the deal. I had a rotten hand, but it was the only one I was dealt and I was going to play it.

"Láuren?"

"Yes?"

"Why did you come back to my room?" She didn't answer. "When you got the money," I said, "Why did you come back to my room?"

"The truth?" she said.

"If you can manage it, yeah."

She looked up into my eyes and turned on that old love machine. "You're a great guy Bockhorn. And you're fun in bed. You're everything a man ought to be. You're even a good Fleet Agent." She was starting to cry now. "I want to be in New Mexico with you, or Florida or Tashkent or God knows where, anywhere. But I can't. Don't you see? I can't."

She was blubbering now. I grabbed her by the shoulder and shook her.

"Leave her alone!" T.J. shouted.

"Sit down!" I shouted back. Then I turned to Lauren Potter from whom I wasn't getting the answer I wanted. I wanted at least a lie, at least an attempt to make me take her back. She didn't have to love me all the way. Just a little. But lie dammit, I thought, lie at least good enough to show me that you care a little! Give me a reason to give T.J. Janes to Obermeir. Give me something! A faint rumble in the bay structure signalled that the "Pride of Peoria" was no longer attached to Satcon. "Give!" I said.

"I can't!" she squealed. "I can't anymore!"

"Tell me, Lauren! Tell me why you came back. You had the money. You knew I'd been hit. Did you come back to see if maybe something had gone wrong? That maybe I was still alive. Did you even hope for that? Or think about it!?"

She stopped shaking. She stiffened a bit, got control of herself, squared her shoulders, took a breath. "I came back," she said, "for the Magnum."

For a second I just stood there staring blindly, waiting, hoping for a retraction, a replay. Then I dropped her. It was very unsatisfying. She just sort of floated back into her stay-harness. The game was over.

Lieutant Obermeir arrived. I gave him Lauren Potter. And also a warning. "I have turned over a rock, Obermeir. A space rock, if you will, and under it I have found a heap of squirmy stuff. It is about to be exterminated. Don't stand in the blast. A MA&P Detective Sergeant is alerted and on his way to your office ASAP to pick up Lauren Potter. Be there to meet him." He nodded. I don't know how Lauren reacted. I never caught her eye.

I walked T.J. Janes back to her office. Neither of us talked. Oh, yeah; as we entered the elevator, she did ask what I thought about her turning state's witness, but it went in one ear and out the other head. As we got farther and farther outward toward the perimeter of "A" ring we got heavier and heavier until, when we made the endless hallway of the ring we were at full Satcon gravity again. "She picked you," I said as we got to T.J.'s office door.

"Blow a horn," she sighed. "Goodbye Bockhorn, good luck."

"Goodbye T.J.," I said with as much enthusiasm. I walked back to my billets to collect my gear. Something my father used to say kept ringing in my ear. It was an old carpenter's maxim. "Never stand in the place of a spinning object."

I wasn't sure it applied.

Afterlog

I'd been right about Obermeir. But wrong about Big and Marv. No one met them at Great Lakes Metro. They were back on Satcon. I sat in the big overstuffed chair across from Oxenhorn in his office at our Lunar HQ, reading "my" report.

It seems, according to the report with my name on it, that I had followed a truant (L. Potter) to Orion and discovered the murder of her lover (H. Cobb) at her own hand, then had returned to Satcon where I turned her over to USSC agent James O'Doul, SGT-9, who had the bad judgment to turn his back on Ms. Potter who then murdered him. I had thereupon recaptured her and turned her over to the proper authorities. I was very happy with the case's final resolution.

"But you can't," I said, rising from the chair," the mob is up there right now—"

"Bockhorn," Oxenhorn said.

"What is it, a clandestine operation? You can tell me."

"Bockhorn," Oxenhorn said.

"I stumbled onto something. I loused up something bigger than my thing, didn't I? I got in the way of some ongoing—"

"Bockhorn, shut it off," Ox said. "I'd like to tell you all that but the fact is, no. We had no idea. I certainly didn't when I found out, I tried to get you off the case but there was no way short of sending a man to . . . terminate you."

"Terminate me?"

"I fought them. I fought them for two days. I told them you knew what you were doing and that you were being discreet. They gave me a deadline. You reported in two hours before that deadline."

"There was MA&P money in that bag?"

"Precisely."

"How much?"

"Classified."

"How goddam much!"

"Half of it. When Janes lost it she panicked. All she could think of to do was get one of our Fleet Agents to track that other girl down."

"Half of it! We're subsidizing murder!"

"Oh, Pffgh," Oxenhorn said, "we are doing nothing of the kind. We have gotten involved in a pilot program to see if we could use some form of syndicate authority, unofficial but self-sanctioned, just as has been ongoing on earth for, God knows, the past five hundred years, to bring some order to the sargassonic chaos of space shipping. It is an experiment. To cut through the bureacratic seaweed!"

"Why don't you just cut the seaweed?"

"What, are you crazy!"

"You're goddam right I am!" And then I went on. Ox let me have my tirade. I shouted and I stamped and I knocked over his chair. I banged on his desk and swept his model Boeing-Toshiba Whispertrain to the floor. Then I picked up the chair and sat down, spent.

"I'd rather you didn't retire because of all this. You're a good man. There may be a promotion to Detective Sergeant in it for you Bockhorn."

"Because I can keep my mouth shut?"

"Because you can handle the job."

"Thanks." I said. "What are you going to do about the trial?"

"What trial?"

"Lauren Potter's. Is she going to cooperate? What if she leaks something that leads to an investigation. How are you going to—?"

"No trial."

"But you don't hold her indefinitely."

"No trial."

"But you have to do something. She can't—"

"Bockhorn, a report has just come in from Satcon. There was a freak accident in penal. Just this morning. A fall down a ladder. Very careless. Lauren Potter, she died. Broken neck and massive head injuries. It was relatively quick. I know that you two had become close. I'm sorry. I'll leave the office if you'd like a couple of minutes to—"

"Penal is in half-G!"

"I told you it was a freak accident," Oxenhorn said.

"Spit!" I screamed. I took my badge and threw it on his desk. I pulled my Stoner and tossed it on his lap. Then I lifted from my boot my .357 Magnum, still never fired. I pointed the cannon end right between the lobes of his forehead. His eyes widened.

"And you can have this too," I said, and dropped the Magnum on the desk top. Then I walked out.

I went to my quarters and whipped up Oysters Rockerfeller, and Oysters Bienville and Oysters Szechuan—there'd been a sale on oysters—I'd bought far too many for me to eat, and I ate them. I switched on the term and looked for some old movies. I'd seen everything. I watched a little of "*Thank you, Mr. Moto,*" but caught myself dozing.

I looked around my place. Silicaform chairs in patterns that didn't match. A nice white couch with a conspicuous patch over a hidden cigarette burn. Some early spacesapes on the wall. My framed "Certificates of Commendation." My "Valorous Performance" medal in a lucite box. A ceramic leopard. A worn carpet. A stack of cook's gear. A wall full of genuine books, mostly detective fiction or culinary in nature. It wasn't exactly my fantasy place in Santa Fe. But then my fantasy place in Santa Fe was . . . a fastasy. I called Ox and asked her for my job back.

Then I struck myself in the hottest bath I could stand. I was the law again. Maybe a bigger part of it then before. Maybe a Detective Sergeant's part. I needed a rest. I wanted to start clean.